BDG 12/73

Yuo

Nine Seven Juliet

Nine Seven Juliet

A MYSTERY NOVEL

BY LAURENCE LAFORE

GARDEN CITY, NEW YORK

DOUBLEDAY & COMPANY, INC.

1969

Library of Congress Catalog Card Number 69-20084

Printed in the United States of America

First Edition

Contents

To Carol and Jacques with love

Introduction

The city of Buchanan and Van Buren County bear some general resemblance to Iowa City and the beautiful country around it, but the details of the geography, physical and human, are imaginary. With reference to Chicago, St. Louis, and Kansas City, Buchanan cannot be where Iowa City is—or any place else, for that matter. Buchanan Municipal Airport has some of the characteristics shared by several thousand small airports throughout the country, but in important ways it is unlike any of them I have ever known, and the Van Buren County Flying Service Inc. is fortunately in all ways unlike any Fixed Base Operation I have ever encountered. N-9397J belongs to me, but there are other Nine Seven Juliets in the world, and I hope their owners will forgive any small notoriety I may bring them, and the peculiar uses to which I have put their namesake. Professor Payne's farm and his opinions may seem faintly familiar to the friends of a friend of mine, but his remarkable character so far transcends any tribute that I could contrive in the form of a portrait from life that I should never consider attempting it; and none of the other characters in this book bear any resemblance to any real people I have ever known.

Nine Seven Juliet

CHAPTER I

Short Field Landing

After Mrs. Sommers' funeral, Professor Payne went back to the farm with a very strong thirst for a very dry martini. He had been experiencing the thirst every afternoon during the forty-odd years since dry martinis had first come to his attention. Today, however, it was stronger than usual. He was eighty years old and had attended more funerals than he liked to remember. They had never moved or edified or even amused him, and the nearer his own approached, the less cheerfully could he tolerate those of others. He regarded death, like most things in life, as interesting but absurd, and he had no wish to encounter it. Old age had modified but not diminished his capacity for enjoying life and strengthened if anything his inclination to shock the world. He regarded every funeral as a meaningless bore and said so.

This kind of judgment on most human affairs had been the source of the considerable fame he had once enjoyed. He had been known as a wit and an iconoclast. His reputation, amounting in *avant garde* quarters to idolatry, was achieved in the second and third decades of the century, when reputations for iconoclasm were easier to come by. Still, it had been impressive by any standard, and he had exerted a substantial influence on his generation. The name of Walter Washburn Payne had been nationally known. So had the nicknames "The American Gawaine," among idolaters, and "The Sour Sage," among his more numerous but less educated detractors. He had brought national attention to the state university where he taught and to its seat, the city of Buchanan; both regarded their prodigy with perturbation, outrage, and pride. Even conventional people had a grudging respect for the man who could so easily shock them. The Goliath of middle-class America asked for flagellation from Payne's verbal slingshot, and got it. Then Goliath cried out with pained shrieks, denouncing Payne's mockery of military glory and his cold contempt for capitalism, lubriciously shivering at his advocacy of sexual emancipation, the more awful for its forthright assumption that sex was neither sacred nor dirty but fun. Goliath moaned when Payne denounced Prohibition not as unworkable or meddlesome but because temperance was immoral.

His books, scholarly studies of nineteenth-century American authors, achieved the sales and reputation usually associated with a *succès de scandale*. The best known, *Emerson the Corrupter*, was denounced from pulpits and podia throughout New England. But the most inimical critics were baffled by the propriety of his private life. There was literally nothing that could be held against him beyond the fact that, after a lifetime of moderation, he began to drink as a protest against the folly of the Volstead Act. His life was not merely respectable; it was model. He was a substantial citizen and a good husband to a devoted, worthy, and unexciting wife. He lived quietly on a farm near a small city, and the propeller over the farmhouse door testified to his dedication to the most dashing branch of the nation's defense in the First World War. It was clear, in short, that his nihilism was not an expression of contempt for the world but a protest against bigotry.

He was also strikingly handsome, and even his most devastating assaults were phrased in language that conveyed the same great elegance and charm that delighted his students. The nickname of Gawaine accurately suggested an affinity with gallantry and glamour.

His opinion of funerals reflected all these elements of a fame now long past. Having, in his salad days, dryly derided them, he continued to do so, deliberately behaving as an *enfant terrible* in the belief that the nation's need for *enfants terribles* so far exceeded the supply that even an octogenarian one was indispensably useful.

It had been, however, with special doubts that he had attended Mrs. Sommers' obsequies and (with even greater doubts) the Viewing on the previous evening. He went to show that his derision was a matter of public policy, not private conscience. The distinction, sometimes unclear to his public, was perfectly obvious to him. But in the case of Mrs. Sommers there was a personal complication. He had disliked her. He had, however, liked her late husband, a former colleague of his, and in the end loyalty had led him to pay conventional deference to the widow.

The distasteful memory of the ceremonies would have quickly dissolved in the first martini had it not been for the curious circumstance that his sixteen-year-old great-nephew, himself lately bereaved, showed an interest in them.

"Did you have a good time at the funeral, Uncle Walt?" Richie asked.

His phrasing and the slightly elaborate courtesy with which he asked the question suggested parody. But Professor Payne played it straight.

"I *always* enjoy funerals," he said untruthfully. Then he chuckled. "They serve to remind me that I am alive. At my age, it is something I find useful."

He watched Richie as he said it. The boy's face, immobile throughout the months since his difficulties had commenced, at first showed no identifiable feeling. But after a moment's silence, he smiled.

Encouraged, Professor Payne went on. "It was all pretty *fancy*, as a matter of fact. The floral tributes, as I believe they are called, were particularly lavish. There was one—I studied it quite carefully last night—fully five feet tall, made entirely of lavender gladioli. There were also innumerable sprays." He chuckled again, as if the word conveyed to him some private and pleasantly improper association. "Dolly Sommers was the most disliked woman in the county, so the munificence of her mourners must represent a triumph of guilt over thrift. Especially since she was cremated."

Richie smiled again, more definitely. "When they cremate you, do they cremate like the coffin and the flowers and all? A package deal?" He paused and added thoughtfully, "A burnt offering?"

This was more than Professor Payne had bargained for. The cremation of Richie's parents was after all only eight months past, and this was Richie's first reference, however oblique, to their death. He tried not to hesitate; he said squarely, "Yes. I believe they do."

"Oh."

Richie smiled for the third time—disagreeably, Professor

Payne thought. He averted his glance from the boy's face to his martini glass and considered once more the problem that had been distressing him for months.

Professor Payne was an expert at understanding young people. His success as a teacher, like his reputation as a gad-fly, had been the product of understanding youth and young ideas, of saying things that young people believed and liked to hear. His gift for this arose not from any mistaken clinging to his own youth; it was instead like a gift for languages. He learned the idiom of each generation and with it the key to understanding its culture and its view of itself.

For all his iconoclasm he was a little sentimental, for all his toughness, a little wistful; and these traits had completed his triumphant bridging of generations. Despite his retirement fifteen years before he was still followed and sometimes surrounded by former students and even occasionally by respectful undergraduates. Richie was a year or two younger than the youngest of those in whom Professor Payne had assiduously implanted skepticism for conventional judgments besides a fondness for literature. But during the previous summer, which Richie had spent at the farm, he had been conversible, companionable, and, so far as any adolescent boy is likely to be, confiding. In the intervening winter he had suffered the accident that had cost him much more than his parents, and his silently rendered image of betrayal and despair not only showed Professor Payne how complete was his failure to help him, but shook his confidence in his understanding of young people. Richie's sullen silences made him feel as if age had at last deprived him of the talent that had been his pride and his career.

Richie's disagreeable smile, however disconcerting, had been the first flicker of a sympathy between them. Professor Payne resolutely determined to go ahead. "It was, as I say, a good funeral. Which is to say, it was a terrible one. All funerals are vulgar. When the universal unpopularity of the deceased is expensively veiled in floral tributes, funerals become odious as well as ludicrous. Fortunately, today we were spared a view of the deceased. There was nothing but the box of ashes. Last night, we were spared nothing at all—we had a lush exhibit of the embalmer's art. The cosmetic work was quite dramatic, and so was the costuming. The corpse's hair-do was exquisite. It was wearing jewelry and glasses. There is something particularly striking about a well done-up corpse with its glasses on. I wondered about the jewels, as a matter of fact. Some of them looked as if they might be worth something, and I imagine the Sommers girls have a normal, healthy respect for pawnable objects."

This time Richie laughed. The reaction might be ghoulish, but it was definite and spontaneous. Professor Payne, who had no strong objections to ghoulishness, warmed to his topic. "The most odious thing of all was the conduct of the heirs. At least of the oldest daughter, the only one of the gals I know at all well, Merry Berger. I say 'gals' because that's how Merry refers to herself and her sisters. She likes to talk about 'We Sommers gals,' although she is fifty if she is a day. A gal, in Merry Berger's book, is distinguished from a girl, a lady, a woman, or a human female, by the qualities she believes herself to possess—sense and sanity. She was being sane but wet-eyed today—tears at parental funerals being for her a necessary form of decorum. Which I suppose they are, if you feel no sense of loss."

He was looking very closely at Richie, but he saw nothing beyond the persisting shadow of a smile. He was deliberately probing the boy's feelings. If there had been signs of distress, he would immediately have abandoned his probe, but there were none, and he thought it essential—indeed urgent—to find out what he could, now that Richie at last showed signs of a break in the wall with which he had surrounded himself. "And I doubt, frankly, if any of the sisters do. Merry, at least, is frankly preoccupied with outward shows and their cost. She told me she spent $12.95 yesterday at the Lovely Lady Shoppe, getting her own face and hair fixed for the Viewing. She got back from Europe only the day before and looked, she said, a wreck, after all day and all night on planes. And now she was crying and destroying the investment. A sense of filial obligation," Professor Payne said carefully, "can be quite expensive."

"What did you say to her?"

"I reproached her for extravagance. Then I untruthfully said, 'Merry, you look fine. One of the things I've always respected about you is your ability to cry whenever you want to without ruining your make-up. You ought to have been on the stage.' Merry said, 'Walt, it's funny you should say that. On the plane coming back from Paris I sat next to a theatrical producer and he said exactly the same thing to me.' And I said, 'Merry, you know, I've known you since you were born, and I always said to myself, 'There is a woman who is cut out to play Lady Macbeth.' " Then her husband came and took her away, but not before she'd told me how much supplementary fare it cost for a plane ticket when she had to give up her charter flight reservation and cut her trip short to get back for her mother's funeral. In point of fact, she's barely spoken to her mother for years. Not since Dolly told her it was her own fault when her husband got mixed up with the usherette at the Palace and there was the business about who would pay for the new chandeliers."

Richie was now looking not only interested but mildly impressed as well. Professor Payne pushed further. "It's true I have some respect for Merry's histrionic abilities. False feeling isn't easy to make convincing. On the other hand, I don't know whether she entirely realizes that it is false. She believes it to be proper and therefore true. But that does not make it less degrading, I think. It's the worst thing about funerals—they make false feeling seem positively virtuous, at least for fools. I am comforted, Richie, by the certainty that if you had been able to go to your parents' funeral you would not have thought it necessary to cry."

Richie laughed again. Professor Payne wondered whether the boy was not only unwracked by sorrow but untouched by it.

If he was, it was not surprising. Professor Payne had always considered Richie's parents, Howard and Dolores Payne, uninteresting people and marginally unsatisfactory parents. They had treated their only child as a sort of well-trained domestic animal, worthy of applause for his accomplishments but more conveniently kept out of sight while they gratified their own taste for an incessant indulgence in outdoor activities. Their seasons were distinguished by shooting, skiing, golf, fishing, sailing and tennis. They moved from one to the next with the determination of devout but ill-tempered monks proceeding from matins to vespers. Since their son had in recent years spent only a few weeks a year in their company, it was not to be expected that he would be drastically downcast by their disappearance. Since the age of eight, he had grown used to being independent.

Professor Payne had reached these slightly chilling conclusions much earlier. That afternoon he had conveyed them, in a somewhat cleaned up version, to his surviving nephew, Jeffrey Payne, who was Richie's legal guardian. Walt and Jeffrey had stood together in front of the church on Tyler Street after Mrs. Sommers' funeral, and Jeff had chosen this moment to inquire about his ward's welfare.

He was convinced that grief was the principal cause of the trouble. Professor Payne had always insistently disagreed. He did so again, although with a certain tentativeness. A funeral was not the best occasion for denying the impact of death. And his own position was weakened by the fact that three weeks at the farm had done nothing to relieve Richie's sad passivity.

"Well," Jeffrey had said, "I still think it's a mistake for him to be out there. He ought to be with other people. Kids his own age. It's bad to hide," he added with the assurance of someone who had never felt any need to hide. "There's nothing the matter with him except that he mopes."

"But that is surely precisely the point." Professor Payne had been irritated. "There *is* something the matter with him. He is crippled."

"His leg would get better if he'd forget about it. Start doing things. He needs to be taken out of himself."

"I agree. But he's afraid to try doing things, and I don't blame him. And when he went back to school, how far out of himself was he taken? He didn't really go to pieces until he went back to school. When he was living," Professor Payne pointed out, "with you and Laura."

"He's brooding about Howard and Dolores." Jeffrey shared the widespread belief that the way to disprove other people's opinions was strenuously to assert his own. "The only thing wrong with him is that he can't face being an orphan."

There was, Professor Payne realized, an element of what psychologists called transference in this. Jeffrey himself could not face the fact that his nephew and ward was permanently crippled. He was a man who required happy endings; he looked on physical infirmity as repulsive and a little disreputable. There was nothing incurable in losing your parents and grieving about it; a show of resolution could cure that malady. But sickness of the soul pursuant to lameness was doubly morbid. Jeffrey, like his late brother, was disposed to the form of mental myopia Professor Payne had spent his career combating, the substitution of proper sentiments for real feelings. "That psychotherapist at the clinic didn't know what the hell he was talking about," he continued ferociously. "And anyway, Richie didn't start worrying until a long time after he was out of the hospital."

"And long after Howard and Dolores were dead and buried," Professor Payne said, staring at the clusters of mourners around them. "He certainly showed no signs of missing them."

"In the last few months he hasn't shown any signs of

anything. He must miss them. After all, they were his parents."

"A great many people dislike their parents."

"You're so damn—bitter, Uncle Walt." Jeff was angry, and he forced himself to remember that his uncle was a very old man and could not be held altogether responsible for his own wickedness. But he could not resist the temptation to make a further reproach. "I don't think you ever really *liked* Howard and Dolores."

"No, I didn't. I thought they were uninteresting hedonists."

"That's a hell of a thing to say." The mourners were dispersing and Jeffrey and Professor Payne were walking toward the parked cars. "I don't like to hear evil spoken of the dead."

"I don't like to hear anything untrue spoken of anyone." Professor Walter Washburn Payne had replied with gentle condescension.

Now, two hours later, he was assured that Richie was not lamenting his orphanhood. His real trouble was much more intractable.

Professor Payne leaned back in his chair, looked at his now empty glass, and contrived to sound as off-hand as possible. "A funeral is very tiring. As a *memento mori*, it is wearing on the soles of the feet. And the calves. It is more wearing than a day's work on the farm."

He covertly studied his great-nephew. The smile was gone, the usual set expression had returned. He was a nice-looking boy, with a rectangular face, dark, smooth complexion, and the broad shoulders and big hands characteristic of the athlete he would not be. He wore the regulation summer uniform of the monstrous regiment he belonged to, white pants, blue shirt with tails out and sleeves rolled up, and hair long on his neck and forehead. His Uncle Jeffrey regarded the uniform as that of an enemy army and had imprudently blustered about it. Professor Payne had seen a dozen generations of youth pass before him and had long given up the hope that any of their members would show any individuality in their way of dress. He merely noted with tolerant relief that the pants and shirt were clean and the hair carefully combed. Perhaps too carefully; he had the impression that brushes and combs occupied an inordinate portion of Richie's day. He was sitting bolt upright, as he often sat now, as if he expected a lurking menace to come at him from the shrubbery.

"The things I find tiring are not the things that involve physical exertion," Professor Payne went on. "I can work hard in the garden all day and feel fine at the end of it. But half an hour spent in company with Mrs. Sommers' ashes in a church, followed by another half hour of hearing fools tell me how beautiful the Rites were, makes me feel ready for bed. Didn't you used to find," he continued with a not altogether successful attempt to sound casual, "before the accident, I mean, that physical activity was less exhausting than boredom? Or than a protracted mental effort? Or than an act of will?"

Richie winced, and his eyes narrowed in almost physical pain. Beyond that he did not at first move; then, after a moment, unconsciously it seemed and certainly involuntarily, he put his hand under his right thigh and shifted slightly the position of his leg.

The new knowledge that these small reactions yielded

cost Professor Payne a pain as great as the boy's. He felt himself helpless in the face of this kind of despair.

It was in some ways other people's fault. The boy had fought to buy his parents' approval by being good at sports, and he had succeeded. Then the icy road and the bridge abutment that had killed his parents had broken his right leg in so many places as to justify the description "shattered." For a while there had been talk of amputation, which might, as things turned out, have been better. There would have been no false hope that way. Professor Payne was sure now that it had been false hope provided, perhaps inadvertently, perhaps by design, by surgeons and nurses and therapists that had caused the psychic disaster.

Professor Payne felt a sudden need for some sort of action that would shake Richie out of his immobility. He issued an order, knowing that only orders brought sure results. "In short, Richie, I'm worn out. Will you go get me another drink. There's a martini already mixed in a pitcher in the refrigerator."

"O.K." The boy stood up, and limped laboriously across the terrace, into the house. Jeffrey had once accused him of malingering, and Professor Payne was obliged to admit that Richie did nothing to hide the effort that walking cost him.

The trouble had come, Professor Payne was sure, when Richie decided he had been lied to. They had told him heartily, the surgeons, nurses, and therapists, that it would be a long time before he would be playing any more football. After several months of anguish bravely borne, Richie had begun to realize that it would be forever. The false suggestion conveyed by the heartiness and the phrase "a long time" had, Professor Payne now thought, almost certainly been deliberate. A similar deception had been practiced on Richie's relatives, who had been told that prognosis was uncertain, that you could never tell what to expect with multiple fractures. They were, the doctors said, reserving judgment.

But in fact they had already made it. When Richie left the hospital, on crutches, they congratulated him on having escaped a lifetime in a wheel chair. When he reached the point of discarding crutches, they congratulated themselves on the triumph of medical skill that had unexpectedly brought him to the point where he could walk by himself, limping badly, with his leg in a brace. It was tacitly accepted that no more triumphs could be looked for. Nothing more was said about how long it would be before he played football again.

Richie, bereft, found he had also been betrayed. He had acted like a man and been treated like a child. After he realized what had happened he refused to see his friends, refused to stay in school, refused almost to talk.

He now came back with the martini pitcher. He followed instructions to the letter. Told he must swim for two hours and walk for a half an hour, he obeyed, minimally and silently, just as he had obeyed the order to produce the pitcher. He handed it, without speaking, to his great-uncle.

Professor Payne poured his second martini and said conversationally, "I thought of calling the Haineses and asking them over after dinner. Maybe Jean would want to come swimming."

The Haineses were his nearest neighbors, on the next farm. Their daughter Jean was a pretty contemporary of Richie's. The summer before, the two of them had spent a good deal of time together. He had not seen her this year, and now he said quietly, in an absolutely even voice, "O.K. I can go up to the room and look at TV."

Walt swallowed his second martini at a gulp, a protest against the decisions of fate and the medical profession.

He cooked the dinner himself, and they ate it on the terrace. He had taken up cooking after the death of his wife, ten years before. She had been an amiable woman, born and raised in White Bear, Minnesota, in a tradition that placed much emphasis on "setting a good table," and she had served her husband wholesome and abundant food at three meals a day as long as she lived.

Professor Payne had never troubled to learn the difference between a soup ladle and a garlic press. But in France, in 1918, he had learned with tolerable assurance the difference between a *Clos Vougeot* and a *Richebourg*, and immediately after her death he became an adept of *quiches lorraines* and, what was still more startling to Buchanan, *escargots bourguignons.* The pleasure he took in preparing them owed something, he realized, to the knowledge that his wife would have been horrified by them. She was well-enough educated, but her literacy stopped short of sauces, and she had disapproved of what she called fancy foods. Professor Payne's cooking, like his other attainments, was partly an expression of dislike for prejudice. It was likewise part of his creed that the satisfying of bodily appetites should be transformed into a fine art and thereafter luxuriously gratified. His wife had died when he was seventy; not without wistfulness he had bowed to destiny and exchanged the pleasures of the bed for those of the table.

In happier times his great-nephew had shown a commendably exploratory attitude toward food. Unlike most of his contemporaries, Richie had not been constrained by the loutish orthodoxy of hamburgers. The summer before he had tolerated snails and applauded a *bouillabaisse* rather overpoweringly garnished with *aïoli*. His tolerance was unimpaired, but this year applause was lacking. He ate in silence what was put before him.

What was put before him tonight was simple. Professor Payne had given up trying either to attract attention with provocative dishes or to make conversation. Tonight they ate Irish stew in customary silence.

It was extremely oppressive, perhaps as a baleful aftermath of Mrs. Sommers' funeral, perhaps because of a sense of finality in Richie's gloom. Professor Payne was more conscious than ever of the passing of time and its costs. The contrast of their moods to their surroundings heightened the sadness. The summer evening was clear and very beautiful. Birds sang. The old house, where Professor Payne and his father before him had been born, was solid and handsome. Overhead, oaks older than the house sheltered them, and below the terrace extended the superbly tended garden.

The intimations of survival and renewal around them led Professor Payne to another effort. "Listen," he said, putting down his fork and leaning forward. Richie looked obligingly up, his eyes determinedly unquestioning. "Listen. Nobody knew that your leg was going to be as bad as it turned out to be. They told me it would help if you had the most favorable possible idea of the prospects, and I went along with that. But *I* didn't know that the idea we were giving you was positively misleading. I suspect *they* may have, but I don't know for sure."

Richie said nothing. He looked as if he might be about to go back to the Irish stew. Professor Payne went hurriedly on. "What matters now is to see things as they are. You were misled into seeing things as they were not. But I talked to the doctor two weeks ago. He gave me what I think was a straight story. I haven't told you before what he said because he asked me not to, and because I didn't know how to go about it. But this is what he said, and he's pretty definite. You're not going to play any more football or basketball, or to ski. You'll be able to walk better, and farther, without getting tired, but you'll always be lame. You can already swim, and there are other things you could do now if you wanted to. You could drive a car. You have a license, and I'd be glad to go out with you and see how it goes. Then you could use my car if you wanted." He hesitated and said, "It's going to be tough. But it's nothing to be ashamed of, it's not going to affect how anybody feels about you except yourself. It's not going to bother girls, it's not going to stop you from doing pretty nearly anything you'll want to do, after another five years. People don't play football or basketball after they leave college. There are none of the important things that you won't be able to do."

Richie still did not speak. He was looking down at his plate. He had glanced up momentarily at the mention of the car, but he had shown no other response. He seemed rather to regard it as a sort of attack against which he could not defend himself, and after a moment he went back to his dinner. Professor Payne realized he was himself experiencing the sort of reaction he most strongly censured in Jeffrey. He felt that Richie was being deliberatly annoying and was affronted by his silence; but silence, blacker than ever, resumed.

It was broken just as the last of the stew was eaten by the distant sound of an airplane. It came closer, but there was nothing sufficiently arresting about it to make either of them look up. In any case, the trees around the farmhouse were too dense for them to see much if they had. But presently the plane approached too near to be disregarded. The buzzing had become a roar, and through the leaves they caught a glimpse of white wings very low above the treetops. Then, astonishingly, the sound of the engine abruptly stopped.

They were both on their feet, reflexively, moving toward the lawn where the ceiling of branches gave way to open sky. They were in time to see the plane, a quarter mile away at the level of the treetops on the hill, turning in a steep bank. It lost altitude rapidly and sank, noiseless, out of sight.

"I'll be damned," Professor Payne said.

"He must have landed. He must have landed in the field at the top of the hill."

"He may have. We'd have heard it if he'd crashed, I think. But he might have gone down in the trees."

"He's got to be in trouble, doesn't he? Nobody would want to land in that field if he didn't have to."

"I shouldn't think so. It's not very long. It would have been long enough for the kind of planes we flew fifty years ago, but for the ones they make now I expect it's short."

Professor Payne spoke anxiously, but his anxiety was not really for the anonymous aviator but for Richie. The boy had moved, and spoken, with greater spontaneity than he had in three months. He had moved not more than twenty feet, but he had covered them, it seemed, with more ease and speed than he had done anything since the accident. There was benign calculation behind Professor Payne's next sentence. "I guess we better go up and find out what's happened. Even if nothing's wrong, I'd like to know what he's doing in my wheatfield."

Still calculating, carefully avoiding a backward glance, he started across the lawn to the track that led up into the woods, listening intently not for signs of activity from the wheatfield but for Richie's footsteps behind him. For a moment he heard nothing and then, to his large satisfaction, there came the sound of the boy's uneven stride.

The farmhouse, surrounded by its trees, stood halfway up a wooded hillside rising from the river to a long low ridge. The flat top of the ridge formed a plateau and there the trees had been cleared for a rectangular field, bordered on all sides by woodland. Earlier generations of Paynes, careful and efficient farmers, had taken advantage of every corner of arable land on their farm, and this stretch had been found fertile.

They climbed slowly toward it along the lane, not much more than a pair of ruts cut by farm machines, as it wound up through the trees. The going was rough, and their progress was not very fast. Still, it was faster than Professor Payne would have predicted ten minutes earlier. He himself was in excellent condition, but he had in recent years learned to move with deliberation over uneven ground. Even then he had to moderate his pace to let Richie keep up with him, but the boy was walking resolutely and, it was obvious, with curiosity.

When they reached and opened the gate that gave onto

the field they saw that the plane had landed safely. It was a little surprising; the field was less than a quarter mile long, and the trees around it were tall. The plane was at the far end, and the tracks of its wheels were clearly visible in the stubble of the newly cut wheat. It had touched down a third of the way along the field and run a straight course to the opposite end.

"It must be quite a trick to have landed it in that space," Professor Payne said consideringly to Richie. "The planes I used to fly landed at about thirty miles an hour, but nowadays they're much faster. They need a much longer—" he paused, grasping for the phrase, and found it, "roll-out. Whoever it is must know how to fly. And must, as you say, have some very good reason for landing here."

They opened the gate and started along the field. It was a small, single-engine plane painted red and white, with low wings. It looked in good order, but there was one surprising thing: there was no sign of a pilot.

They approached and studied the plane with interest. It was remarkably neat, Professor Payne thought. Compared to what he had been used to, it was smooth, sleek and compact. Plaques on the fusilage identified it as a Cherokee 180, which meant little to either of them, and there were large red figures N9397J painted on the side, which meant even less. The door, giving onto the top of the wing, was wide open. They could see the whole of the cabin, and it was empty.

"He has probably gone to look for a telephone," Professor Payne said. "It must be fifteen or twenty minutes or more since we started up the hill. Of course he had no idea anybody saw him come down, and he probably didn't notice the house or barn, since they're pretty well covered by trees in summer. So he started off on his own in another direction, looking for civilization."

Richie considered. "He's going to have a long way to go, no matter which way he's gone. There's no other house within a mile, is there?"

"Almost that. The Haineses is nearest. He picked the loneliest part of the county to land in. It's odd; he must have been able to see that from the air. Whatever way he was coming from, he would see bigger fields and more houses before he got here. Something must have happened suddenly."

"He maybe ran out of gas. You read in the papers all the time about guys doing it. You'd think"—Richie was examining the aircraft—"that they'd have more sense. Man, I'd make sure I had plenty to get where I was going if I was in one of these. Suppose this field wasn't there?"

"It's not too bad, landing in trees, if you know how to do it." Professor Payne found he took some satisfaction in his command of this field of knowledge. "The small branches slow you down and the big ones hold you up. You have a good chance of walking away. I did it once, in the Argonne." He leaned back against the plane in a casual pose. He looked remarkably young. He had kept his lean figure and his hair, now steel gray. His face was deeply tanned and his muscles still tight. Standing still, his bearing was almost that of a young man, and from a little distance he might still have been taken for the dashing airman who would shortly put on his helmet and goggles, rev up his engine, and take off over enemy lines. "I'd run out of gas myself. But not through improvidence. The Germans had shot holes in the tank. I made it over our lines. Just. Still, I'd rather not do it again. Not if I could avoid it by checking a gas gauge."

"Did you have gas gauges, like a car?" Richie asked reverently.

"No, we certainly didn't. I used a stick to measure it. We had nothing much more than a deck chair lashed to the lower wing, and a machine gun. But I imagine they have gauges now. Along with ashtrays, heaters, decorator colors, and such-like decadence. The age of the pioneers ended a long time ago. There are a lot of women and children flying now who probably treat an instrument panel as if it were something on an automatic clothes washer." And Professor Payne, in a gesture that suggested he was merely confirming a random guess, did what he had been wanting to do since they first came up to the Cherokee. He climbed onto the wing, pulling himself up by the side of the door, and clambered into the cabin.

For someone eighty years old and not used to it, it was a slightly clumsy process. Inside, space was restricted, but he maneuvered himself into the seat furthest from the door, on the left of the plane, and began to examine the instruments. Glancing over his shoulder, he saw that Richie was trying to follow him.

It was a bad moment. To get in he had had to put one foot on a step, another on the wing, then kneel down and crawl onto a seat lower than the doorsill, with minimal legroom. Even with help it would be hard, perhaps impossible, for anyone with one stiff leg.

Professor Payne stared straight ahead out the windshield at the sky, listening tensely. He heard two false tries and, with some relief, a muttered curse. Then the sounds of more scrambling. From the corner of his eye he saw that

Richie had completed the first stage; he was standing on the wing. Then, awkwardly, he knelt down, holding onto the door. The next part was slow, and he was breathing hard. But he managed it at last, pulling the bad leg in behind him and settled himself in the seat beside his uncle. There was an expression of beatific intensity on his half-opened lips, and as he put one hand gingerly on the wheel and stared at the instruments he said in an undertone to himself, "Goddam, that's cool."

It was so, in the lexicons of both occupants. Professor Payne, suddenly relaxing, had the curious physical sensation of someone who has lived through a hot spell so protracted that he had lost awareness of how nearly intolerable it was and then, suddenly, felt a cool breeze blowing. It was the first time Richie had tried anything on his own initiative, and he had succeeded. It was the first time he had shown interest in anything, and his interest now was engrossing and sustained.

For a moment neither of them spoke, and Professor Payne studied the panel in an effort to quiet his slightly trembling hands and heart. It did, in fact, divert him. For someone whose last occupancy of a pilot's seat was almost half a century past, what he now saw in front of him was intimidating. A pang of sorrow touched him. It had been a long, long time ago, that heroic age, and he would never fly a plane again. The instrument panel showed him he belonged to a different era. For all that he could read of their meaning the score or more of dials and switches might have belonged in a hundred-seat jet liner. Where they were identified, it was in an alien language, faintly Slavic, as unintelligible as Croat. *Com, Nav, Mag. Vor, Sql,* and *Obs.*

Richie, still reverently fingering the wheel, asked after a long reverie, "Could you fly it, Uncle Walt?"

"Good God, no."

"They do have gas gauges. Two of them. They both say empty, but then they probably don't register if the ignition's off. Where's the ignition."

"I don't know, Richie."

"Turn that key and see what happens."

"Don't be absurd. It might be the starter."

"Think so?" Clearly Richie did not regard this as a reason not to turn it. "Where do they keep the gas tanks?"

"I haven't any idea."

"In the wings, maybe?"

"Possibly."

"What's that?" He pointed to a dial on the far side of the panel.

Professor Payne was glad to be able to answer a question at last. "It's an altimeter."

"Al*tim*'eter? Not alti-*met*'er?"

"Al*tim*'eter," Professor Payne said authoritatively. "It gives the number of feet above mean sea level if the barometer is set right."

"O.K." Richie peered. "*If* it is, this scene's eight hundred and ninety feet above sea level." He paused. "*If* what you're supposed to read is the minute hand."

"It is." Professor Payne was a little taken aback. He had been trying to work it out himself. "You must be right. External evidence confirms your reading."

"Meaning you know the elevation?"

"Roughly." He looked again at the altimeter and found it still confusing. "You're learning to fly very fast."

"So what's this one?" Richie pointed to another dial, in front of him.

"Tachometer." Again he was pleased to be able to answer.

"Tach-*om*-eter." Richie repeated it after him. "And what's it do?"

"It measures rpm's."

"Revolutions per minute. They've got *them* on racing cars. So what's this one?"

Professor Payne gave up. The sense of superannuation gripped him again. "I don't know, Richie. It's been a very long time." He shrugged his shoulders. "I probably know less about flying than you do. You people"—he meant Richie's generation—"absorb the air age through your pores." He was talking more naturally to the boy than he had for months. But now he paused. Reminded of his age, he was reminded of the need for caution and prudence. "I don't think we ought to be here."

"Why not?"

"If the pilot comes back, he might complain. We are trespassing on valuable property, after all."

"So's he," Richie said logically. "What are the foot pedals for?"

The catechism was intensely serious. Professor Payne settled back again. "They work the rudder I imagine."

"So what's the rudder do?"

"It steers the plane, more or less. At least as I remember, it changes the direction the nose is pointing in."

"What's the steering wheel do?"

"If it works like a joy stick, it lowers the left wing when you push it to the left. With the ailerons."

"So what happens when you pull it out?" It seemed to be this feature of the controls that most interested him.

"Again, if it's like the stick, when you pull it back toward you it makes the nose point up. Then you climb."

"O.K.," Richie said approvingly, rather as if his great-uncle had passed some sort of test. He let go of the wheel, leaned back and studied the instrument panel in silence.

After they returned to the house a half an hour later, they heard the plane take off, and a moment later saw it through the trees, climbing steeply and then leveling off and disappearing over the sunset horizon.

"We didn't miss him by much, did we?" Richie was still alert. "What do you think he could have been doing? He *wasn't* stopping for gas. He didn't have time to get anywhere he could have found any."

Professor Payne considered. "It is certainly extremely curious."

"Maybe he was like digging for buried treasure." A faraway look, betokening sixteen's fancies of romance, came into Richie's eyes, and he added dreamily, "Or else he was in the bushes, making out with some girl."

CHAPTER II

Ground Run

It was one of Professor Payne's sustaining traits that he always woke up early with his mind already at work, his thoughts thoroughly engaged by the day's prospective purposes and the ways in which he would undertake them. The morning after the airplane's visit to his upper wheatfield, his first waking moments were attended by inspiriting thoughts of cultivation: the harrowing of corn, the maturing of squash, and the massacring of gnawing insects.

Not more than half of the agreeable few minutes he allowed himself for planning his chores had elapsed, however, before he was distracted by thoughts of the events of the previous evening, and first of all of Richie. He had lived too long to believe that psychic transformations took place suddenly, but long enough to know that a concatenation of circumstances might produce surprising results, the end-product of a process invisibly developing. He had no great hopes that the morning would find Richie in the same state of rehabilitation in which he had left him the night before. But if it had happened once, it might happen again. A break in clouds did not indicate fine weather to come, but it was much better than a constant overcast.

Richie's wholly unself-conscious excitement had been, if nothing more, a break in the clouds.

The circumstance that had produced it was however a good deal less satisfactory to a mind that disliked unsolved puzzles. The more Professor Payne thought about the red and white Cherokee, the more peculiar its presence seemed. A romantic association, which for a moment became a romantic confusion, formed in his mind: he had a brief image of a Brave, menacingly painted with red and white stripes on his face, brandishing a tomahawk in the upper wheatfield.

It was certainly time to get out of bed and begin the day. Images of Red Indians had not affected him since he was ten. But in the course of dressing, he found himself still concerned with the problem. He tried to put it in rational terms: a pilot in a small plane, which was demonstrably in good flying condition, had landed in a small field surrounded by high trees in a part of the country exceptionally, almost uniquely, sparsely settled. This was, in a way, the most striking feature of the situation. There was no settlement nearer than a crossroads village two miles away. The inevitable conclusion was that the pilot had been seeking not company but privacy.

Privacy for what, Professor Payne wondered as he tied the laces on his work shoes. It was barely possible that Richie's ribald suggestion contained some part of truth. But the oak woods had nothing but isolation—and that in excess—to recommend them as a trysting place. It was extremely unlikely that anyone should *plan* a landing there for amorous purposes, however beguiling it was to imagine a pilot overcome in midair by an urgent, irresistible passion for his passenger.

He considered other explanations. It might possibly have been the simplest of all emergencies, answering the call of nature. He remembered from fifty years ago, several precedents for such an emergency, some behind enemy lines. But it was very unlikely. Buchanan Municipal Airport was not more than fifteen miles away, a few minutes by air. The plane could have got there almost as soon as it could have made the exploratory circles preparatory to landing in the wheatfield.

There was Richie's other suggestion of buried treasure. Treasure, in the form of doubloons, was quite as unlikely an explanation as a sudden access of lust, but it fitted the circumstances well enough. The pilot had been gone from his plane—Professor Payne made the calculation with some care—just about an hour. It had taken about twenty minutes for them to reach the field from the time he landed. They had spent another twenty-five inside the Cherokee, and fifteen more on the downhill walk back. That was time enough for digging up doubloons.

Walter Payne's imagination did not in general tend to extravagance. But now, standing in front of his bedroom window, contemplating the familiar aspect of his garden and meadow, a series of exhilarating fancies came to him. He was pleased by the idea that his woodland might be an exchange point for ancient coins. There were grave objections to the hypothesis, but then, as he reminded himself, there were grave objections to any other hypothesis as well.

If some such hoard had indeed been dug up, the pilot must have either brought a shovel or known that one was there. He must also have known exactly where to look for the treasure. It must not have been a very deep hole—as a gardener, Professor Payne knew that even small excavations invariably took more time and sweat than anticipated —and it could not have been very far from the perimeter of the wheatfield.

He ran his hand through his hair. Perhaps the treasure had not been buried. It might have been hidden in a hollow tree trunk, or concealed under a rock. In that case the shovel could be dismissed and the range of action considerably extended. But burial seemed most probable: the woods were not absolutely isolated. The high road ran, invisible but audible, a few hundred yards away, on the far slope of the ridge. If the treasure were to be at all secure from casual walkers or farm workers, it would almost have to be buried. And—he returned to his point of logical departure—this meant that traces of its disinterment would be evident. A hurried excavator could not possibly conceal such traces from a practiced eye.

Professor Payne liked to start the day with a good breakfast. Now, however, he yielded to powerful curiosity and within five minutes was making his way up the lane to the wheatfield.

The woodland looked, when he reached the field, dauntingly vast. There was not the slightest possibility of exploring it all. It would take several men a full day to cover even the shallow circumference of it. He had—which was rare and embarrassing for him—yielded to a wholly unreasoning impulse. The whole notion of buried treasure, suggested in irony by a sixteen-year-old boy, should have been dismissed with a smile. But he was here, and some of his curiosity outlived his disenchantment. As he stood inside the gate, he saw again the tracks of the Cherokee's wheels on the spikes of the cut wheat. They had multiplied;

at the end, where the plane had been parked and turned, the stubble was flattened, and an irregular trail led up the side of the field, crossing a few feet in front of him to the far end. There, it was easy to see the traces of the ground run and to tell where the plane had lifted off, halfway down the field. This suggested that footsteps might also leave their mark. He looked for his own and Richie's and after a moment found traces, faint and fragmentary but definite. Somewhat encouraged, he walked to the spot where the plane had stood. If there were signs of footprints in any direction but the one he had come, they must belong to the occupant or occupants of the plane, since he and Richie had walked nowhere else in the field.

It took close study and perhaps a touch of imagination, before he saw them. His eyesight like his powers of observation was in good repair. He squatted down like a golfer prospecting a difficult putt and found that from that angle the marks were much clearer. He could, indeed, see enough to observe tracks going in the direction of the nearest point of the woodland. He could not make out footprints, merely the indication that someone or something had passed back and forth.

Bending low to maintain the perspective, he followed the tracks to the border of brambles and bushes on the line between the sunny field and the shady forest. Here there were undoubted signs that someone had passed. A certain amount of forest craft, the heritage of every farm boy in his generation, was at Professor Payne's command; at least his eye for signs was very sharp, and he was sure that someone had broken through the barrier of bushes. He followed the trail into the woods and found that it led to his objective in a matter of yards. The disturbance in the forest bed of leaves and lichens ended abruptly in a pile of twigs and leaves clumsily stacked—an attempt by someone who knew nothing of nature to imitate the natural appearance of the forest floor. Much excited, he kicked aside the amateurish covering. Beneath it was raw black earth irregularly heaped and dug over, an area some three yards square. The operation had been, after all, a fairly extensive one.

He felt a moment's apprehension, as if the airborne digger might be lurking behind a massive tree trunk. It was dispelled not so much by the light of reason as by an even more arresting thought. The contours of the excavated area were very uneven, but the larger part was well above the level of the surrounding ground. It had not, for some reason, previously occurred to him that the pilot's mysterious occupation might have been burying, not unburying. It now seemed obvious, and it made everything simpler. There was no need to speculate how he could have known where the treasure was, or how long it had been there.

He stared speculatively for a moment longer, and then he started rapidly back toward the house and the shed where he kept his shovels.

He had got one and, sweating a little, was starting up the hill again before he thought of Richie. It was the first time the boy had been off his great-uncle's mind since his arrival, and pausing at the bottom of the lane he wondered whether his forgetfulness could be ascribed to the exciting discovery in the woodland or to a new confidence in Richie's ability to take care of himself. Regretfully he concluded that the former was more likely. In any case, he had to tell him what was going on. He turned back to the house and found him stretched out flat on a chaise longue on the terrace, staring at the sky.

"I've got distracted from breakfast," Professor Payne said. "Are you hungry?"

"Yes."

It was unexpected. Richie's recent style had been more in the way of a numb and courteous acquiescence in everything. But the definiteness was not so much demanding as dreamy. It was as if he were answering a question loudly put by fantasmal voices.

"I'll get you some shortly. In the meantime I am going to go dig in the woods."

"O.K.," Richie said, still listening to the inaudible voices.

"Our invisible pilot last night was burying something. I've found the place he was digging. I'm going to dig up whatever it was."

"Oh? Yeah?" Richie sounded surprised and pleased by this news, but it obviously did not interrupt his own train of thought. It was decidedly a new phase. Professor Payne was disappointed. He had been hoping the boy might throw himself into the investigation with the same zeal he had shown in hoisting himself into the plane. But he showed nothing more than concern with his own thoughts —which was doubtless better than showing no concern at all. His expression was quite different from the opacity of recent weeks. The sinister word "withdrawn" still applied, Professor Payne decided, but the withdrawal was into something in the nature of concentrated study. Richie was frowning abstractedly, with a sort of other-worldly concentration.

His uncle wondered, not for the first time, whether he could have got hold of drugs somewhere. But this was most improbable. He did not appear turned on. He looked more like someone planning a bank hold-up.

Slightly disturbed, Professor Payne set off alone with his shovel. He grew more disturbed, for different reasons, as he approached the site of the dig. His mission seemed an act of folly; humbling phrases—"a wild goose chase," "a fool's errand"—formed in his mind. But he banished doubts with exercise.

The soil was damp and heavy, and the irregularity of the mound left him unsure about where to begin and how deep to dig. After tossing up a dozen shovelfuls of earth he began to wonder whether Richie's exertions of the evening might not account for his present state. He had taken more, and rougher, exercise than he had since the accident. His prone position and abstracted state of mind might be the consequence of exhaustion.

Professor Payne shrugged his shoulders, which was a mannerism of his, a substitute for the custom of those old people who talked aloud to themselves, and returned to his digging. His mind was still as much occupied with Richie as with buried treasure, and he was startled when he felt the shovel strike something solid. He knelt down to feel with his fingers in the soil, burrowing for a moment, finding the object, raising it, and shaking the dirt from it.

Richie's conjecture had been right: he had come on buried treasure. What he saw was a number of rings set with stones that glittered as the dirt fell from them. So surprising was this confirmation of a romantic guess that not until the second instant of his discovery did Professor Payne take in a much more surprising fact: the rings were on fingers, and what he had pulled from the ground was a human hand attached to a human wrist.

He stood bolt upright. He was neither superstitious nor squeamish. In his day he had seen many bodies, not all of them in the good state of preservation in which this one, judging from what he had seen of it, appeared to be. Still he could not help realizing, in a flash of realism, that he was a very old and unarmed man, and that no help was nearer than a quarter of a mile away.

The knowledge that he was old, the awareness of infirmities that attended age, came each time as new, distasteful surprise. He regarded age as a man of thirty might regard inoperable cancer. He hated it as an unwanted, unbelonging presence, and when he remembered it he felt not so much depression as a sort of lonely anger. It was this emotion that now momentarily overcame him, as if years had suddenly enfeebled him, making him vulnerable to the hazards and complexities that his discovery brought. For he could not avoid the judgment that he must be in the presence of a crime that was, beyond doubt, both heinous and grotesque. His sense of loneliness was overpowering; he felt bereft not only of allies but of human goodness.

He continued his digging. The grave was very shallow. Indeed, it was not a grave at all. The body had been laid on the ground and covered with earth dug from the surrounding area. It had been done, obviously, by someone in a hurry, and by someone remarkably careless, who knew nothing of graves or of forests.

He had by now taken away most of the earth on top of what he supposed, from its shape and location, was the rest of the body. He could not dig further without risking putting the blade of his shovel into it and this he very much preferred to avoid. He resorted, therefore, to pulling.

It was not easy, but it was not much harder than pulling up recalcitrant weeds or unwanted hollyhock plants. He strained at the horribly limp hand. The body finally moved —he was relieved to see that it *was* a body, evidently intact. He shook off some of the soil that disconcertingly clung to it and with an effort obliged himself to inspect it. When he did he got much the worst shock he had yet received.

The body was that of an elderly woman fully, indeed elaborately, dressed in gray satin. It was perfectly preserved, with the false, sweet perfection of embalming. The hair was set in wiry, lacquered, tight white curls. The lips and cheeks were heavily rouged. The color of the rest of the skin was an apricot travesty of sun-tan, harlequin glasses were still set over closed eyelids, and there was a pearl necklace around the throat. The whole effect was made as gruesome as possible by the fact that a good deal of muddy soil still stuck to the satin dress, the white curls, the pink cheeks. But what unnerved him as completely as anything had unnerved him in his eighty years was the corpse's identity. He was looking into the face of old Mrs. Sommers, over whose supposed ashes, the afternoon before, he had heard a minister invoke the eternal life of the soul.

He observed that he had exaggerated the avarice of the Sommers gals. The rings he had come upon were the ones he had guessed they would remove before bidding final farewell to the remains of their mother. But then, he concluded, the stones were probably not precious after all.

He reached home at a half-run with just enough breath left to shout loudly for Richie.

There was no answer, and a brief inspection showed no sign of him. Professor Payne was gravely perplexed at this, but there were more immediate matters to be dealt with than a search for his great-nephew. A former sheriff of Van Buren County was, like half its literate citizens, a former student of his. Since his undergraduate days, Russ Mallery had been a friend; he would have good advice to offer, and he would be glad to offer it. At the moment, both a friend and good advice were urgently needed. Professor Payne went to the telephone.

Russ whistled with gratifying astonishment and said he would drive out to the farm immediately. "On my way to the office," he added detachedly. He had the habit of mitigating good deeds with irony: since he had been defeated for re-election as sheriff he had practiced as a lawyer in Buchanan, and the visit would mean a thirty-mile detour.

"It's good of you," Professor Payne said. "Is there someone local I should notify?"

Russ, moodily contemplating a half-drunk cup of coffee rapidly cooling on a table six inches beyond arm's reach, considered. "No, not yet, Walt. Let me get out there and think about it. It isn't a case of . . ." He stopped. "It's hard to say what it *is* a case of. There are laws against grave-robbing and body-snatching, of course, but this body hasn't been robbed, and it hasn't indeed been snatched from a grave either. At most from the portal of a fiery furnace."

Professor Payne had always found Russ's astringencies stimulating even when, as a freshman, he had defended fundamentalist interpretations of the Book of Genesis. He began to feel better.

"Until we are sure a crime has been committed, and what crime, in whose jurisdiction, and when, I see no reason not to let sleeping dogs lie. Meaning no offense to my successor. Jim Fess is a son of a bitch, though, and since he's a lazy son of a bitch he's probably still asleep, so let him lie. Lying is what he does best. You were quite correct to consult your attorney first, and I shall now come give you professional advice. O.K.?"

"O.K." Professor Payne was on the whole pleased by the professional advice given so far.

"I'll see you in twenty minutes," Russ said with increased cordiality. He had just maneuvered his outstretched fingers around the handle of the coffee cup.

Professor Payne thought of adding, "By the way, my nephew has disappeared, too." But he did not really think that Richie had, in any except the most literal sense, disappeared. He had probably gone down to the river to swim, after giving up hopes of breakfast. Instead, he said, "I'm much obliged."

He hung up and went to conduct a more thorough investigation of the disappearance. He was not, it presently turned out, in the house or at the river, and he began to feel more uneasy. Then, on the chaise longue where he had last seen Richie, weighted by an ashtray, he noticed a small piece of paper torn from a learned journal devoted to comparative literature. "Dear Uncle Walt," it read, "I have taken the car for a while. I will be careful with it. Hope you don't mind. Yours, Richie." There was, at the bottom, an arrow pointings sideways. On the reverse, between printed lines that read, "the ontological motif of much of Grabenstein's early wo—" and "—con of youth, but rather a telic preoccupation with dea—", Richie had written in very small letters indeed, "Also borrowed $23.56 off your dresser. Will pay you back. Hope this is O.K., R."

Professor Payne's reactions ran like a film run at high speed: relief, concern for his car, concern for Richie, irritation, amazement, disbelief. He studied the note and reached the reasonable conclusion that since there was nothing he could do about it, he had better have some breakfast. He was finishing his coffee when he heard Russ Mallery's car on the drive.

The "Russ" in his name was a contraction not of Russell but of Russky, which schoolmates in first grade had called him. His signature on checks was Porfiri P. Mallery, and the "P," he would explain when asked, stood for Petrovitch. He told people that his mother, who had been an English teacher in South Dakota, had been frightened during pregnancy by *Crime and Punishment*. "Badly frightened." And, when he had still been sheriff, he would gravely add, "It decided both my name and my career."

It had decided his temperament as well. He was a hunter; his vocation was the apprehension of criminals. He required adventure, and he liked—as if by compensation for a nature outwardly composed and contemplative—intimations of danger and violence. A law practice consisting mainly of the peaceable preparation of wills and the transference of titles to real estate made him feel like an efficient hound chained up in a public library.

His loss of office rankled. There had been accusations of incompetence in the unpleasant political wrangle that preceded his defeat, and he was much troubled by the suspicion that they were well-founded. In fact, his friends supposed, it had not been incompetence so much as the gap between the inner impulses of a hunter and the outward manner and appearance of a sedentary professional man that had lost him the voters' support. At forty-five he was slight, but with a pronounced paunch. He had small, rather finely formed features, thin, questioning eyebrows, buttony eyes, and a shiny forehead that reached behind his ears. He chain-smoked compulsively, and his fingers and teeth were stained. His wary astuteness displayed itself to the public as a slightly cynical lethargy. To those who knew him, he revealed not only zeal for the chase but a quickness and flexibility of mind that they respected. Despite his youthful dedication to the belief that the earth had been created in six days, Professor Payne had admired him from the beginning and given him A's in four successive literature courses. At fairly frequent intervals since then they had gotten drunk together.

This morning Russ accepted a cup of coffee, inspected his former teacher with a solicitous eye for possible bad effects from his grisly experience, found nothing to alarm him, and sat down on the edge of the chaise longue lately vacated by Richie. "In matters of this sort, Walt, I have found that it is best to begin at the end and proceed to the beginning. Tell me about this morning."

He was told.

"And you formed the impression that the—remains—had been buried, or, to put it exactly, covered, by someone who was, *a.* amateurish in his handling of dead bodies in woodlands, *b.* careless in his workmanship, *c.* in a hell of a hurry? Any of these, or any combination of them, would be possible. But you would feel that these three are both exclusive and inclusive?" He asked the questions with rapid-fire incisiveness.

"Yes." Professor Payne hesitated and asked, "Do you talk to all your clients this way?"

"No. It saves a good deal of time when I'm able to, though. I'll go up and look at the body myself, so we needn't inquire into its aspect. Unless of course someone has gone by in a balloon with a grappling hook and taken it away. I take it you noticed nothing untoward about it?"

"No, unless you call being dead and embalmed untoward."

"It looked roughly the way it did in the casket?"

"Yes."

"And the Viewing took place where?"

"Stanley Brill's. You know Stanley, of course. He was a few years ahead of you in college, but still of your generation, if I remember correctly."

"You always do. I know Stanley. We had professional interests in common when I was sheriff."

"He laid Dolly Sommers out very prettily. Roses in her cheeks, glasses on her nose, rings on her fingers, dead, all dead. Mourners came in force to say farewell to the pretty corpse among tactfully flood-lit potted palms at 784 South Polk, six to ten P.M."

"You make it sound loathsome."

"It was."

"Do you have any idea when they closed the coffin for the last time? Or when the cremation actually took place —or was supposed to take place?"

"No."

"It doesn't matter at the moment. I can ask Stanley. Did you know Mrs. Sommers well? I knew her only by reputation, which was poor."

"I knew her quite well. She was an abominable woman." Professor Payne settled himself comfortably into the deck chair and sipped his coffee. "Perfectly abominable. I knew the late Benjamin H. Sommers intimately. He died considerably before your time at the university. Knowing them both, I always thought he died in self-defense. He was a very sound classicist. Interested in Thucydides. A good scholar and a most likable fellow, poor old Bimbo. A few years younger than I, but I saw a good deal of him. After he died Dolly stayed on in Buchanan and was active in community affairs. In much the way that a virus is active —energetically doing things that no one wanted done. I continued, against my will, to see her, at parties that people felt obliged to ask her to because they disliked her so intensely. I would not say that I kept up with her, and I should hate to think that it could be said that she kept up with me, but something of that sort took place."

"What did she die of?"

"Spiritually, an enlarged spleen. Medically, cancer."

"There's no likelihood that anyone pushed her? A few extra pills, or something?"

"I doubt it. I was told several months ago by her eldest daughter that 'the end was a matter of time.' Disregarding the fact that that is a statement that could be made of anybody, I interpreted it to mean a matter of weeks. So I doubt if anyone pushed her into the grave, although apparently someone did pull her out of it."

Russ tapped his foot, then he said, "I know there are daughters. Who else survives?"

"There is Dolly's sister, Agnes Creston."

"I thought she died years ago."

"That's what everyone in Buchanan thinks about everyone who moves away. Actually, she's been living in Paris for years. When I spoke to Merry Berger after the funeral, she told me she had seen her quite recently."

"Merry is the oldest daughter, isn't she?"

Professor Payne nodded. "She was traveling abroad when her mother died."

"Traveling abroad?" Russ raised his eyebrows. "Surely rather unfeeling, in view of her mother's illness."

"No one except Merry has ever believed that Merry had much in the way of feelings. She did come home for the funeral. The three daughters, with families, were all on hand, so any one of them may be . . . implicated." He had chosen the word with care. "And that is not the end of the implications, in both senses. Thinking over what I know about the Sommers family, while waiting for you, I perceived a much larger and more sinister peculiarity. Something very suggestive indeed. However, I shall come to that in due time."

"I'd like to get the daughters and their husbands straight first of all. I know the Bergers slightly, and I've met the rest of the family, but I don't remember them. The merciful operation of memory's censorship, no doubt."

"There were four girls. Merry, Joy, Gay, and Patience."

"There seems to have been a change of mood at the end."

"Poor old Bimbo was hoping for a son." Professor Payne sighed. "He never had one. And Joy died young."

Russ drew heavily on the stub of his cigarette and lit a new one from it. "And Merry, Gay, and Patience were at the funeral, with respective husbands and children and the late Dolly's circle of grieving friends?"

"Her circle of friends was infinitesimal. The circle of

people she had intimidated was, however, large. Most of them were present."

"For the moment we better concentrate on family."

"First the Bergers. Merry and Glendenning."

"I know him as Glen. I didn't know he was Glendenning. Glendenning Berger. He sounds like an inferior meat dish, made of ground up glendennings."

"A similar thought occurred to others. He was known in youth as Ham. A name his wife cannot abide. How well do you know him?"

"I've been acquainted with him for years, from a safe distance. Gilded middle age, I judge, of a sadly tarnished sort. His wild oats have been, as it were, frostbitten. I see him at the club sometimes on Saturday nights. Occasionally with odd company. The only other thing I know is that he used to be an officer of the Corn State Bank but is no more. A sort of Leading Citizen who never led, just as he's a Lothario *manqué*. I have met and disliked the wife. I know nothing else about them. Are there children?"

"A son, about thirty, named Beaufort. There was a Confederate general of that name whom Merry fancies as an ancestor. The family had faint pretensions to long-lost elegance. Not typically middle-western. The pretensions were very hazily substantiated, and possibly mythical. I should say that Dolly was an *arriviste*."

"At present it would be more accurate to call her a *départiste*."

Professor Payne disregarded this. "Years ago Merry and Glen were good-looking, and cheerful at evening parties. I used to see them fairly often. But they have grown old ungracefully. However, I must say that however ungraceful they are I don't really picture them as criminals. Certainly not Glen."

"I agree. He doesn't *look* as if he had enough enterprise to take up ghouling. Or enough imagination for necrophilia."

"It's true that he disliked his mother-in-law, but who doesn't? He had good reason. Dolly's favorite form of needlework was embroidering stories of his depravity. It was one of the things Merry and her mother had public quarrels about. One of those interesting human situations where the only thing that could make Merry pro-Glen was Dolly's being anti-Glen."

"An edifying household. Are the others in the family less dismal? Have you any arresting data on Gay—she's married to Pershing Custer, isn't she? Or Patience, whoever she is married to?"

"If by arresting you intend a pun, the answer is, no. I know Gay slightly and Persh hardly at all. I find her as uninteresting as Merry, but in a different way. She is in some ways the opposite of Merry. Instead of fancying herself sane and stable, she thinks of herself as deliciously madcap. If you know Persh, you know that they look to be rather mismated."

Russ had taken out a pencil and some four by six cards and started to write. Now he looked up. "Decidedly. I know Custer, but again slightly. Do you suppose he was known in his youth, in line with Ham Berger, as Frozen?"

"It would be apt."

"It would. I have rarely heard him utter more than a virile grunt. Have *they* a family?"

"A daughter, who must be about twenty. I have not seen her since infancy."

"And Patience? I don't even know whom she's married to."

"She married a foreigner. That is, I think he came from Colorado. I have never met him either. I believe there are several young children."

"It all sounds disappointingly routine and unsuspicious. Like half the families in town." He laid down his pencil. "But—" he looked up. "Perpend. I see a connection."

"I thought you would. An aerial connection."

"As you say. Persh runs the airport."

"He does. I remembered it when I was waiting for you."

"And runs it very badly, if the stories are true. A strong, silent type with no head for figures. He moved in a long time ago, after the war. He'd been a retired air force officer, and made a deal with the city. Of course, there are a lot of airports in the world."

"Still, it is a coincidence. And what is a good deal more of a coincidence is something else I remembered. Beaufort Berger is also an aviator. He spent some time a while back as a flight officer in the Navy. The story was that he was discharged dishonorably, but this may have been suggested by the fact that most people in town would like to have discharged his mother and grandmother dishonorably from *something,* and chose Beaufort as a surrogate victim. In any case, Beaufort is now working for his uncle as a pilot at the airport. Or—again, if gossip is to be credited—he is not actually working but merely employed. And I think someone said that Patience's husband works there too. It seems to be very much a family business."

"The coincidence becomes more and more remarkable." Russ was writing again. "So remarkable that I am tentatively prepared to presume that it is not a coincidence.

Body removed from its legal resting place by air. Grandson and sons-in-law of deceased fly planes. Presumptive proof, though not for a law court. And a motive eludes me. Especially not the obvious motive where an old woman is concerned, which is money. I can't see how any of the family pilots would profit by burying a matriarch already deceased in an oak forest. And in any event, these people are, I believe, all reasonably well off. The airport doesn't make much money, or didn't when I knew about its finances. But I take it there is no sign of actual penury."

"I should judge not. Merry likes to say—or rather, to shout, since she shouts everything she says—'Walt, we've never been rich, but I've always seen to it that my boys' —which means Glen and Beaufort—'have the best of everything. That's my job, and I'm proud to say I've always done it well.'"

Russ shuddered slightly. Professor Payne's voice had taken on a peculiar quality, at once stentorian and whining, that suggested a rarely exercised gift for mimicry. "Pending further information, then, we may suspend the question of money. And I can't imagine any other motive. We return to method. Do you think you could identify the plane if you saw it?"

"I don't know how many there are like it. I would recognize the general outlines, and the fact that it said Cherokee 180, and a long number beginning with 'N.' It was painted red and white. A monoplane."

"That's not exactly final," Russ said. "All light planes have registration numbers beginning with 'N.' There have been nothing but monoplanes made for the last twenty years or so, and thousands of them may well have been Cherokee 180s, for all I know. And no doubt many of them are red and white. Still, at an airport the size of Buchanan, the chances are you wouldn't find more than one that met those requirements. It might be a lead, although we'd have a rough time proving that any given person did or did not transport a body in it on the evening of July 18 from the aforesaid airport to a wheatfield belonging to . . ."

"I suppose it would be conclusive evidence of something, at any rate, if I were sure of the numbers. But I have no recollection of them beyond the 'N.' On the other hand"—Professor Payne's voice suddenly changed—"Richie might. I had forgotten Richie. He has a good memory. But he's disappeared."

"Disappeared?"

"He took my car while I was unearthing Dolly Sommers. I don't mind his taking it, but he oughtn't to be driving. It's really quite worrying. He'd only had a license a month at the time of the accident, and he hasn't driven since."

Russ stood up, and said with sudden professional briskness, "You should have mentioned this before, Walt. You should notify the police."

"There were other things on my mind. And I wouldn't want him pulled in," Professor Payne said. "Or anything else that would discourage his initiative. Up until now he's done nothing except when actually ordered to. It's better to have him doing something."

"It might be, if you knew *what* he was doing. He may be endangering the public. Under the circumstances, he is certainly endangering himself and your car."

Professor Payne considered this. "It is, of course, possible. But I should not want him followed, let alone arrested. If he is to act like a responsible adult, he mustn't be treated as an undependable child."

"I think we better get the police on it, nevertheless. I know the chief very well, and I'll tell him to make sure his men are discreet. What's the make, model, and registration, please?" He disappeared in the direction of the phone and returned a few minutes later.

"They'll send out a radio call and probably locate him in an hour or so. Unless he's in trouble, they'll just keep a tactful eye on him. The cops are not, as a group, wholly incapable of subtlety."

"As you are not incapable of decision." Professor Payne was not accustomed to his former student's displays of professional efficiency. "What decisive action will you take in connection with our other mystery?"

"I have already taken it," Russ said. "Total silence for the moment, pending cogitation and some private investigation. It's irregular, of course. But suppose we did call in Jim Fess. It would be all over town by lunchtime and on the front page of the *Courier-Bee* tomorrow. That would be like dropping eight wasps' nests in the middle of a crowded movie theater with locked doors. And it looks as if whatever offense *was* committed was committed within the jurisdiction of Buchanan City, not Van Buren County. It may be against the sanitary regulations or something out here to bury bodies on a private enterprise basis, but the major offense was taking, not burying the body. By the way, you didn't notice anything *except* the corpse in your treasure trove?"

"No, aside from the jewelry."

"It's interesting, that. Is it valuable, do you think?"

"I don't know. There was a diamond engagement ring

and several others, and a pearl necklace. Possibly more—I didn't notice. Dolly liked jewelry."

"So do most people. After we locate your wandering great-nephew, I'll stroll up the hill and have a look at the rings and other possible features of interest. When I have inspected the situation and drawn such conclusions as may occur to me, I'll take the shovel I will have carried up and decently cover over the remains. Perhaps dig a real grave and cover it to a greater depth than the original interment. I don't propose that it should be left there very long, but I think we should keep it as safe as possible."

Professor Payne, accustomed throughout a long life to appearing the most cold-blooded person in any group, was slightly taken aback. But he said, "The corpse is, after all, inanimate organic matter. It can do no harm to bury it a second time."

"You can't have too much of a good thing. Let's put it like this—if we have to put it at all, which God forfend: a body twice buried is twice blest."

Professor Payne smiled. "It dropped from heaven, certainly. But not as the gentle rain."

The telephone rang. Russ said, "That may be the cops with some news of the boy."

He was gone very briefly, and when he came back he was looking thoroughly baffled.

"They discovered his whereabouts in ten minutes. Do you know what he's doing?"

"No, of course I don't."

Russ scratched his head. "This is going to surprise you," he said.

CHAPTER III

Climb-out

The terminal building was set at the edge of a large parking lot, an indeterminate area of cracked asphalt and cinders enclosing an irregular circle of dusty weeds in front of the main entrance. An old automobile tire, painted yellow and also filled with weeds, stood in the center of the circle by way of decoration. There was a surprising number of cars parked randomly about.

The terminal was a small, one-story, flat roofed building of dirty stucco, overshadowed by a hangar and several large sheds. Over the door a shabby sign said, *BUCHANAN MUNICIPAL AIRPORT*. On the wall beside the front door a slightly newer sign said MIDWEST AIRWAYS FAST DAILY SERVICE TO CHICAGO, KANSAS CITY, AND ST. LOUIS. At the corner of the building, pointing toward the sheds, were two arrows. One said *Ladies* and the other, obscurely, *Link*. On the main door was a red plaque, the only one of the signs in good condition, which said COCA-COLA. In worse condition of all was a large board on a post near the ornamental yellow tire which read, in peeling letters, VAN BUREN COUNTY FLYING SERVICE INC. RENTALS. CHARTER FLIGHTS. INSTRUCTION. SIGHT-SEEING RIDES, $2.00 UP. Richie, studying it, was considering the final item of these offerings. "And how much Down?" he asked himself.

He had parked in front of the terminal and switched off the ignition. Now he was dully contemplating the sign. During much of the fifteen mile drive he had been breathless—but not, for the most part, from alarm. More often, from triumph. Habits half-formed in a driving school almost a year before had proved reliable. His memory, and certainly his reflexes, skipped safely back to before the accident. There had been little traffic over the country road, but by the time he had come to the end of it his confidence had been so far restored that he would have welcomed more.

The first few miles had been bad. He had at first doubted —and then only very gradually realized—that his leg would work. Weak, scarred, and misshapen, with an uncontrollable knee and the weight of the brace adding to the difficulty of maneuvering it, it still had responded to the instructions he hesitantly gave it. At first he had had to lift it and press it down with his hand, to regulate the gas. A few miles later he was working the accelerator with his foot without thinking about it.

This was the best thing that had happened to him since he had left the hospital. The refusal of his leg to obey orders had from the beginning filled him with rage and, more than the searing fatigue or the shambling limp, with grief. He had come to feel that the leg had stopped being part of him and had become an appendage, alien and inimical. At times he had had to curb an impulse to strike it with his fist. It forever reminded him of the weakness he feared.

But the weakness was not physical. Professor Payne had been largely correct in his diagnosis: Richie's despair came from having been misled, or, more precisely, from his feeling that he had been administered moral medicine suitable to children. Above everything else he was afraid of being turned back to childishness. He was not at all sure he could count on himself to avoid infantile behavior with each successive revelation of infirmity, each addition to the list of things he would not be able to do again. The list had looked like being endless, and he was certain now that it was permanent. He was prepared to face the limitations, but he was not sure he could face them without flinching.

But this instinctive fear of losing a manhood barely achieved was now, for the moment, forgotten. Everything was changing.

He had started out from the farm in a sort of trance, after a night spent in half-waking visions of airplanes. He had not previously taken much more than a passing interest in flying. But the plane over the terrace had detonated something in his mind, and the visit to the field had filled him with a powerful appetite of the electric, restless, unmanageable sort that he associated with sex. It was not immediately clear what consummation would release the passion that had come on him in the cabin of the Cherokee; but in the course of the night he had realized that flying a plane was something he had to do.

In the slightly eerie fantasies of the early morning he had lost sight of what had actually happened in the wheatfield the night before, just as he had later lost sight of both the morals and practicalities of appropriating an automobile and his uncle's money. But he had a perfectly reasonable plan in mind. He had reckoned that if he were able to drive to the airport, he would have proved himself competent enough to inquire whether it was at all plausible for him to try to fly. If the question was received, as he had cautiously prepared himself to expect, with a friendly, sober, pitying answer, that teenagers with bad legs were not acceptable as students, then at least he would have the cushioning consolation that he could successfully drive a car.

He was, in the darkest of his moods, never without realism, even a certain calculation. He planned that if he came home disappointed, he would fail to mention where he had gone with the car. So far as his Uncle Walt, or anybody else, went, he would simply have tested his ability to manage a car and won a small, bold, illicit triumph.

Sitting in the parked car, however, he looked about him with misgivings. The expanse of other cars reminded him that the ability to drive one was, after all, a very small accomplishment. The array of planes, distantly visible beyond the terminal, had an equally dispiriting effect, though of an opposite sort. They looked large, intricate, and powerful. A single one in a wheatfield had been wonderfully exhilarating, but in such numbers they belonged to the secret society of adults. Richie wished passionately to press his claims to full membership in the ritual-ridden lodge that ran the universe, if only so he could defy its sovereignty. But he was sometimes aware of over-reaching himself. Membership in the club was arranged, he recognized, in degrees. At the moment he was disposed to think of people who flew planes with the same modulated sense of equality with which the president of the Corn State Bank of Buchanan might have regarded the president of the Chase-Manhattan.

In an odd way the slovenly surroundings strengthened his doubts. The citizens of the Van Buren Flying Service

Inc., Richie considered, must be so deeply involved in celestial tasks that they could spare no time for their front yard.

Still, the airport was the gate to a magic kingdom. The obstacles might seem more formidable, but his state of mind was similar to that with which, in autumns past, he had approached the kick-off of a football game. He was nervous, tense, and determined. Disregarding butterflies in his stomach, he opened the door of the car with decision, pushed his bad leg out and, as he had been taught to do, stood upright with the help of one hand on the car door, heard the click as the knee joint of the brace locked, and set off across the asphalt with a reasonably exact likeness of an easy stride. He was breathing a little hard when he reached the door, but he had been walking better, he knew, than he had walked for eight months.

Inside he met with anticlimax. The room was empty. Not much more in the way of money, care or taste had gone into the decoration of the lobby than into the landscaping. There was torn linoleum on the floor, two broken wicker sofas, and an end table piled with dog-eared magazines. Full ashtrays and several vending machines purveying food and beverages, a large teletype machine, a counter with several filing cabinets and a cluttered desk behind it, a bulletin board, and an arrow marked *Men* completed the furnishings.

He realized as he looked around the empty room that he had half-imagined that there would be someone there to greet him—as if he were an expected guest.

"Hi," he called. "Is anybody around?"

There was no reply.

He resolutely stiffened his spine and followed the arrow

that said *Men.* When he came back, the lobby was still empty. He opened a door which led to an inner office and found it also vacant. He went on, opened another door, and found that it led to the field and a panorama of aircraft. But still there was no one.

He went back to the lobby, sat down, picked up from the table a magazine called *Today's Pilot,* and opened it, at random, to a full-page advertisement. It featured a photograph of a dial, much like those that had fascinated him in the Cherokee, here much enlarged and staring at him like a vast eye. The copy read ". . . another dynamic Navairco *first!* TRI-MATIC YAWL, ROLL AND PITCH ELIMINATOR. The Concept: 1. Basic stabilization; 2. TC 100 Turn Coordinator. EQUALS Turn Control, Attitude, and Trim Roll Functions to maintain straight and level flight with cushioned actuators. INCREASES IFR AND VFR PROFICIENCY."

He felt, as he looked at it, a shudder, at once of cold alarm and hot lust. But alarm prevailed. He started to leave, and thought better of it. He was suddenly very hungry and remembered he had had no breakfast. He postponed his departure to buy an Arctic Sandwich, formed of gelatinous ice cream between two chocolate wafers, and ate it standing in the middle of the lobby. He felt much better when he had finished it, and after a moment's thought he bought a second one.

He was finishing that when the front door was opened by a young woman. She glanced at him in passing as she entered, said "Hi," and went behind the counter to the disorderly desk, where she began to study the papers. Richie was considering how to approach her when she looked up and said, "If you're waiting for Midwest, they're going to be an hour or so late getting in. They called up a while ago, so I went down to the diner for some coffee. The stuff in that thing," she added confidentially, waving at a vending machine, "tastes like stewed mud."

She went back to the papers. She was, Richie thought, very attractive indeed. A woman of maybe twenty, twenty-one, he guessed, with very large, deep, dark eyes, and the kind of figure he especially liked, slender and yet well-developed, that had showed to its best advantage as she walked across the room in her very short dress. He was studying her with some calculation, about to speak, when she unexpectedly sprang to her feet and said, "My God, the unicom, I forgot the unicom," and switched on a radio on top of the filing case. The room was immediately filled with a loud confusion of mushy noises, none of them intelligible except for the words, ringing out with mystic, clarion distinctness above the babel: "Beech seven one papa our active is eight." Then, abruptly, there was total silence.

Richie walked to the counter, leaned one elbow on it, and spoke lazily in a voice that he thought was at once casual and maturely appealing, "What I want is to talk to someone about maybe taking some flying lessons." He sounded, he hoped, as if the flying lessons were a matter of less interest to him at the moment than she was. In fact, she and flying were blending into one indistinguishable excitement.

She glanced at him and then at the clock. "Well," she said, "the chief left early this morning on a trip, and Cheese hasn't come in." She had a quick, taut, rich voice, as if everything she said mattered intensely to her, and she said it with the same intimacy as she had spoken of the coffee and the unicom, as to a colleague of long-standing. "And Doc's still sick. Bud's up with Jack right now, but he's been gone for quite a while, so he'll probably be down soon." She swung her chair around to study a blackboard on the wall behind her. It was divided into squares, with obscure notations in chalk. "I don't think he's scheduled until after ten, so he might give you some dual when he gets down. Why not sit down and wait a while, if you have time."

"O.K." He was a little tentative, affected by the glib obscurities of her conversation. But the jargon, if it baffled him, also exhilarated him. It was the tongue of the magic kingdom. "O.K. I'll wait for a while. My name's Richie Payne."

"I'm Lisa," the girl said.

"Hi," he said.

"Hi." She smiled brilliantly, but there the conversation ended.

He waited uneasily. He tried *Today's Pilot* again and came to a feature headed "Accident File," with the boldface subhead: "*Careless Preflight.* Plane: Mooney Mustang. Pilot: Professional pilot, age 37; 6,540 hours, commercial license. Results: Plane destroyed; fatal injuries to pilot and three passengers." The text began, "The flight left Ozark Field, Pinkerton, Missouri, at 1641. Pilot contacted Jefferson FSS following take-off to activate flight plan . . ."

He gave it up. After a long wait, while Lisa typed, came the sound of a plane overhead, fading and then, a minute later, roaring on the runway just outside. Then silence. Lisa looked at the clock and said to Richie, "That's Norm, I guess. He's early this morning."

Norm appeared shortly through the door from the field.

He carried a briefcase but except for that he looked more as if he had come from a cornfield than a runway, and a tractor than a plane. He was middle-aged and looked like an ill-tempered farmer, bald, fat, and sunburned. He had an oddly intense expression however, as if he were perpetually aware of dangers to be fended off by a pose of lassitude.

"Hi, Norm," Lisa said.

"Boy," Norm said, "you almost didn't see me at all today. I thought I was never going to get off the ground this morning. Waited for half an hour on the taxiway between a one fifty and a Bonanza, and finally Ground Control said to the one fifty, 'Six six Juliet cleared for Romeo proceed cautiously, cleared for Quebec proceed cautiously, cleared for Papa proceed cautiously, cleared for Oscar proceed cautiously, hold in position at November and await clearance.'" He spoke in a fast falsetto, full of disdain. "He's really giving it like a machine gun, see, and this one fifty, probably he's some kid from the boondocks, doesn't move, doesn't even answer. So after a while Ground Control says, 'Six six Juliet do you read taxi instructions?' and after about two minutes this one fifty answers, 'Ground control, this is six six Juliet and I read your taxi instructions but I don't know what the hell they mean.' So then Ground Control gets mad and they have a fight. Jeez," Norm said, "I thought we'd be there all day." He turned to Richie. "I never been held up that long for take-off before, anywhere." Then he added to no one in particular, "Kind of bumpy under two thousand. Cheese got a student?"

"No. He isn't in yet. Bud's got Jack up. He ought to be down soon."

"I got to get into town. I got a big day lined up."

Lisa said nothing, and Norm did not move. Instead he stood leaning against the counter, studying first the blackboard, then the clock, then, with the same measure of mild interest, Richie. He considered him for a minute as he might have considered a billboard advertising some product which he had no intention of buying, and then he went to the coffee vending machine and bought a cup of coffee. He drank it slowly and said, "It gets worse every week, this stuff."

"Yes, it does," Lisa said. "You've been socked in in Chicago quite a while, haven't you?"

"It's been as thick as this coffee for a week. I never seen nothing like it. Stationary warm front. Nobody got off the ground at all except one crazy guy who hit the power lines and killed himself. That was Tuesday." He paused, and seemed to reflect on the peculiar reprehensibility of hitting power lines on Tuesday. "They said everyday it was going to be clear tomorrow. Until yesterday. Then they said the fog would stay another week. So last night it cleared up. CAVU this morning. The weather boys'd be O.K. if they was *always* wrong. The trouble is you can't count on them. Last March, once, they was right."

"Buchanan Unicom this is five four Lima what kind of wind have we got right now?" the radio said.

Lisa stood up, looking questioningly at Norm, who said, "Down the slot. About one zero zero I guess."

She picked up a microphone and said into it, "Five four Lima. This is Buchanan Unicom. The wind is one one zero at—" She put her hand on the microphone and grimaced questioningly at Norm.

"Oh, say six, eight."

"At seven," she continued crisply into the microphone. "It's shifted. Barometer is, let's see, two niner niner eight. They're using one one now."

"Be seeing you. Five four Lima," the radio said.

Richie had been listening carefully with the fascinated hope of learning.

"Bud?" Norm asked.

"Yes. He usually calls up when he's out in the morning. The wind tends to shift. It's hard to tell anything from the sock. They keep talking about relocating it."

"They better," Norm said. "It doesn't mean a thing, with that hill behind it. I've seen 'em trying to land from opposite ends at the same time. Jeez! *You ought to get a tet.*"

There was silence. Indeed, a state of suspended animation seemed suddenly to have intervened in strong contrast to Richie's rapid pulse. Lisa was motionless over her desk. Norm leaned on the counter. The unicom was silent.

After five minutes came the sound of another plane. Animation resumed. Norm pushed open the back door and looked out. "He's got the twin," he observed vacantly.

"Jack's working on his rating." Lisa, unlike Norm, showed interest in everything she said. "They'll be in in a minute." She turned to Richie as if she were giving him a present.

"The student must of landed it," Norm said. "Ballooned. Terrible." He closed the door and resumed his place at the counter. "I'm in a hell of hurry. I got to be getting on my way." But his pose suggested a well-trained watch dog loyally obeying orders to stay put.

Richie felt a new surge of excitement. He stood up,

partly in preparation for meeting Bud, partly in the belief that when he was on his feet people were less likely to notice that there was anything wrong with him.

Two men came in from the back door. One was a young Negro, the other a tall, very lean man with black hair in a crewcut and a narrow, deeply lined, expressive, sardonic face. He had narrow black eyes that moved as if he were surveying a hazardous world. Not a hostile one, like that suggested by Norm's fixed, blue-eyed stare, but one full of traps inadvertently laid by fools.

The young man said to the older one, "Coffee, Bud?"

"Sure, Jack, what the hell," Bud said. "I been thinking about how they make that stuff. They got their factory hooked up to all the dishwashers in the county. Then they dry out the dishwater and put it in vending machines mixed with warm mud and powdered chalk. And we pay a dime for it, right? But you build up immunity." He took the paper cup the Negro offered him, sipped it, and said out of one corner of his mouth, "How's things, Norm?"

"Busy as hell," Norm said, without moving. "I got a big day scheduled in town. Never been so busy. You know where Cheese is?"

"Who ever knows where Cheese is?" Bud said. Richie thought that Bud didn't like Norm much. Bud started to say something else, but Lisa cut him off in what looked like a tactful diversion.

"You're early," she said. "Earlier than usual. In spite of the one fifty."

"Tail wind," Norm said. "Hey, Bud, I was telling Lisa and this kid what happened when I was leaving. The traffic got piled up on the ramp and Ground Control couldn't handle it, and this one fifty . . ."

He retold the story of Six Six Juliet. At the end Bud said, "Yeah?"

"Yeah," Norm said. "I thought that would give you a kick."

So far they had disregarded Richie. Not, he thought, neglecting him, but treating him, as Lisa had, as though they had expected to find him there, as though he were always there. Another silence ensued. Norm, still leaning on the counter, and Jack, silently drinking coffee, were passive. But there was some slight indication of business activity on the part of Lisa and Bud, the one contemplating her desk, the other an open drawer of the filing cabinet. Richie, growing more tense each minute, thought that if he did anything to direct their interest to himself, he might be interrupting something important.

After several minutes Bud closed the file drawer without apparently having done anything except stare at its contents from a distance and sat down.

"Bumpy under two thousand," Norm said.

"Yeah. It's nice higher up, though," Bud answered.

Then Lisa said, "Bud, this guy here has been waiting for you to see if you can give him some dual this morning."

Bud glanced first at the blackboard, then at Richie, entirely unsurprised by either of them. "O.K.," he said. "I got some time. You want to go right now?"

"Sure." Richie's voice was a little thick.

"You done any flying?"

"No."

"Right. First lesson. Lisa, you got a log book for him?"

From a drawer in her desk she pulled out a small black

book, asked his name, wrote it on the page ends, and handed it to him. "Remind Bud to make the entry, when you get down."

Richie looked at it. On the cover, in gold letters, it said *Pilot's Flight Record and Logbook.* His heart beat faster with astonished pride. For a moment he held it in hands that he hoped were not noticeably trembling. Then, with all the control he could summon, he faced the hardest task of his life. He swallowed hard and said to Bud, "I better ask you first. You see, I got this bad leg, and I . . ."

He faltered. Bud, looking directly at him for the first time, had glanced down. He said, "You walked in here? Right?"

Richie managed a grin. "Yes, sir."

"They say, 'If you can walk up to the aircraft you can learn to fly it. If you can walk away from it, you *have* learned to fly it.' Right?"

"I can drive a car O.K." He knew this was unnecessary, but he could not stop himself from adding it.

"O.K. You walk, you drive. So you can fly. Right?"

Norm, without shifting position or looking up, said, "Kid, I got a brother left a leg in a reaper and binder when he was fourteen. He's been flying thirty years with a tin one. No problem."

Bud said, "So let's get under way. What did you say your name was?"

Richie heard them as if their voices had come from a long way off. He answered with sudden buoyancy, as if things would come easily now, as if he were swimming, floating, on the foam of seas that dissolved his uncertainties, and he followed Bud out the door.

They walked across an expanse of oil-stained concrete.

"The one-forty's on the other side of the ramp, there," Bud said. Then he stopped and yelled to a youth in a gas truck, "Hey, Earl, did you get the one-forty topped?"

"Yeah, Bud. It didn't take much."

"Right." He turned back to Richie. "Earl's our new line boy. Just starting. Like you."

Richie was aware of a slight feeling of envy of Earl. "What's a line boy?" he asked.

"He works on the line." Bud seemed surprised. As if Richie had said he had never tasted waffles.

"What's the line?"

Bud answered with a gesture toward the planes parked on the grass. Then, as they walked toward the one-forty, he casually asked, "What happened to your leg?" He made it sound as if he were inquiring about a bad bruise.

"Car smash. Last Thanksgiving."

"A great time to have it. How old are you, Richie?" He had apparently dismissed the leg.

"Sixteen. Seventeen month after next."

"Right. You married?"

Richie was impressed and flattered. He hesitated a moment before he answered, "No."

"If you're under twenty-one and unmarried, you'll have to get written permission from your parents when you apply for a license. Right? But you don't have to worry about it for a while."

"My parents are dead," Richie said. "But I got a guardian."

"He'll do," Bud said. "Here's the one-forty. It was out this morning so we don't need to preflight it. Next time I'll show you what you'd do if you were going to take it out cold. Right?"

"Right." They had approached a plane that looked to Richie very similar to the one in the field, and he saw on the fusilage the word Cherokee. But this one was painted blue and white instead of red and white. Bud leaned forward and opened the door. "O.K. You get in first. Take the left seat." He watched as Richie approached the plane. "It may be a little tough for you. Hard enough to get in and out even with two good legs." He put one hand under the boy's elbow to help him up. "Easiest way will be to crawl in. You'll get used to it, after a few times."

Richie had been dreading this, remembering the false starts the evening before. But with a small boost from Bud, he found himself quite easily installed in the seat, with his hands again fingering the wheel, staring at the instrument panel. And now the magic of yesterday reasserted itself, combined with almost unbearable excitement. The enormity of what was about to happen overcame him. It was unthinkable, unbelievable, terrifying, beautiful.

Bud swung himself in beside him and fastened the seat belt. Richie, to his intense embarrassment, was shaking. Bud pushed knobs, turned switches, and yelled to the world in general, "Clear." Then he leaned across Richie, pushed a button, and the engine started, coughing for an instant, and then roaring smoothly. "I'll get it off the ramp," Bud said. "Then we'll see how you make out taxiing it." His left hand on a knob before him, his right surprisingly lying in his lap, he neatly maneuvered it out from among the other planes onto a straight roadway of concrete. The plane halted.

"O.K., Richie," Bud said. "Put your right hand on the throttle. Here. Push it in, you get more power. Pull it out, you get less. Handle it easy. Right?"

"Right." He was breathless, but his voice and, more important, his right hand were under satisfactory control.

"Now. You steer with your feet. Hard to get used to after you've been driving a car. Keep your left hand off the wheel. You got to break the habit of steering with your hands, the sooner the better. Right? Push the left pedal, you turn left. Push the right pedal, you turn right. Right? O.K., give it a little power. See what happens."

Richie was very tense, far too excited to think about the muscular movement by which, with only small assistance from his hand, he lifted his right toe onto the pedal. Then he put his left toe in place, put his right hand on the throttle and the left on his thigh, and carefully gave it a little power. The plane, to his incredulous delight, moved smoothly forward.

"You want to taxi about the pace of a fast walk," Bud said. "Take it easy 'til you get with it. You need a little left pedal."

He gave it a little left pedal. The plane headed sharply left and he reflexively corrected its direction with his right toe. Bud had inconspicuously glanced down as he did so and then silently nodded.

They were, astoundingly, in the air.

"We'll get her up a couple of thousand feet, above this turbulence, and give you an idea of how she flies," Bud said. After a moment he pulled back his feet, took his hands off the wheel, lit a cigarette, folded his hands in his lap and said, "O.K., Richie. You see what happens?"

Nothing happened, and after a moment he was bold enough to say so.

"Nothing happens," Bud said. "So the plane is flying

itself. That's what it's made for, to fly. It *likes* flying. Right?" Bud put his hands and feet back on the controls.

"Right." The take-off had exhilarated him. But at the same time he had felt his hands and knees shaking. It was odd; he had no consciousness of fear.

"O.K. Now get your left hand back on the stick and your right one on the power and your feet on the rudders." Richie, noticing that the terms had changed since they left the ground, obeyed. "O.K. You push your stick forward, your nose goes down. So you pull your stick back, your nose goes up. Right?"

"Right."

"O.K. So you can do anything you want with it, but whatever you do you got to do it easy. Very, very easy. Right?"

"Right."

"So you want to make it fly straight and level, you don't do anything except make adjustments. Like keeping a car on the road. Right?"

"Right."

"O.K. Now look over your nose at the horizon, Richie. You see how far it is over your nose?"

"Right."

"Remember that. As long as it stays the same, then you're flying level. Look out at the horizon on each side. You see how far the horizon is above your wing tips?"

"Right."

"Remember that. As long as those distances stay the same, you're flying straight. So O.K., fly it straight and level for a while." He abandoned the controls again. "It's your airplane, Richie."

The pressure on the wheel and pedals slackened as Bud

let them go. Richie took them and felt the plane point downward toward the earth. He glanced at the nose, and seeing the spread between it and the horizon slowly widen, pulled back the stick. He pulled it back too hard; in an instant the horizon had disappeared under the nose, and he had to push forward again. But in a moment it was back to level flight. And Bud had not said anything.

He did not say anything now. Richie, glancing hastily from wing to wing to nose, manipulating his left hand, felt himself suddenly, exuberantly, alone with the plane. There was the steady roar of the engine, a presence rather than an accompaniment, the hard pounding presence of power and assurance. There was the undoubted but unbelievable fact that when he pushed forward with his left hand, the plane pointed earthward. He was in charge, not only of the plane, but more completely than ever before of himself, his universe and his destiny. He was lord of the skies. It was far, far better than he had imagined. His breath caught in his throat and then, to himself, he whispered, "Beautiful."

It went on for some time. Both of them were silent. The sky was clear and very blue, with snatches of cloud far above them. Beneath, when Richie snatched a glance, the land was spread flat, like a big gray-green map, it's landmarks suddenly transposed into ordered patterns. But it was not the earth but the sky and the engine and himself that fascinated him. He leaned back in his chair and felt the muscles in his arms and legs relax.

"O.K." Bud was brusque, as if rebuking them both for an overlong indulgence in idleness. "Try turning it. Remember, right stick lowers your right wing, right rudder turns your nose. Give it a little of each, and keep on holding the stick."

"Right." He followed directions and felt his muscles go taut again, his exaltation fade with the new concentration required.

"O.K. Now roll out. Give it some *left* stick, and some left rudder until your wings are level again. Right?"

"Right." He did it. Indeed overdid it. The left wing dipped and the plane started turning to the left. With a trace of embarrassment he felt the pressure on the wheel stiffen as Bud took it.

"O.K. Now, we'll try a one-eighty. You got a barn with a lake down there on your left. Right?"

"Right."

"O.K. Make a left turn. Easy, like you did before. You give it some left stick, and some left rudder just at first. Then hold it, until you've gone around the barn and are heading the other way. Right?"

"Right." Tensely he did it. It was interminable. At the end of what seemed minutes he saw with desperation that he was only halfway round. And something, he was not sure what, but something wrong and alarming, was happening to the plane. He was aware of a troubled suggestion of dizziness, and of queer feelings in his stomach.

"You're losing altitude," Bud said. "What do you do to regain altitude?"

Richie pulled back harder than he intended, and in the process inadvertently leveled the wings. Then he started to turn again, holding back this time to keep the nose up. And now the turn went faster. He was around the barn before he expected it. And this, along with the prodigious effort of concentration involved in doing several things at once, had made him more tense than ever and brought sweat to his forehead, so that his hair was wet against it. He wiped his hands across his eyes and then, watching the horizon, leveled the wings.

"You knew when to roll out. Good. Fly straight and level again for a while. Right?"

"Right." It was easy now. His tautness faded and was replaced not by a renewal of the incredible elation of a moment earlier but by a relaxing sense of facility. Competently he resumed his study of the horizon, lowering a left wing infinitesimally high and raising the nose that had infinitesimally lowered beneath the invisible line below the horizon.

"Try another right turn and remember to give it a little back pressure, so you won't lose altitude in your bank. Right?"

"Right." He swung capably into the right turn.

His feelings when he reached the ground were chiefly that it had been much longer than an hour and that he was exhausted. He climbed out of the plane after Bud with a leaden fatigue and stood limply watching him kick triangular blocks of wood under the nose wheel and tie ropes from rings in the ground to rings on the wings.

But the exhaustion was momentary. He wiped his forehead and then, as they started back to the terminal, he found the courage to ask, "How'd I do, sir?"

"My name's Bud." He looked at Richie in surprise. The question, if not improper, was evidently a strange one. He stopped walking, scratched the black crewcut, and said, "There've been worse students than you." He considered this. "In fact, a lot of them. You'll make a pilot."

As he started walking again toward the terminal he added casually, "And about that leg. It's not going to get in your way. Don't worry about it. Right?"

"Right."

In the terminal, nothing had changed except for the addition of another person. A worn-looking man, pale, with thin reddish hair, was staring bleakly out the window onto the parking lot. His bearing was gloomy and apprehensive, as if he had been recently bitten by a dog and had information that the same dog was again in the neighborhood. Jack was sitting on the wicker sofa, drinking a soft drink from the can. Lisa was at her desk, her beautiful eyes frowning at a pile of mimeographed forms. Norm was leaning on the counter. As they came in he tonelessly said, "Hi, Bud. Hi, Richie." And then he resumed his study of the clock, apparently expecting that, if he waited long enough, it might reveal something to his advantage.

"O.K., Richie," Bud said. "I'll enter this in your log book and you can pay me twenty-two bucks. When do you want the next one?"

Richie was still in the air, and he said a little dreamily, "Tomorrow?"

"O.K. Ten, right? You want to schedule it, Lisa?"

"O.K.," she said to Bud, "Cheese's here."

"I see him," Bud said. The red-haired man looked over his shoulder and then resumed his study of the parking lot.

"What's wrong, Cheese?" Bud asked. "I decided you weren't coming today. You love us so much you can't stay away? Or are they cleaning your cage?"

Cheese said ill-humoredly, without turning, "Mother's got to go over to Pierce City for lunch. So there was no time for anything else this morning. She's making me fly her. I don't know where the hell she is. She told me to meet her here half an hour ago. They got thunderstorms between here and Pierce. Probably tear the plane to pieces."

"Cheerful fellow," Bud said to Richie, waving toward Cheese. "We keep him around to brighten the place up. O.K." He took Richie's money. "See you in the morning, ace."

Lisa said to him, "How did it go, Richie?"

"O.K., I guess."

"You liked it?"

"Yeah." His code warned against showing enthusiasm, particularly to women. But Lisa was smiling at him with a misty intimacy that tended to confirm his first impression that she liked him almost as much as he liked her. "It was beautiful."

"I'm really glad," she said seriously. Then, "There was a guy here looking for you."

"Looking for me?"

"For one Richard Payne, driver of a '65 green Chevy with 6604-R plates."

"Who was he?" He was incredulous; having assumed the citizenship of a new country, he had forgotten that there was any other.

"The police. He came in a prowl car. Wanted to know if you were here."

Lisa was telling it straight, giving him information she thought he ought to know. But he saw that the others were looking at him with amusement. He was embarrassed and annoyed. His great-uncle must have called the police, treating him like a runaway child. He flushed.

"What were you doing, Richie?" Norm asked with

heavy, genial humor. "Stealing money to pay for your dual?"

They all laughed, except Lisa, who said, "He just wanted to know where you were and what you were doing. He wasn't about to pull you in."

Richie nodded silently. The exuberance had faded. He had been lord of the skies. Now he was re-entering the land where the fuzz kept track of lost teenagers.

"I told him you were flying," Lisa went on. "He laughed and said not to bother. He said, 'I guess that baby can take care of himself.' Then he left."

Richie looked at her with thanks. He felt better again. Better, conceivably, than he had ever felt. He laughed and strode easily to the door, out to the car. He started to get in when his eye caught the planes on the line, a sight that had seemed awesome an hour before. Now, instead, it was irresistible, and he walked slowly back around the terminal building for a last look at them before he left.

CHAPTER IV

Angle of Attack

"Excavation," Russ Mallery said, "is not usually thought of as setting off a chain reaction. But it works that way. Our unknown aviator dug last night. You and I dug this morning. I dug this afternoon. Your great-nephew perhaps will dig later, although so far today his movements have been in the opposite direction." He was unwontedly excited. Something had pleased him very much.

"Your digging this afternoon," Professor Payne said, "was, I take it, metaphorical. If so, it doesn't count. The aviator and I worked hard."

"Material in the morning, metaphorical in the afternoon; work is where you find the holes in your clothes. I worked hard, too, at both kinds of digging."

They were sitting on the terrace. A bare twenty-four hours had elapsed since the sound of an aircraft engine had first broken into the dismal tenor of the summer.

"I worked hard," Russ repeated, "but I am tortured by the lack of official standing. I wished I could turn back my lapel, flash the silver badge of cowardice, ask embarrassing questions, and demand compliance and relevance from witnesses. Instead I am obliged to accept the role of accessory after the fact."

"Are you indeed? And I?" Professor Payne spoke dryly.

"Am I not the fact itself? Am I not in a position, to paraphrase Louis XIV, where *Le fait, c'est moi?* An uncomfortable position, especially when I am placed in it by my legal adviser. Against my better judgment." He did not look as if it were against his better judgment. He looked as if he were enjoying himself. "You assured me that my conduct was not merely innocent but a civic duty. Have you now discovered—or merely decided—that we are accessories after the fact?"

"I speak as I dig—metaphorically. Contrary to lay opinion, the status of accessory after the fact is very rare in law, and in any case the fact after which I am an accessory doesn't involve you at all. But something I have done may conceivably be a felony. It is a moot question. Being moot, it better remain mute as well. By the way, I assume your great-nephew got back safely."

"He did, and apologized politely for stealing my car and my money. I agreed not to press charges. The pardoned criminal ate a hearty lunch, followed by repose, swimming, and an even heartier dinner. He is at the moment on his pad studying volume *Aar* to *Bep* of the encyclopedia."

"Then all is well."

"Not entirely. There are problems. First of all the matter of what I should tell his legal guardians. I am sure they would disapprove—not on grounds of any reasonable objection but from a feeling, common among parents, that anything Richie wants to do must be bad for him. There is also the question of finance."

"Finance?"

"Today's aeronautical venture was paid for by petty larceny. From now on, more regular means of financing must be found. He made inquiries. At best, this will cost somebody seven hundred dollars. Howard left a fair amount, but unfortunately, Jeff controls his inheritance absolutely, and Jeff is likely to react to a request for funds for flying lessons in the same spirit as he would to a suggestion that he give the boy a pot allowance. Richie speaks of getting a job to pay for it, and he may have to."

"That's a change, isn't it?"

"Yes indeed. And he is, God knows, no longer uncommunicative. I have been bored to the point of madness with details. Precisely how he went about turning his plane a hundred and eighty degrees to the left. *And* to the right. One obsession has been replaced by another." Professor Payne seemed irritated rather than worried by this. "Another thing. One would suppose that a red-blooded American boy would take an interest in corpses *qua* corpses, especially when dug up by his great-uncle a few hundred yards from home. But his chief interest in the account of my morning's discovery seems to lie in the fact that he, like the gravedigger, flies a Cherokee."

"Still," Russ observed, "his involvement in Buchanan Municipal Airport is, from our point of view, fortunate. We need an informer. And I have certain evidence in my possession which makes the matter one of high importance. I think we must summon him to hear testimony, if we can prize him loose from *Aar-Bep*. We must inform him that *his* obsession is indispensable to gratifying ours."

Professor Payne hesitated. "Do you really think it is wise to have him take part? Or likely to be useful? I am reasonably confident of his discretion, but his judgment is not, at the moment, detached."

"Is ours?"

"Relatively. Richie acts as if he had just come back from

a trip up Mount Olympus. He spent an hour in the care of a god named Bud." Russ looked up quickly. "Bud Hermes. There is also a girl, a receptionist I gather, named Lisa—Lisa Artemis." Russ gave him a sharp glance, which he ignored. "A detective is likely to be handicapped if the suspects are deities."

"Nevertheless," said Russ, "I think we better have him."

"Perhaps you are right. It would be an impertinence to exclude him."

Professor Payne rose, and presently returned with Richie, who was carrying *Aar-Bep* and a can of Coke.

Russ greeted him with gravity. "We need you. Walt has told you we are conducting what might optimistically be called a private investigation of recent events in the wheatfield?"

"Right." He looked more interested than Professor Payne's remarks had led Russ to expect. In fact, he seemed positively eager to take part in the discussion.

"You can help us in your capacity as airman."

Richie was startled. "So, I've had one whole lesson."

"I think you have thereby become an airman, legally speaking, in the eyes of the Federal Aviation Agency. It's not really your technical skill we need, however. But unless everything I've heard is misleading, it looks as if we are going to have to take an interest in the airport scene. In fact"—he exhaled a cloud of smoke—"I think the Death Plane came from Buchanan Municipal and probably went back there."

Richie had sat down. "You sure about that?"

"It looks that way. There's no other airport for . . ."

"I don't mean that. I mean about my being an . . ."

"An airman? Yes, I am. You are."

"Right." Richie sank back happily and gave Russ his flattering attention.

"As I was telling Walt, I spent the day exploring the circumstances attending Mrs. Sommers' death and burial. Turning stones as I happened upon them in the course of ordinary business. Turning *stones*," he repeated with emphasis, "both literal and figurative. Some of them were quite surprising stones. To take the least surprising first, I interrogated my secretary, who knows everything. My wife, who knows most things. A mildly paranoid cop I happen to know, named Big Frank, who stopped me on his beat to talk about the problem of beer cans. He believes that the population of Buchanan devotes its early morning hours to throwing beer cans at him from speeding cars while he is patrolling Washington Street between Second and Sixth. I have also talked to Hal Daniels, a city hall habitué who is a client of mine. He came to me with some provocative tales of goings-on in the Prothonotary's office." He was counting them off on his fingers. "And with an eminent professional man of the city, whom we'll get to in a minute.

"Except for the professional man, I met them all in the normal course of the day's work and brought up the death of Dolly Sommers casual-like. The most significant conclusion I draw from my findings is that the dog did not bark in the night."

"They showed no interest?" Professor Payne asked.

Russ shook his head. "Among my interviewees are some of the most gifted gossip-mongers in Greater Buchanan, the Heart of the Fast-Growing Tri-County Area, and I'm pretty sure that none of them has heard anything gossip-worthy about Dolly's death and supposed cremation. But they all knew something about her and her family. A surprising lot, in some cases. Most of it hearsay. In a city of fifty thousand, most people know *something* about *some* other people, but the Sommers family enjoys a special notoriety. However, as far as I can see, none of it was at all helpful in explaining the abduction of the mortal remains. Incidentally, I did some quick legal research on the problem of removing an embalmed body from a casket for private burial. It will take more time than I had to get the full picture. There's a lot about who has a right to embalm a corpse, and so on, but the law is complicated, as it always is; obscure, as it frequently is; and archaic, as it sometimes is.

"So I'm working in a legal fog. But I have collected a lot of facts that must bear on the situation, though I've no idea how."

He took from his pocket a substantial pack of filing cards, riffled through them, and began methodically to sort them. He put one in his teeth and, continuing his sorting, said a little thickly, "You know some of this, Walt, but I'll give a quick runover for Richie. Dolly Sommers was seventy-seven. She had cancer of the stomach. She was operated on two and a half years ago, but it recurred, and they told the family almost a year ago that there was no hope. There really seems to be no question at all about this. She herself knew it from the beginning and talked about it to everyone. She died attended by nurses in her own apartment in The Harrison, on North Harrison where she'd lived for ten years, since Patience got married. She paid, if it's any interest, a hundred and sixty-five for a comfortable, not deluxe, apartment. She'd been a widow for thirty-one years. Except for her daughters, her only near living relative is her sister Agnes Creston, who is eight years younger. Also a widow. Her husband, Moses Creston, was a farmer over near Monroe Court House. They had no children. Creston's been dead twenty years. Agnes came and lived for a while with Dolly, but, predictably, that didn't work out, and she went traveling. She finally, as you know, settled in Paris, where she's had an apartment for the last ten years. Never came back, but various citizens have dropped in on her there and found her quite changed from Buchanan days." He sorted the cards again. "It is reported that she calls herself Mme. Agnes Bates-Creston. She is alleged to tell visitors that she cannot tolerate the thought of submitting herself to the barbarism of American ways and hence will not come to visit her Loved Ones. So, my secretary says, her aunt says her sister-in-law said after a trip abroad in 1963.

"The money for all this came from Harold J. Bates, the father of Dolly and Agnes. He was a local boy but he set out to make his fortune in Chicago in the eighteen-eighties, and made it. On hog feed. Old Harold devised a formula for mixing glue with sawdust or something that doubled the normal weight of boars. This was very big around the turn of the century. He retired early and devoted his life to work in the fundamentalist cause. He was a deep-water Baptist and a fanatical foe of Darwin. He hit the anti-evolutionary lecture circuit and produced his little daughters on the platform, shouting hoarsely to the audience, 'Do you believe that these lovely, golden-haired, innocent girls are descended from baboons?' Very effective oratorical device, I am told, but perhaps better for the Cause than for the little girls. He was called to continue his ministry in higher spheres many years ago, when Agnes and Dolly were young matrons. Nobody knows how much he left, but it was quite a lot. Glen Berger has been handling business affairs for both sisters. That was the ostensible reason he retired from the Corn State Bank—he was too busy with his mother-in-law's money to bother with anyone else's.

"So much for Dolly. Now as to the girls. First, Merry Berger. Again, nothing strikingly at variance with Walt's judgment. Opinions differ. Women claim to admire her; men mostly don't. My wife thinks she's efficient and courageous and has 'put up with a lot without being got down,' as she tersely put it. Big Frank, on the other hand, says she's a loud-mouthed bitch who probably beats her husband. There's a corresponding variety in Glen's reputation, although in his case there is agreement on certain points." He sorted a number of cards, evidently putting them in alphabetical order. "It is unanimously affirmed that Ham Berger is: *a.* a notable failure on the golf course; *b.* a failure; *c.* a rather squalid amateur Don Juan; *d.* a bore. Women think he's a dismal monster. At least wives do. Men seem to think he's kind of a nice guy, and a victim."

He broke off to light a cigarette and looked, a little uncertainly, at Richie over the flame of his lighter. The boy was listening carefully but otherwise inscrutable. "What the Bergers seem to live off of—officially, as it were—is commissions Dolly paid him for running her affairs. Dolly owned the house the Bergers live in, and they paid her rent for it. What they have really been living off of, I rather think, was hand-outs from Dolly.

"Next, Beaufort Berger. It turns out that everyone except his parents call him Cheese, which is logical enough."

Richie looked up, started to speak, and thought better of it. "He is twenty-nine. He wandered off from the university to become a navy pilot, and he wandered off from the navy into total obscurity for a year or so. His parents said they had no knowledge of his whereabouts in that period, but it was rumored that he was in trouble of some sort. Then he wandered back to Buchanan a couple of years ago. His uncle Persh gave him a job at the airport, but he doesn't do much work. He is reported to be a good pilot but in all other respects resembles his father. 'A chip off the old blockhead,' to quote Hal Daniels, who views the family unfavorably. He is also"—Russ flipped another card—"reported to be afflicted with sullenness and incurable pessimism."

"Right," Richie said. "He is."

The other two turned to him with interest. "You met him this morning?" Russ asked.

"Right."

"Good. Accounts tally. Anyway, he's back in the parental fold, which in this case is Dolly's former residence, a big, nineteen-twenties house on Harding Road. But Cheese is rarely in evidence. He keeps out of his parents' way, or tries to. It is thought that he must spend most of his time at the airport—'to keep away from his mother.' But he doesn't usually succeed."

"Right," Richie said. "He said today he had to fly his mother to Pierce City for lunch or something."

He spoke like a board member making a helpful contribution to high level discussion.

"Good," Russ said again. "You seem to have learned as much in an hour as I did in an afternoon. The rest of the family invites less comment; people don't seem to take sides about the Custers and Ramseys. But certain observations recurred among my sources. All of them live well, but none of them is notably prosperous. And Persh and Bud Ramsey, who is Patience's husband, apparently depend entirely on the flying business."

Richie sat up straight. He looked startled and disturbed. Professor Payne said, "Bud is Patience's husband?"

"Yes. I'll come to them in a minute. First the Custers. Persh, as we know, is founder and president of the Van Buren County Flying Service Inc.—what is known in the trade as a Fixed Base Operator. I know something about this part through city hall. The city bought the old airport after World War II, when Custer was looking for a job, and as a result of family influence, the two came together. It was a sort of concession. The city people had dreams that Buchanan might become the air crossroads of the nation, but that hasn't worked out. There were never any big airlines that cared to serve Buchanan—as you know, there's only Midwest's one flight each way daily to Chicago, Kansas City, and St. Louis. Persh's operation is quite independent of this. Hal has been in on some of the negotiations. He says many fixed base operations are marginal, and Persh has not shown notable enterprise in building his up. Hal says that pilots, like fish and birds, tend to operate awkwardly on the ground . . ." He broke off again and glanced doubtfully, at Richie, but he was smiling as if the remark had pleased him. "Indifferent businessmen. The company is not affluent."

"In short, nobody connected with the airport business is exactly rich?" Professor Payne asked.

"No," Russ said.

"It checks out," Richie said judiciously. "Things look

kind of poor out there. Like they were waiting for next Christmas to pay for a paint job."

"There seems to be nothing particularly interesting about the Custers," Russ went on, "except perhaps their daughter. They have a daughter named Lisa."

Richie looked up and then, quickly, down. He had grown progressively more attentive as Russ's report had approached the airport. Now he transparently displayed intense interest and an effort to conceal it.

"Lisa is a very good-looking girl of twenty. But she's packed a certain amount of adventure into a short life. She went East to college when she was seventeen, ran away and got married to a sophomore in the middle of her first year, was abandoned by the husband, a character named Burton Peel, and thereafter came home and got a divorce. She works as receptionist at the airport. Hal told me all this. He says Lisa is the brains of the outfit. Has more practical sense than all of the men in the business put together."

"Right," Richie said.

He said it with so much feeling that Russ went on rather hurriedly. "There remain the Ramseys, Patience and Bud, who are both under forty. They live in a ranch house out in Eisenhower Crest. According to my wife, who works with her in the second grade PTA, she is 'the better type of blonde,' which I take it is high praise. Bud is a professional pilot and has been since youth. He came here from Denver about twelve years ago when he answered a want-ad for a pilot that Persh had put in one of the trade magazines. He stayed on and married the boss's sister-in-law. He's chief pilot now, and owns part of the business. He gets a salary too, but Hal says it's not huge. He is reported"—Russ gave Richie a sidewise, questioning look—"to be a good pilot and a good guy."

"That's true," Richie said, with feeling undiminished.

"You get the message, I take it: all these people seem to be substantial citizens, but none of them has much in the way of visible substance. From which we must conclude that the old lady had been contributing largely. This I find surprising, after what I've heard about her character."

Professor Payne considered. "I'm not sure about that. She was a sour-minded egoist who quarrelled with her daughters. But she was preoccupied with appearances. It would have been a terrible humiliation for her to know that her grandchildren couldn't boast of having color TV in every bathroom. She was frugal herself, not to say stingy, but I think she might well have paid to indulge the sin of family pride."

"In which case," Russ said, "you'd think they'd have every interest in cherishing her. And if they couldn't keep her alive—" He broke off, puzzled. "Well, to move ahead, I dropped in at the funeral home of my old college chum, Stanley Brill. Smooth and soothing, he asked if I was anticipating the loss of a loved one. I like Stan, but he gives the impression that he has been practicing the art of embalming on himself.

"I told him, no, but that I have always had a broad, cultural interest in cremation. I'm afraid he didn't altogether believe me. But he did his best, or at least tried to give the impression that he was doing his best, to be informative. He is inscrutable, partly because he uses pancake make-up. Even as a freshman he had a terrible skin problem. He also wears tinted glasses and has the kind of false teeth that hold the lips rigid with just a hint of a smile. So it's hard to tell what's going on in his mind.

"To sum up his account: Corpses are normally brought to his shop as soon as the certifying physician permits them to leave the death bed. They undergo extensive chemical operations, followed by a beauty-shop phase. This usually takes a day or so, unless, as Stanley said, there are 'special problems.'

"We now come to what are obviously the crucial data. Cremation usually takes place *after* the funeral, unless the remains have to be shipped somewhere. He was evasive about this, but he insisted practice varied sometimes one way, sometimes another. If the cremation is to be done between the end of the evening performance and the matinee, as it were, it is done in the morning. When the viewers have left, an attendant pushes the casket, which is on a wheeled conveyance like a large tea-table, out of the Viewing Parlor, into something called the Waiting Hall. There the casket is closed. Since the furnace is shut down at the end of each working day when the furnace-man goes home, the remains awaiting incineration are left in the Waiting Hall until nine-thirty the next morning. The furnace-man then stokes up his furnace, which is actually something like a large electric kiln. When it is hot enough, he introduces the coffin onto a moving belt which runs it into the kiln, and it is consumed by intense heat. When the moving belt comes out the other end, there's nothing left of the coffin except feathery ash, which is placed in the small bronze casserole and then in a black box and taken to the church."

"Why don't they save the coffin and use it over?" Richie

asked. He seemed as interested in this phase of Russ's report as the earlier one.

"That isn't the creed of Stanley Brill. He's like an automobile dealer. He's interested in selling new coffins, not used ones. The coffin-makers are his allies; he wouldn't want to damage their business by flooding the market with second-hand coffins. And I must say," Russ went on thoughtfully, "much as I despise all the sentiments considered appropriate in this profession, I have a creepy feeling that I'd rather not be laid out in a coffin that previously belonged to somebody else."

"Does the furnace-man look into the coffin before he consigns it to the kiln?" Professor Payne asked.

"No. I specifically asked that."

Professor Payne tapped the arm of his chair with a finger. "How tightly locked up is this Waiting Hall during the night?"

"That's the question that was tormenting me. But I couldn't think of a way to ask without making Stan even more suspicious than he was. But I looked. I requested a conducted tour of the premises. The doors, both interior and exterior, are substantial. I assume they are locked after business hours. The windows in the Waiting Hall, giving on to the parking lot in back of the Funeral Home, are just ordinary windows, with double-hung sashes. The catches were all locked when I saw them, and since the place is powerfully air-conditioned I imagine they stay locked."

"Still, windows can be jimmied open. Or a pane broken and then replaced. The Waiting Hall *must* have been entered somehow. Between ten-thirty or so and daybreak the next morning." Professor Payne appeared a little annoyed by Russ's determination to present him with an impenetrably sealed room.

"Unless, of course, it was an inside job."

Professor Payne replied with skepticism. "You think Stanley Brill stole his own handiwork?"

"I don't know. There's something peculiar about Stanley."

"Of course there is. Any professional mortician must be peculiar, from the point of view of non-morticians anyway. But body-*snatching* is the very misdeed one does not expect of someone whose business is body-catching. Where would be the point of it? And I can think of several objections. For one thing, Stanley is not an aviator, surely. And I really don't see how he could stroll up to the airport and say he wanted to secure the services of a pilot to fly a freshly embalmed corpse out to the country and bury it in a handy forest."

"There is, of course, that objection. But when I spoke of peculiarity, I meant his position."

"His position? In relation to Dolly Sommers?" Professor Payne found this surprising.

"Exactly. You see, I didn't mention Mrs. Sommers to him at all. But at the end, Stanley was nervous. He thought something must have happened on the premises to attract my professional interest. I suppose—" Russ leaned back and lazily lit a cigarette. "I suppose every man has a guts quotient, which he expends in different ways. I couldn't work as an embalmer. As a matter of fact, I'd be too scared to fly a plane too." He looked seriously at Richie. "But I could maintain my composure better than Stanley did if somebody came around and started asking questions about how I did my job. Anyway, Stanley lost his presence of mind to the point of saying, 'If you think there was anything funny about the Last Services for Dolly Sommers, Russ, you're dead wrong.'"

"Hey," Richie said.

"It's not as if it was the only corpse he's dealt with in the last few days," Russ said. "There were a couple of other burials and at least one other cremation. I looked it up in the *Courier-Bee.* So he must have had Dolly on his mind—very much on his mind."

"What did you say when he said it?" Professor Payne asked.

"I feigned a look of utter astonishment and said, 'Did you think it was *Dolly Sommers'* funeral I was interested in?'"

"I have no hesitation," Professor Payne elaborately folded his hands in his lap, "in pronouncing you a credit to my career as a molder of men. What the hell did he answer to that?"

"He said, 'Oh.'"

"Disappointing. But natural."

"So *I* said, 'Stan, old man, what made you think I thought there might be something funny about Dolly Sommers' funeral? Are you having some kind of problem? I ask it as a friend and an attorney, anxious to help you, Stan.' He laughed nervously and said that he must have misunderstood something I said, but I pushed him and asked, 'Was somebody else around asking about Dolly Sommers' funeral, Stan? Or what makes you worry about it?' He just kept shaking his head. I think I convinced him that it wasn't Dolly I was interested in, but he was too scared to ask what I *was* interested in. He's up to something."

Richie said thoughtfully, "In his business you could be up to anything. You know, like he's got the perfect scene for a murder ring. Like cremating three stiffs to a box."

They considered this. "The situation appears to be the reverse of that," Professor Payne said. "Like cremating no stiffs to a box."

"A situation I suspect that Stanley may be aware of," Russ said.

"That won't work," Richie said. "So suppose he did take the old lady out to make room for some other stiff? Like one he smashed late Monday night. He might have a murder gang going. He smashes somebody every Monday and takes their wallet and puts them in a legitimate box and steals the real stiff. Maybe Van Buren County is full of real stiffs under piles of leaves. Or maybe he normally puts two in one box, but the old lady's box was too small. Or like that."

"You show remarkable prescience. As I shall reveal shortly. But there are some difficulties." Russ was seriously interested. He certainly did not dismiss Richie's hypothesis out of hand. "The most considerable difficulty is that there haven't been that many people disappearing. In fact, nobody's disappeared."

"So he's bringing them in from Chicago. Or anywhere. All over the place. Like he's running a central stiff disposal depot. He may have corpse pipe-lines all over the country. Advertises in porno magazines: 'Unwanted bodies? Let us take them. Parcel pick-up provided.'"

Richie was getting a good deal of satisfaction from this, and it occurred to Professor Payne that it had perhaps been a mistake after all to bring him into their counsels. A boy in his position might very possibly be led astray by his and Russ's ways of approaching death, embalming and cremation. Richie's enjoyment of his theory suggested a degree of enthusiasm for the subject that might be described as morbid. But on consideration, he relaxed. A show of toughness in such matters was, at that age, the indispensable condition of adulthood. The first thing boys learned to enjoy about their own minds was the power to use them for butchering sacred cows. Properly considered, Richie's rather grisly imaginative processes were nothing more than an unreflective protest against sham sentiment. And—Professor Payne paused here with a sense of mild shock—the same could be said of his and Russ Mallery's. *They* had no claim to object to morbid flippancies on grounds of its unwholesome immaturity.

"In a way, it fits, personality-wise." Russ was also enjoyably dallying with the idea of a nation-wide corpse disposal service. "Stan is quite capable of something like that, I think. For kicks as well as money, you know. I suspect that he's frightened by live people and works it off by manipulating dead ones. But the trouble is"—he scratched his head—"the operating expenses would be very high per transaction."

"Right." Richie accepted the objection good-humoredly. "So it doesn't have to be bodies. Anything. He'd be real well-fixed to run a *general* disposal service, wouldn't he? 'Send me your incriminating documents for cremation. Lowest prices.'"

"People are capable of disposing of most kinds of incriminating evidence by themselves. They'd rather not get mixed up with third parties. Can you think of anything that you'd require Stanley's professional services to get rid of *except* a dead body?"

"Counterfeit bills that the feds were on to? A trunkful of pot?"

"Perhaps. But then we almost have to give up the idea of a regular business and come back to an isolated act. What could Stan have wanted to get rid of, for himself or on commission, so badly that he'd pull out Mrs. Sommers' body and hire a pilot to go bury it? And why a pilot? Why not a car?"

"Do we know for certain that Stanley Brill is not a pilot? Or, what is more likely, that he is not intimately connected with someone who is?" Professor Payne asked.

"Hypotheses are always dangerous, and I try to avoid them," Russ sententiously began, "but let us suppose Stanley Brill, perhaps as part of a regular professional side-line, has something to dispose of, something that must be immediately and utterly destroyed. Counterfeits or pot or records revealing embezzlement of public funds by the Bishop of Buchanan, or what-not. He calls up a pilot he knows, over whom he has some powerful hold, and says 'Stop by with your car at the back of the Waiting Hall at four A.M. and I'll have some goods for you.' But it does seem a pretty striking coincidence. Furthermore, knowing Stanley, I can't guess what hold he could have over anybody. And there's a complication. Someone, we believe, was moved by a need to destroy something. They were also moved by a need to preserve something. Do you happen to have any guns here?"

Both his listeners were startled by this apparent change of subject. But Professor Payne responded emphatically, "No. I dislike guns."

"Could you use a revolver if you had one?"

"No." His emphasis was even greater.

"I could," Richie said hopefully.

Professor Payne turned to him sternly. "No doubt you could. But while you're here, you won't. What do you mean by this, Russ? Do you think that a person or persons unknown are going to change their minds and decide it would be better to have Dolly cremated after all? Or that perhaps the whole arrangement was temporary, that she was left here while some other body was keeping her place —cold?"

"No, I don't, although it's possible. What I do think is that the gravedigger might come back again to recover some property."

Professor Payne started. "The rings and so on? You really think so?"

"Something more." With the furtive melodrama of a movie thief producing the Take for his colleagues, Russ opened his briefcase and brought out a handful of glittering gold. Rings, earrings, necklace—a very substantial token of buried treasure between his fingers. "These are what Dolly Sommers was buried in. I thought we better put this stuff in a safe place. Tomorrow I'm going to see a jeweler, a discreet man I know over in Jackson Rapids."

His eyes were gleaming, and so were Richie's. He held out his hands silently, and Russ put the jewelry into them. The boy studied them. "You think this airborne cat will remember he forgot and come back for them."

"I doubt if he forgot. I doubt if he was much interested in these. I may be wrong. My discreet friend in Jackson Rapids will tell me if I am. What I think he will come back for is something he didn't forget." He paused pregnantly. "There are matters of more magnitude involved. My afternoon's investigations were devoted mainly to an attempt to find out something about them. I failed. But I think that what is at stake is large enough so that the villain will certainly return, and will be armed when he does. If you were, too, you might be in a position not only to defend yourselves but to catch him." He tapped his left armpit portentously. "I carry a gun." He said it with pride and added, nostalgically, "I used it once, when I was sheriff. And even a simple lawyer meets strange people, sometimes."

Richie said, "Uncle Walt, I . . ."

"No."

Richie settled back. "O.K., O.K."

"And what are these matters of magnitude?" Professor Payne demanded.

Russ, having achieved an atmosphere of climax, spoke offhandedly. "In the course of my researches under your oak trees this morning, I undertook, as promised, to provide a more suitable grave for the deceased. In the course of excavation I found, under the body—this."

Again he reached in his briefcase and brought out a small canister. It looked like a tin for baking powder. He unscrewed the top, took out some absorbent cotton, and then a small cloth bag which he opened, rolling the contents onto the palm of his hand. There were six small blue pebbles. "I would, I think, be justified in saying, '*Eureka.*' "

Richie looked at them and whistled.

Professor Payne said calmly, "They would appear to be star sapphires."

"They certainly look like star sapphires, and big ones. The man in Jackson Rapids will know, but considering where I found them, it's unlikely that they're paste." Russ replaced them in the bag. "If they are real, they are worth quite a lot. Perhaps fifty or sixty thousand dollars. My wife wanted a star sapphire ring once. I priced them. She is still wanting one."

"It is curious," Professor Payne observed, unstirred by the dollar signs, "that we have been considering what the culprit might have been trying to get rid of. Now, as you said a moment ago, we are obliged to consider what he wanted to preserve. The two problems seem mutually exclusive."

"Maybe just separate," Richie said. "Maybe Brill works two businesses at the same time, burning up some things, keeping other things."

"It is possible that these stones belong to Dolly," Professor Payne said. "Or, now, to the estate. Elderly women sometimes like to keep tangible assets at hand. Like gold coins in a mattress. One heir might be trying to appropriate them, steal them, in effect, from the others. If, say, Glen Berger knew his mother-in-law had them, and nobody else did . . . It is, I admit, an obvious rather than an illuminating hypothesis. But this surely puts a different light on *our* position. Stealing a corpse is unpleasant, but in itself it doesn't do anybody any damage. A corpse is not exactly stolen *from* anyone. Money is." Professor Payne was at once cynical and sincere.

"The matter is one of degree. A corpse, like its worldly belongings, is the property of the heirs."

"In any case, we are compounding a much larger felony if we conceal this from the authorities. And from a moral point of view, a much less defensible one. Do you still suggest that we should pursue a—private investigation?"

"Temporarily." Russ was much pleased with himself

and was correspondingly authoritative. "I think the moral issue is irrelevant to our concerns; we will, of course, in due time restore the sapphires to whoever owns them. I think we have a better chance of doing it than Jim Fess would. The thief is bound to come back; that is the most important thing we have learned. He might leave a body to rot, and he might even disregard the rings and necklace and so on. He is not going to leave fifty thousand dollars permanently buried. And there is a chance you will know it when he does come back. That is why I suggest a gun. We are not," he concluded frowning, "playing for peanuts."

"You suggest, in short, that we leave the body as bait, while keeping the oak trees under surveillance?"

"Something of that sort. Of course, nobody can *patrol* the oak trees. Jim Fess couldn't station a deputy there, any more than we can. And there is no reason to think the thief will necessarily come by air the second time. I can't imagine why he did the first time, as a matter of fact. But if he does, you'll know it. I think I can get some leads. I may have some already. In the interests of justice I think we should hold off for a few days. We are much better placed to see that justice is done than Jim Fess is. By circumstance and by IQ. Do you agree?"

Professor Payne considered. "I agree." He looked at Richie, who nodded.

They were silent for a moment, contemplating justice. But all their expressions suggested conspirators, conspirators inspired by cheerful hunger and lust, rather than judges. After a moment, Professor Payne said, with the appearance of a man attempting against odds to be reasonable, "I take it that by circumstance you mean, among other things, that you can privately exploit your own contacts in a way that Jim Fess cannot. Do you think that your contacts include people who are really likely to be helpful in a crime, if that's what it is, of this sort?"

"It undoubtedly involves a crime, and our position, which permits us to act silently, will undoubtedly be helpful in exploring it. As to contacts, mine may not be directly helpful. But I have a great many sources of information, and access to more. Lawyers can ask questions without provoking the same kind of uproar as a sheriff or the same kind of obstruction as a private citizen. And I can find out matters-of-record as easily as Jim Fess, although I doubt that matters-of-record are going to tell us much. I can find out, for example, if Stanley Brill has a pilot's license, by asking the FAA in Oklahoma City. Which I'll do tomorrow morning. Of course, it won't mean anything if he doesn't. A man who wants to fly dead bodies and star sapphires from place to place isn't going to fuss about flight rule violations. For all we know, Stanley may be a defrocked pilot who got his license lifted for flying under-age girls across state lines. I can also find out what's in Dolly Sommers' will, although I'll bet you that won't tell us much either. No provision that everything is to go to a home for retired dachshunds if her body should be cremated. What we need is not matters-of-record, which a sheriff can get, but gossip, which he can't. Not a computer, but Mrs. Grundy."

Professor Payne said, "Mrs. Grundy we happen to have. Would you like me to ask her to dinner?"

"Mrs. Berger? It might be useful. Although she, of all people, is not likely to allow herself the luxury of indiscretions if her relatives are involved."

"She is so fond of talking that she'd take the opportunity

to do so even if the only subject for conversation was that she had just poisoned a family of eight. She likes to be a heroine. Even, as I told her at the Viewing, if the heroine is Lady Macbeth." Professor Payne laughed grimly. "You are cordially invited to dinner. . . ."

"Not me." Russ stood up. "The presence of a stranger might make her suspicious. Especially if she is colluding with Stanley Brill, and Stanley happened to mention to her—as he certainly would—that I had dropped in for a little chat. But invite her by all means, and see what she says. The points of inquiry that would seem to be most promising are (a) any mention of star sapphires, especially as an investment by her mother; (b) any intimations of large, unidentified objects that it was imperative to have cremated in place of the body; (c) any connection between her, or her relatives, and Stanley Brill."

He stood silent in the deepening night, as if to emphasize these points. And then he thought of another. "Also, (d) any evidence of a connection between Stanley, the airport, and the Death Plane."

Richie said casually in the darkness, "Well, as a matter of fact I can help you on that point. The Death Plane was out at the airport this morning. Parked on the line"—he produced the idiomatic phrase with some pride—"at like ten A.M. I noticed it just when I was getting ready to come home."

"My God," Russ said. "Why didn't you say so before?"

"I was kind of saving it up. Like you with the sapphires."

Russ cleared his throat, "Are you sure of this? How do you know?"

"I could tell the model. And the number. I happened to notice last night. A red and white one eighty, *nine three*"—

again his voice betrayed satisfaction in the idiom—"*Nine Seven Juliet.* Juliet for J."

"Bravo," Professor Payne said.

"You don't know anything else about it?" Russ was businesslike. "Whose it is, or anything?"

Richie stretched out in his chair. "No, not yet. But I'll find out tomorrow. If the weather's O.K."

CHAPTER V

Airwork

The weather was O.K.

Richie reached the airport the next morning early. Scheduled for dual—another term he savored—at ten, he got there at nine-thirty.

The terminal was empty again. The telephone was ringing unanswered, the Unicom gabbled into space. He considered answering the phone himself, but he hesitated, and it stopped ringing before he made up his mind. The next few minutes he spent, as he had the morning before, standing uncertainly, surveying the shabby scene. But this morning the place was, for him, friendly, and he was comfortably at home in it.

He waited a minute and then strolled composedly out onto the ramp. Stretched out on the concrete, his shoulders against the landing gear of a small plane and shaded by its wing from the warm sun, Earl, the line boy, was taking his ease with a comic book.

"Hi," Richie said.

Earl signified that he had heard with a barely perceptible movement of the index finger of his right hand.

"Phone was ringing."

"I heard it."

He still had not looked up. It was like trying to talk to a turtle. "Where's everybody?"

Earl pointed his left thumb to the sky, a movement so slight as to be hardly noticeable. It did not interrupt the progress of his finger across the page, digitally underlining each word as he read it. And he read not only with his eyes and fingers but his lips as well. He had a very bad complexion. Richie, whose own was good, felt conflicting emotions about this affliction—sympathy, revulsion, and a primitive apprehension that smugness might suddenly bring on an unsightly rash. But for the most part mild disdain predominated in his view of Earl, fortified by Earl's articulation when he presently spoke. He spoke fast and sloppily, as though conversation were physically painful. "Cheese's in the Bonanza and Jack's up for dual with Bud in the twin Beech and Persh's in town and Doc's still sick and Lisa's taking some dame to Pierce in the Mooney." It sounded remarkably like the Unicom talking, Richie thought. "Somebody might come back after a while."

Richie walked away. He had come early with a purpose, on the chance of finding exactly this opportunity to pursue the investigations he had been charged to conduct by his Uncle Walt and Russ Mallery.

He studied the airport. Except for Earl, no human being was in sight. The blue and white 140—*his* plane he now considered it—was parked at the near end of the line. He limped toward it in a leisurely way, memorizing its number, N5721W, contemplating its profile with pleasure. He tentatively wiggled an aileron, as if testing it. It was always possible somebody was at a window looking out at him, a mechanic or one of the anonymous part-time citizens who seemed to hover around the place. He studied the rudder with an appearance of concentrated interest while he covertly looked for the red and white one eighty. With a small explosion of excitement he saw it, tied down, five or six planes from him, the registration number, N9397J, boldly legible.

He devoted a moment more to Two One Whisky's rudder, then walked on with elaborate aimlessness, pausing to consider each intervening plane.

The morning was hot, the sky cloudless, the air still, the silence unbroken. There was still no one else in view. But he moved cautiously, tense and alert now. The solo investigation, now that he was engaged in it, seemed more of an adventure than he had expected. Corpses and crime were remote from the silent field and sky and the line of planes, but the intimations of violence were the more alarming for that. And they were complicated by an elusive, biting sense of treachery, as though merely looking at the 180 might involve him in a conspiracy against people whom he wanted to look on as both comrades and heroes.

And so he hesitated. But while he might be imaginative and in some ways oversensitive, he was also resolute, and after a moment's reluctant immobility he climbed onto the 180 wing, opened the door, and after a last quick look around the field got into the cabin.

There were no threads of gray satin on the doorsill, or anywhere else he could see. There seemed, in fact, to be nothing out of the way at all. He opened the glove compartment. It contained a small glass bottle, empty, a rag, a wrench. He felt in the side pockets and pulled out three aeronautical charts of predominantly green and purple hues, unintelligible to him, another rag, a dog-eared card with a list that began "1. Mixture rich." He turned the seats forward and in the pockets on the backs of them found official documents of esoteric significance.

As he was replacing these papers, he noticed what he thought might be considered a clue. On the red carpeting, between the front and rear seats, were blackish smudges. Then he saw in the corner, in the crack between the edge of the carpet and the cabin wall, several very small crumbs of earth and part of a half-rotted leaf.

The traces were infinitesimal. The rug had evidently been vigorously brushed, and the smears were barely visible. The substantial evidence could easily have been held in a coffee spoon. But it had a decided effect on him. He had not previously doubted that this was the plane that had landed in the wheatfield: his confidence in his recollection of its aspect and number was complete, for his memory was not yet spoiled by the clutterings of time; he had been certain that Mrs. Sommers' body had once occupied it and had been buried by its pilot. But the connection was now tangibly proved. Nine Seven Juliet was beyond all reasonable doubt the Death Plane.

He took from his pocket an envelope containing an urgent plea to him to subscribe to a periodical called *Teen Male*, which had arrived that morning. He scooped the crumbs of earth and the leaf into it and put it back in his pocket. He was a little sheepishly aware of a thrill as he did it. Coolly considered, this was a kid kind of melodrama. But he continued exploring with his fingers under the seats, and almost immediately a clue more solidly melodramatic than clods of loam came his way. Under the front right seat he found a diamond ring.

At least he concluded, when he dislodged and studied it, it looked like a diamond. It was a rather small stone, small enough to make its genuineness plausible. It had to belong with the Arabian Nights-type handful of jewels he had been fingering the night before. A graphic picture came to him: an old woman's body, opulently dressed, propped limply in the passenger's seat and held in place—he shuddered slightly at this and then laughed at himself—by the seat belt, with its left arm dangling downward beside the seat. He stared incredulously at the ring.

And then he heard a plane in the air. He jammed the ring in his pants pocket, got out of the cabin and climbed down to the ground. The plane overhead was still far enough away to be unidentifiable to him and he, therefore, was certainly unidentifiable to it, but it was bound for the airport. He started rapidly back to the ramp, watching as it turned in beyond the end of the field, sank fast and smooth toward the ground, and rolled along the runway. It had all been remarkably quick. Earl had stood up, cramming the comic book in his pocket, and was ambling toward the taxiing plane, waving his arms in gestures that struck Richie as not only amateurish but inconclusive.

It was the twin Beech, and when they parked it Bud and Jack got out.

"It's a good day," Bud said to Richie, as if they had been interrupted a few seconds before in the middle of a long conversation. "You can see about a hundred miles up there. We got dual today?"

"Right."

Bud looked at his watch and sighed resignedly. "Right. I'll be with you. Tie down the Twin, Earl."

He and Jack went into the terminal. Earl looked at the Beech without enthusiasm and kicked a chock under the nose wheel. Then he languidly looked around the concrete for the ropes anchored in it. Richie strolled away to wait by the 140. He found Earl's apathetic approach to his duties disagreeable to observe.

He also found the presence of the diamond ring in his

pocket, with its implication of divided loyalties, disagreeable. But the 140 had a tonic effect. He put his hand on the wing; the excitement of physical contact with his plane submerged other excitements.

Bud was a long time coming back. When he finally reappeared, his casual approach contrasted a little provokingly with Richie's fervor. He walked in no particular direction, in a relaxed, loose-jointed stride, pausing to speak to Earl and then to study, with the same enigmatic concentration he had devoted yesterday to the filing case, an oil stain on the concrete. The casualness, while it made Richie a little impatient, increased his admiration. Precisely such offhandedness about important things was a quality he strove, without much success, he feared, to achieve.

"How are you, Ace?" he asked, speaking now as if he had not seen him before that morning. "Myself, I'm terrible."

"I'm O.K."

"I been spending so much time working my kids don't recognize me when I go home. They think I'm a burglar. 'Mom,' they yell, 'make that man go away.' I been flying every night for the past week, and pretty near all day. Hundred hour work week. Jack and I just spent two hours up there trying to get him ready for his multi-engine rating so he can fly the Beech for us." He shook himself slightly, as if to wake up, although he did not look tired. "So today we learn how to preflight it, right? It keeps you out of some kinds of trouble. Nothing you can do will keep you out of *all* kinds of trouble."

"Right."

"Birds' nests," Bud said, staring at the propeller.

"Birds' nests?"

"They get into the cowling and build a nest. Over night. Then it catches fire after you been flying a while. If you don't land and get it out, the gas tanks blow up, right? So you want to give a look for them. In summer, anyway."

"O.K." Richie peered behind the propeller under the cowling and perceived no birds' nests.

"Prop. You want to *feel* the prop." Bud ran his fingers along the blade, and went on briskly with his catalogue of disasters. "A pebble gets thrown up when you're taxiing and hits it. Nicks it. You get upstairs. That steel's under a hell of a lot of stress when it's going round at twenty-five hundred rpms, right? So one end breaks off. Either it hits you in the face, or you hit some cornfield in its face. Either way it's not good.

"Right."

"Wings. Test the wings to make sure they're on tight. If a wing falls off, you have trouble flying the plane. You find yourself driving along at five thousand feet in a two-door hard top, and you're in trouble. Right?"

Richie laughed dryly.

Bud shook the end of the wing gently. "Gear." He squatted and stared appraisingly under it. "If the gear falls off when you're in the air, you mightn't notice it. Causes trouble when you try to land." He untied the ropes from the rings on the bottom of the wings. "The struts"—he pointed to them—"ought to be roughly two, three inches up. And you want to remember to untie the bird when you preflight it. Otherwise you'll be pulling the whole damn ramp behind you. Makes it hard to taxi."

"Right."

"Drain sumps." He opened a valve under the wing, let

gasoline trickle over his fingers, sniffed them, and closed it. "You get water collecting in the bottom of your gas tank and it gets into the carburetor. The engine doesn't run so good on water."

"No," Richie was trying to memorize these precautions.

"*Then*"—Bud stood up, and unscrewed a cap on the top of the wing—"gas. You run out of gas when you're over downtown St. Louis, and you got a problem. Right?"

"Right."

"Oil." He pulled up a small lid on the cowling and examined the oil gauge. "Ought to run six, seven quarts. You forget to look at the oil, you run out, and the engine blows itself to pieces. Or else there's a leak that catches fire and the plane explodes, leaving"—he frowned ferociously—"nothing but some molecular garbage. Right?"

Richie nodded. He started to answer, "Right," but checked himself. He didn't want to seem to be aping his instructor.

Bud clapped him on the shoulders. "O.K., Richie. You ready to fly? Feeling relaxed and carefree?"

He grinned, with an effort. Bud went on, "Carefree, Ace, is what I want you not to be. Guys get carefree and after their next flight we're acting as pall bearers."

"You lose many?" Richie asked.

"A fair number," Bud said imperturbably and followed him into the plane. Richie settled into the pilot's seat and fastened his seat belt. He felt some mild satisfaction in his riposte. The second lesson was well begun: he was a veteran.

An hour later he had learned to make climbing turns, power let-downs, and steep banks. Or at least he had performed them; he had no clear recollection of how they were done. Now, at the end of the hour, Bud had taken over for the landing, and he discovered that, as he had been the day before, he was soaked with sweat and very tired. He leaned back in his seat.

But the lesson was not finished. Bud prodded him. "You see the numerals?" He nodded toward the runway which lay a long way away on their left. At its nearer end big figures were painted white on the asphalt.

"Twenty-nine?"

"Two nine. Right. That's the runway number, which is also the direction you're heading when you land on it. Two nine zero degrees—a little north of west. Right? When you can take the plane down with the power off and put it home on the numerals every time, with the nose up in a full stall, you'll have learned to fly. Right? O.K., Richie, follow me through on the controls while we try doing it."

He pulled out the throttle and the noise of the idling engine sank to a hum. Richie put his fingers and toes on the controls and followed the two slightly dizzy right-angle turns and then through the last straight glide down toward the runway. A second later the wheels were three inches over the numerals, and the plane stalled out smoothly on the asphalt.

They walked slowly toward the terminal. Richie could feel a phantasmal yoke and pedals still under his hands and feet; he was on a concrete cloud.

"Your turns are kind of ragged," Bud said. "And you overcontrol. But hell, everybody overcontrols." He looked at him gravely. "You're doing O.K."

Richie was working hard, steering his cloud. He nodded a little absently but not without pleasure.

Inside he paid his bill, and Bud, making the entry in his log book, looked up to ask, "When do we go again?" and turned to consult the blackboard where squares representing days of the week were arranged in columns, downward under the registration number of each plane. He ran his finger across the horizontal row of squares that represented Thursday and said, "Tomorrow's no good. I got an all day trip to make in the one eighty." His finger had stopped in the square under 97J.

It reminded Richie of the ring in his pocket. He shivered. And then he noticed that the schedule for the preceding days of the week had not yet been erased. Here was possible evidence. Whoever had scheduled the 180 for Monday night might have reserved it and might have thought, after his mission in the wheatfield, that it would attract more attention than otherwise to erase his name. Richie wished he had thought of this earlier, so he could have studied the blackboard at his leisure when the terminal was deserted. He said, "Any time. Day after tomorrow?" But he was looking at the Monday square under 97J.

Bud's back was still turned as he bent over to study Friday's schedule. Over his head, Richie read the chalked message: *6–10 pm Bud.*

"Not Friday either, Richie. Busy all day again. Saturday? Say ten?"

Richie swallowed hard and said, his throat dry, "Right." Bud wrote *10–11 Bud dual Richie.* Then he turned back, "Want some of that adulterated swamp they sell us for coffee?"

"No thanks, not right now." His voice was hoarse, but it was under control. Bud, walking to the coffee vending machine, seemed to notice nothing out of the way about it. Richie, as he started for the door, put his hand involuntarily in his pocket, feeling for the ring. It was still there, a talisman of betrayal.

"How *is* Beaufort?" Professor Payne courteously asked. "It's too bad he couldn't come."

"Oh, he's busy down in the cellar all by himself as usual." Merry Berger laughed. "Projecting color slides from his pornography collection, I guess."

She leaned back in the chaise longue and sipped her rum punch. Her voice, as Professor Payne had told Russ, was loud and assertive. She spoke each sentence like an auctioneer aggressively persuading buyers of the inner virtues of items that had little outward appeal. There was, he considered, no sensible reply that could be made to her explanation of her son's absence. Since he tried to avoid saying things that were not sensible, he said nothing. And, as he had somewhat maliciously expected, there was an embarrassing silence. Merry had counted on his jocular contradiction. In its absence, she was made to appear merely salacious.

Her sister, Gay Custer, was the only one who cared to attempt a conversational rescue, although it didn't look as if Merry realized one were needed. "Oh, *pornography*," Gay cried. "Pornography shmornography, as long as it keeps his mind off sex." She had a mop of dyed blonde curls which she frequently shook. She shook it now.

Again Professor Payne made no comment. The silence was, as he intended, even more embarrassing this time. Glendenning Berger finally broke it, not apparently in any effort to ease a social situation but because his mind, lumbering, had at last assembled a sentence ready for utterance. He was a bald, fat man whose face looked as if it had been carved out of prune whip. His delivery was the opposite of his wife's, mumbling and hesitant in a way that suggested he was pronouncing each syllable twice. Between each word he ran his tongue around the inside of his mouth, as though lubricating it. "We fixed up a den for Beaufort in the basement. He studies down there."

"Ooh," Mrs. Custer said.

"What does he study?" Professor Payne asked.

Mr. Berger thought and said, "Dynamics."

"Ooh," Mrs. Custer said again. "Pershie, you've got to tell them about that man we met in Louisville, you know the one, the one in dynamics. I just adore him, he was so sort of, I don't know. It was when Pershie and I were in Louisville last, when was it we were in Louisville that time? Anyway he was the dearest man."

"You mean Ed Phipps." Persh Custer, the strong, silent man, so confidently expected to be listened to that he didn't trouble to notice whether he was or not. "It's not dynamics, it's cybernetics. It was in Cleveland we met him, in '64. He's . . ."

His wife clapped her hands. "I *knew* it was Cleveland. But it was in Louisville where we met that cute man who was interested in something or other—the cutest thing, I absolutely adored him. Pershie, tell them about it."

"What sort of dynamics does Beaufort study?" Professor Payne asked.

"I hated Louisville," Mrs. Custer said. "The manager of the motel was so *awful*—tell them, Pershie . . . that time in the bar . . . you remember. By the way, Merry, did I tell you we're building a new bar in the family room, instead of downstairs, the ceiling was too low for Pershie. We're going to call the new one *the Pershie Bar!* But anyway, in Louisville, the manager was so awful, I hated him."

Pershie Bar. Professor Payne considered J. Pershing Custer. In appearance he combined the more rugged aspects of a marine sergeant and a lumberjack. If the attraction of opposites meant anything, the Custers' marriage ought to be a happy one.

Merry Berger interrupted her sister. She set down her glass on a flagstone with emphasis, indicating that she found Gay's wisps of babble irksome. *She* was nothing if not consecutive. "Nobody knows what goes on in that cellar of ours. You ought to see it. I can hardly get inside the door to clean it. Beaufort shuts himself up there whenever he comes home. Which isn't often. Persh works him so hard he's never at home in the daytime, and at night he goes off some place by himself. On the tiles. Then he locks himself in the cellar. He never comes out to eat except when everybody else has gone to bed. Nocturnal. Like a bat. Batty Berger I call him. I leave his food and laundry out for him and every once in a while I yell at him to take a bath. I tell you, that boy wouldn't know when to change his underwear if I didn't tell him. Neither of my boys knows how to take care of himself." She laughed. "I practically have to brush Glen's teeth for him. If I weren't around, those two boys would just die of neglect."

"Pershie, when we got to Louisville—you have to tell them what that manager said to me."

"Well." Custer said it as a command, possibly to Merry

Berger to shut up. "When we checked into this motel in Louisville where we were going to stay. . . ."

"They had the most awful *colors* in the rooms," Mrs. Custer said. "The one they showed us—honestly, Walt, you just wouldn't believe it, it was so sort of I don't know, you just couldn't describe it. Pershie, tell them what color it was."

In half a century of being a thoughtful host Professor Payne had not felt a stronger impulse to say "Shut up" to a guest. Instead, he occupied himself with silent lamentations that he had ever thought of asking the Bergers and Custers to dinner. As a social occasion, the party was obviously bound to be—already was—what in his salad days he might have called a "wash-out"—an odd image, its derivation obscure, but somehow forceful. And as part of the investigation only whimsy, he now considered, could have made him think it might be helpful. In prospect it had seemed plausible to imagine that the guests would reveal their inmost secrets. Physically present, fully clad, and occupied with the ingestion of rum punch, they looked, so far as hope the breaching of their defenses went, to be built of granite.

It was even possible, he thought, that their suspicions had been aroused by this sudden festivity. He had explained his invitation on the phone by saying that seeing the Bergers and the Custers at the funeral had reminded him he was in their debt for several dinner parties in the past. But the debts were some ten years old. He supposed even the weakest intellect—and the collective intellect of his guests was, he judged, moderately weak—might see a rather peculiar contrast between the ten years' gap and his cordial insistence that the debt must be repaid that night.

Mitigating the peculiarity, however, was one fortunate fact of which Professor Payne was, characteristically, calmly aware. His dinner parties had come to have a notable fame, a little wider than local. He knew that his invitations were something people managed to work into their conversations. "No, we were sorry, we couldn't go to Betsy's Monopoly party. As a matter of fact, Walt had asked us down to the farm for dinner that night"; this was a formula that wives of university presidents and state senators practiced in front of their mirrors. In the present situation his reputation as a host might exempt him from normal curiosity about the motives of his hospitality.

Still the suddenness must seem rather queer to them. In the case that any of them had anything to conceal, which almost certainly *was* the case, it might make them think about some other queer things. And taken together these might well be giving rise to queries in a guilty mind. There was, most simply, the fact of the location of his wheatfield. Anyone who had interred Dolly Sommers' remains and fifty thousand dollars' worth of sapphires, or arranged their interment, must be disconcerted to find himself dining on the premises. But this he was on consideration inclined to discount; if the guilty party had known that it *was* the premises, he would hardly have chosen it as a burying ground. The pilot had merely picked what looked, misleadingly, like a suitably isolated spot. That was certain. And it was likely that from the ground he would not recognize the spot he had picked. The wheatfield was completely surrounded by woods. Professor Payne remembered enough from his flying days to know that it was often infuriatingly difficult to locate and identify on the ground geographical features that looked salient, even dominant, from the air. Of the guests, only Persh was actually a pilot, and he had certainly shown no sign of startled recognition.

There was also Richie. At the moment he was standing in well-bred silence at the edge of the terrace, leaning against the wall of the house, presumably waiting to pass the olives. His state of mind had turned worrying again; since his return from the airport at lunchtime he had been silent and a little belligerent, summarily rejecting as inedible a luncheon that consisted, admittedly, of an unsuccessful experiment in combining leftover mutton with leftover parsnips. Belligerence was a change—it might be for the better—from withdrawal; it was certainly a change for the worse from yesterday's euphoric good humor—and this accounted in part for Professor Payne's impatience with his dinner guests. But it was not Richie's mood but Richie's presence that troubled him at the moment. Richie's connection with the Van Buren County Flying Service Inc. was as recent and as sudden as Professor Payne's lust for the company of Bergers and Custers. If they knew about his flying lessons—and Persh Custer quite possibly did—they would reasonably conclude that his purpose in taking them was espionage. He wondered if it mighn't put things on a more open and natural basis to bring the flying lessons up himself, but it would be undesirable to draw attention to a connection that might possibly escape their attention otherwise. It was a vexing question, and he frowned as he glanced at Richie, who was also frowning.

Doubts about expediency was not the principal reason for Professor Payne's frown. There remained the more urgent prospect of insensate boredom. Gay and Merry gave him—another colloquialism from a past age struck him as precise—a bellyache. Even if they had been silenced by providential lightning striking them mute, their physical presence would still have depressed him. He disliked the way they looked.

They were very different—so different that it seemed almost that they had deliberately manufactured contrasting appearances, so as to avoid confusion between them.

Mrs. Berger had been handsome as a girl, regally tall and stately, with slightly aquiline features. Now she was dumpy and frowzy, her short gray hair unkempt, her glasses thick, her clothes shapeless. She seemed determined to depict a frump, perhaps as a demonstration that her mind was on higher things, perhaps simply because she was so wrapped up in the sound of her words that she had no attention left to spare for her appearance. Everything about her was either much too tight or much too loose. The curls in her hair were wiry, and her watchband cut into her fat wrist like a sausage link. But her flat, worn shoes were noticeably oversize; she sloshed in them as she walked. And her sagging skirt was too long not merely for fashion but for convenience. She had a mannerism of shifting her weight in a chair and then wriggling slightly into a more comfortable position. The effect was that of a building disturbed by an earthquake.

By contrast, Gay Custer was good-looking. She had the structure of voluptuous youth. But it was synthetic. Her sex appeal was machine-made. Hair thoroughly tinted and tended by experts, as bewitching as chemistry and electrical engineering could make it, rich, soft, golden curls. An excellent figure produced by determination and technology, a lithe, youthful figure, admirably dressed in ways that a specialist would advise for maximum biological magnetism. Contact lenses, capped teeth, miracle creams, a skin elegantly veneered with the masterly reproduction of real-life flesh. There was, it occurred unpleasantly to Professor Payne, a marked affinity between this work of art and those turned out in Stanley Brill's establishment. She was, moreover, delighted with herself, triumphant in the perfection of her creation. She regarded herself with a mother's adoring love.

During these ruminations, the conversation had moved on. "Oh, oh, oh," Mrs. Custer was saying, "that concert Friday, the sweetest little cellist, an albino hunchback, I could have *eaten* him, he was so darling, so I made Pershie take me around afterward to meet him . . ."

Gay piped. Merry roared. She drowned out Gay whenever she had heard enough from her. "I had a real funny experience at a concert in London last month. Nobody would believe it."

As happened so often with her, she got no response from this provocative declaration. It was surprising that she continued to have faith in her power to extract breathless *whats*! But she seemed not to care when they did not come; she merely proceeded without them. "On the plane going over—taking that plane was really a thrill for an unsophisticated gal from Buchanan like me—I started talking to the gal next to me. She was a real smooth number about my age, done up to the chin with pearls. Well, it turned out she was a countess from Yugoslovakia, and her daughter was married to a millionaire lumber magnate from Seattle and she'd been out visiting them. Well, she and I really hit it off and by the time we got there we were good friends, and she absolutely insisted I stay at her apartment instead of going to a hotel. And boy, Walt, was that an apartment. Ten rooms and three maids, right on Grosvenor Square. Well, Helmtrude and I got along fine as housemates and she took me everywhere. So I wanted to do something for her, which was a real problem because she's a gal who really has *everything.* But I decided I could probably find some little thing she'd like—I have a kind of knack for finding inexpensive things that are really just right for people, so I had a talk with Helmtrude's lady's maid—French, my dear, and what a . . ."

The concert, the fragile peg on which all this had been hung, had been forgotten. Professor Payne was normally a fancier of human foibles, but Mrs. Berger's were reversing his appetite for dinner. The strangely unresonant quality of her voice made each word seem like a blow with a wooden mallet. He decided that the kitchen required his attention and departed from the terrace.

She seemed not to notice his going. She went on; and he had an eerie sense that she would go on if everybody left, or if they all dropped dead. But when, after ten minutes' surcease during which he stared emptily at the refrigerator and drank another drink, he forced himself back to the terrace, his return diverted her from her unending anecdote.

"Walt, I've just been thinking about you. You and I are old friends, so I know you won't mind if I tell you something."

"You are wrong. I shall mind."

"Walt, you old fraud, I know you too well." She laughed like a burlesque buffoon at his own dirty joke. "You always like to make people think you're a cynic, but *I* know deep down you're just an old marshmallow. So, do you know what I'm going to tell you?"

He sat down thinking that at least two more hours of this faced him and said, "No, I don't know, and I don't want to hear it." As he said it he caught the sardonic eye of Richie, still leaning against the wall like a bareheaded caryatid. Richie winked. Professor Payne was slightly warmed by a display of fellow-feeling. He waited for her recommendation of a superior brand of floor paint or better quality rum.

"Walt, I think you ought to go to Buenos Aires."

He was taken aback. "Why? Have you been there recently?"

"No." She laughed deprecatingly. "But when I was in Paris—I went to Paris after I left London, you know—I met a man who lives there. I was reminded of him when you asked me about my trip," she added, apparently in the honest belief that this was how the conversation had started. "*I met him in a bar in Paris.*" She paused, waiting for exclamations, thinking that meeting men in bars in Paris must appear so remote from her usual deportment as to be hilarious. When none came she continued, unruffled. "I stopped in for a cup of coffee—I'd been walking for an hour and a half and my feet felt like risen dough. And this man—a real good-looking, well-dressed, smooth-type older man, I mean—came up and said to me, 'Excuse me, but didn't I meet you at Señora Blankdeblank's in Buenos Aires last winter?' Well, Walt, I could have exploded. You *know* what I thought. But it wasn't that way at all, he told me afterward he'd hesitated because he knows what a good-looking woman is bound to think when somebody talks to her in a bar, which was real cute of him, I thought. He really did think he'd met me down there, because he lives on a kind of ranch except he tells me it has twenty bedrooms, and he owns about half the pampas, I guess. So we got into conversation and got along fine together—we really hit it off—and he *insisted* I go out to some fancy three-star place and have dinner with him."

She stopped to sip rum punch. Several people started sentences, but she swallowed rapidly and went on. "He told me all about himself. He'd had a real interesting life. He'd been to Dartmouth College in New Hampshire and used to work in a bank in New York. I'm a good listener, as you know, so I learned plenty. He told me he liked talking to me, his wife is the kind that talks all the time and won't listen when he says anything. He had a lot on the ball, that guy. So I wanted to do something for him, and I asked him around for a drink at Agnes's the next day. The old gal loved having me entertain my friends at her place while I was staying there.

"Walt, you ought to get a load of Agnes's apartment. She's got some old furniture from the sixteenth century, *two* living rooms. *It really is something.*" She looked around and seemed to notice that this graphic depiction of unlimited grandeur had not much impressed Professor Payne, or indeed anybody else. For the first time she took cognizance of the insufficient impact of her narrative and repeated the sentence with still more emphasis, as if her listeners' defective hearing had weakened the impression she intended to make. The effort made her choke slightly and spill her drink. She stood up to brush the drops off her dress. Richie wordlessly moved forward, took her glass, replenished it at the bar, and returned it to her. He was, Professor Payne thought, taking saturnine satisfaction in the scene.

"*Really something,*" she said a third time in admonitory tones. "Thanks, Richie. Well, she's got these priceless antiques. And two Chagalls." She glanced at Professor Payne to see whether he was reacting to these proofs of munificence. He was, instead, staring out toward his garden, half thinking about Crown Borers and the Cucumber Moth. He wondered idly why Merry should care whether he expressed astonishment at how rich her aunt was or not, but he knew the dreary answer to his own question and soothed his sense of the world's folly by contemplating insecticides.

He had not counted on the effect this had on Merry. She seemed to be in a frenzy of frustration at his abstractedness. "Not only that," she recklessly went on, "she has diamonds."

"Aggie is comfortably off, then?"

The response may have seemed inadequate to her, but she did not take it as irony. She went on pounding the same point with her mallet. Failure to secure the desired effect had filled her with ungovernable annoyance with the world in general. "She sure is. She's generous, too. Wanted to know how Mom was making out. She was worried about Mom. She said to me, 'Merry,' she said, 'you mustn't let poor Dolly throw her money away, keeping that damned airplane business going.' And—" She stopped, and then went on hastily, averting her glance from the Custers, as if she had gone rather further than she intended. "Anyway, she liked having me ask my friends in while I was there. You know, Walt, I'm a pretty good judge of people, and as soon as I got to Paris I saw something was wrong with old Agnes, and I figured I knew what it was. She doesn't see any young people. All her friends are tired old millionairesses with nothing to do but count the pearls in their necklaces. So I figured I'd bring something new into her life. I wanted to do something for her, Walt—she did everything for me. Lent me her Rolls-Royce and her chauffeur for two whole weeks, fed me, wined me, dined me, took me to the opera, and to every fancy restaurant in town. So I figured the best thing I could do for Agnes was to bring my friends around for drinks and dinner. Every night we weren't going out, I had some young people my age at her house—I knew it wouldn't be any trouble for her. And she loved it, Walt. She was like a house plant somebody finally waters after a month. I picked up a lot of people one way or another while I was there—you know me, Walt, I love *people*—and I brought them all around. She especially loved Carlton Ritz, this guy from Buenos Aires. Carlton Ritz wasn't his name, of course. He's named Carlton O'Connell, but we all kidded him by calling him Carlton Ritz, since he was staying at the Ritz Hotel in Paris . . ."

Professor Payne stood up. A survey of the other guests indicated that enough was enough. Mr. Berger, his indeterminate features relaxed to the point of liquefaction, looked like a man in narcosis. Gay Custer was compulsively twisting, as she had been since the moment she stopped talking, a very long strand of brightly colored beads. It seemed possible that they had been custom-built for the purpose; so violent were her manipulations that

Professor Payne thought they must be strung on steel. Persh Custer was sitting stiffly upright, his eyes closed. He looked like a man catching a much-needed nap after a hard day on the shores of Tripoli.

Merry did not acknowledge her host's nugatory movement. "I sure put some life into the old lady. My friends all kidded the life out of her, made fun of her for being rich and all, she really loved it. She was about a hundred percent more cheerful after she'd had a houseful of guests for a couple of weeks. And you know, Walt, that made me feel real good. The only thing that gives me real pleasure is doing things for other people."

"The only thing that gives most people real pleasure is running other people's lives," Professor Payne said. "If they can convince themselves that they're doing it for the other people's own good, the pleasure is doubled."

Merry laughed rather doubtfully, and started to say something. But Persh Custer forestalled her. He had finished his drink—his fifth or sixth, Professor Payne had noted—and now thrust himself smartly through the door, as if to lead a bayonet charge on a waiting casserole.

And the casserole, when it was served, had an animating effect on him. He continued to look stern, but he began to talk. And he talked, a little surprisingly, about the stock market. Professor Payne had supposed this was Glen Berger's speciality.

"I've been buying United Gasket," he said. "I picked up a hundred last February when it was down to thirty-one and a quarter, and another hundred a week ago, at twenty-nine. And you know what it closed at today?"

Gay immediately answered. "No, but you must tell

them about that wonderful little man in the broker's office with the ticker tape. Please tell them, Pershie. . . ."

He disregarded her, thereby raising himself in Professor Payne's esteem. "It closed," he went on with measured, majestic accents, as if he were swearing allegiance to something, "at thirty-seven and five-eighths."

This information, as uninteresting as any Professor Payne had ever heard, nevertheless had interesting consequences. Berger's face had been growing darker. His expression indicated with tolerable certainty that he hated Persh Custer's guts. And Merry was replying with what looked like a mixture of fury and disarray. The play of expressions was quite arresting; Richie, circulating with a good Beaujolais whose price Professor Payne now seriously regretted, nudged his great-uncle as he filled his glass, and, when he looked up, directed his glance to Berger's murderous regard.

Persh continued in his obscure but obviously deliberate provocation. "It closed at thirty-seven and five-eighths. After the merger with Wiley-Allardyce was announced yesterday. It climbed six points in one day. Even though everybody on the street had been discussing the merger for six months. *Do you hear that?*"

They had all heard, although not all had understood. "I have an order in to sell tomorrow at thirty-eight. It's sure to hit thirty-eight, and when it does I'll have netted . . ."

"Listen, Persh, why don't you can all that dreary stuff," Mrs. Berger interrupted. She was making an effort to control herself; this was the kind of sentence that passed, in her book, for amiable persiflage.

"Approximately thirty-six hundred and forty dollars and sixty-six cents. Less commission."

Merry lost her temper. "Shut up," she said. He did, possibly because he had said all he had to say, but she did not. "You better leave Glen alone. He has enough to put up with without your yapping." She then pulled herself together and laughed, although hoarsely. "Everybody's always jumping on Glen," she said to the world at large. "He doesn't know how to take care of himself. None of the men in my life have been able to take care of themselves." She laughed again, a little more naturally. "When I was fourteen I used to go with a boy who just got his driver's license but he couldn't go round the block without running into something. Well, I was a pretty good driver, even then, so every time he got his family's car to take me out, I'd do the driving, even though I didn't have my license."

This had no beneficial effect on her husband's morale. He was slouched in his chair, staring at his plate. And Persh, silent and perhaps silenced, was looking as fierce as ever, determined to hold his cryptic beachhead against heavy odds. It was this aspect of things that most interested Professor Payne. An offensive against the Bergers had been launched, although the engagement had ended indecisively. And it was an ancient war; the battles clearly had all been fought before. They were all familiar with Glen's malignant defenselessness, Merry's stories, Persh's assaults. Or, more precisely, Persh's persecutions . . . *Pershiecution.* The phrase slipped horridly into his mind. Professor Payne wondered worriedly if Gay's style might be contagious. Then, returning to more rational concerns, he recalled that Persh had drunk a lot of rum. Was he drunk? drunk enough to open old sores for no particular purpose, with no interesting contemporary implications attached? It seemed doubtful. But what the battle was about was more doubtful still.

He glanced at Richie, and sensed that rather similar thoughts were running through his mind. He was taking this very seriously, watching the proceedings no longer with the air of a saturnine observer of the lunacies of his elders but with the concentrated attention he might have paid to a problem in the New Math.

Mrs. Berger glanced at Professor Payne at precisely the moment he was glancing at Richie, with something of the same intuitive understanding of his thoughts. "You know, Mom used to say a woman's place shouldn't be in the home at all but standing in front of her man on the battlefield acting as a shield against Yankee bullets. I sure am going to miss Mom's sayings, Walt. You know, she always had plenty of courage all her life. She put up with everything that happened to her—and life wasn't always too easy for her—with a smile and a kind word. She never cared about anything except being brave. You got to admire that."

"No, I don't." His feelings were overflowing the vessel of hostly good manners. "I've never understood what use that kind of bravery was. I think I should be on the whole more sympathetic to somebody who screamed with pain or fear when they were in trouble. Cowardice is a much more likable trait than courage. More wholesome, too."

"I know you don't mean that, Walt." She spoke with perfect assurance, but she looked troubled by dissent, as she always did when she happened to hear it. "I may not be as bright as you professors, but there's one thing I am good at, and that's understanding people. You're just a dear old teddy-bear, Walt. I know you'd never believe anything so *wrong*."

"Nevertheless, I do." The heterodoxy, emphatically spoken, silenced them momentarily, and there was no sound except that of Glendenning Berger, mournfully but doggedly chewing on *boeuf bourguignon*. He looked as if he expected the battle to begin again at any moment and was trying to fortify himself with hasty and massive food supplies. It seemed to Professor Payne that the moment was as favorable as any for a probing operation. "Don't you think—" He spoke with great reasonableness and geniality. It was an opening familiar to everyone who knew him, an exasperating one to those who disagreed with him. "That courage is something that everybody is born with, that shows itself in different ways in different people? We all have courage quotients, perhaps, as a friend of mine recently said. Some people face physical pain stoically. Others follow professions like Stanley Brill's."

Mrs. Berger's fork stopped halfway to her mouth and then returned to the plate. Her infallible understanding of people was, he was glad to see, insufficient to this sudden intromission of the undertaker. "Why did you bring him up?"

"He is a man who might not be judged particularly brave by a casual acquaintance. But embalming takes guts."

This aphorism further confused her. She could not tell whether he was praising Mr. Brill or burying him. And apparently she had an interest in the matter. "I didn't know you were a friend of Stan's," she said.

"He was a student of mine. I've kept up with him. I thought of him, of course, because I saw him at your mother's Viewing. Talking about her reminded me of Stanley."

This, blandly delivered, did not at all satisfy her. "Stan is quite a guy, Walt. You shouldn't run him down."

"I wouldn't think of it." He affected surprise. "I've always admired his professional standards. He did a beautiful job."

She relaxed into the jocularity that passed with her grace. "He is *quite* a guy. I tell you frankly, there's nobody I'd rather trust with my own body."

Professor Payne laughed. It was clearly expected of him, and now that he was pursuing a definite object, conversation with her was more tolerable. "Oh, come on. You'll outlive him and all the rest of us. Or did you mean it in a different sense?" He laughed again, insinuatingly, to please her. She was a woman who liked to have her inferences drawn.

"Oh, *Walt*. You really are something. But seriously, Stan Brill is a wonderful human being."

Treacherously he moved in for the kill. "You don't find him a little oily? Perhaps not completely trustworthy?"

Once again she was startled, angry at having misunderstood his intentions. "He is a real mature guy. He'd do anything for his friends."

"Anything?"

"Yes, anything. People don't appreciate Stan. I don't know who you've been listening to, but I know a lot of people around town say he isn't interested in anything except money. But it's not true. He doesn't make as much as everybody thinks. You know, there's one thing my worst enemy couldn't say about me, and that is that I'm not loyal to my friends. I'm proud of that, Walt. Stan is a good friend of mine."

"I hadn't known."

"Oh, yes, he . . ." She checked herself. "Stan and I have been pals for years and years," she ended with a false lightness.

But not quite light enough, her interrogator thought. "Would you like some more stew?" he asked. He was pleased with himself.

"It's not bad," she said, welcoming a diversion. "What's it got in it, Walt? Marjoram?"

He did not answer but instead nodded to Richie for a new round of Beaujolais. And Gay, looking for an opening, said, "I saw the most marvelous old lady buying a hat in a store I took Lisa to for a dress. She was a real little-old-lady type old lady, you know what I mean, and she was just the sweetest, oh, I don't know, but I loved just *looking* at her."

Richie spilled the Beaujolais. It occurred to Professor Payne that he had not, until this moment, fully accepted the fact that this woman was the mother of Lisa, Lisa Artemis. It must come as a shock. He was old enough, however—precisely the best age, in fact—to realize that what mothers were had nothing to do with what their daughters were or might become. He recovered quickly and proceeded on his round. But now that Gay's anecdote seemed to be over, Merry embarked on a sentence that shook him still more.

"If Lisa didn't spend so much time on clothes and things, the airport mightn't be in the shape that it is." She said it brutally, the aggressive purpose wholly unconcealed.

Professor Payne, interested in the cause and effect of

this cannon ball, hoped it might lead to revelations. He hoped even more that it might break the party up completely. Richie, who had reached Mrs. Berger's glass, passed it by and had to be called back. But on the others her remark had a much smaller effect than the earlier, covert exchanges of blows. Gay took up the conversation again as if her sister had merely uttered a polite exclamation. "Speaking of the airport," she said, "Pershie, tell them what you were telling me the other day about that man who wanted a job, oh, I don't know, I've sort of forgotten, but it was really cute."

Persh said to Professor Payne, "I need more pilots. You'd be surprised how much work we're getting now." He was suddenly expansive, malevolently so, as he had been with United Gaskets. If he had been wearing a vest, he might have stuck his fingers in its armholes. "Somebody forgets and leaves their purse up in Pierce City and has to have it right away, so we have to send a pilot up for it." He laughed with unreasonable hilarity, and went on more expansively than ever, in the manner of a successful businessman happy to deliver details of an enterprise in which no one except himself was interested. We get *too* much business like that. We don't have time for really important work. Like boar delivery."

"Boar delivery?" Professor Payne had several half-formed puns in his mind and asked the question politely, to prevent himself from saying any of them.

"Somebody needs a boar for breeding, so we ship it to them. Hogs like to fly," he added sententiously. "There's a hell of a lot of them being flown around the country. We need people for work like that. Being on hog-call, I call it. It mounts up. Most of our jobs don't come to much taken one at a time, but they mount up. Even the women's purses in Pierce. *Providing you get paid.*"

Richie had paused again and was staring. The last sentence had been spoken with sudden venom. Persh was attacking again. Another pershiecution. Professor Payne again followed Richie's meaning glance to the Bergers' faces. Purses and hogs, like United Gaskets, twisted Glen's features into a pasty rage, and his wife looked like an approaching Cold Front. They stared at Persh Custer with feral hatred.

This unseemly, if obscure, skirmish was undoubtedly an act of revenge for Merry Berger's criticism of his daughter, and possibly for the earlier reference to her mother's throwing her money away on the airport. Revenge looked like a familiar, perhaps a favorite pastime of Persh's. And spilling expensive burgundy seemed to be becoming one of Richie's. A small stain spread on the bare wood around Persh Custer's place. But this time his fault was due to lack of attention, not to shock. He had been too much engrossed in the Bergers' expressions to watch where he was pouring.

Persh Custer had a sergeant's taste for bullying. But there was more to it than good, clean sadism. Professor Payne pondered for a moment what it might be. The Bergers had been free-loading, and they had been reproaching Persh for his business methods, or lack of them. That was obvious. But there was a good deal more that had been going on for a long time. Since long, long before Dolly Sommers' death. He reviewed the matter in his mind and then, deciding that his stomach was not strong enough for any more of these impalpables, he offered second helpings from the casserole.

But Persh was well started now, and nothing short of force could stop him. He had a sergeant's voice as well as a sergeant's impulses. "We've been busy as hell at the airport the last few weeks especially. And Doc's been sick, and *of course* Cheese doesn't show up for work, half the time. Lisa's a pretty good pilot, but she isn't instrument-rated yet, and most of our jobs are on instruments. She goes along with Bud when he needs a co-pilot sometimes. Besides running most of the business side of things, which she does damn well." He had worked himself into a fury, driving home his offensive with a series of short explosions of words. "Besides her work in the office, she's been out almost every night this week. Tuesday we had to send her all the way to Monroe, Wisconsin, for a litter of pigs."

Merry said the only thing she could think of, "Boy, I'd sure never trust my pigs to *that* girl . . ."

"The hell you wouldn't," he said with a final explosion. "You'd trust your pigs or yourself to anybody if you can get away without paying for it."

"I found the most marvelous old patchwork quilt in an antique shop in East St. Louis last month," Gay Custer cried. "Pershie, you've got to tell them about that place, it was somewhere I'd heard about from somebody, and . . ."

"Anybody want more wine?" Richie asked. He sounded desperate.

"Give me some," Glen Berger said.

The festivities proceeded under armistice.

CHAPTER VI

Base Leg

"There's no data shortage," Russ said. "In fact there's a data downpour, but all of it unhelpful, or at best cryptic. Like dry rain."

He was sitting at Professor Payne's kitchen table lunching on Swiss cheese on rye with beer, making notes on cards with his right hand while sandwich, stein, and cigarette alternated in his left. The aridity of the data was depressing him, Professor Payne thought. He looked less jaunty than he had two days earlier. He munched gloomily.

"First I'll give you my formless findings." He finished the sandwich and wiped his lips with a paper napkin. "Then I'll hear yours. Mine are pretty easily summarized. I am now able to tell you that (a) the computers of the Federal Aviation Agency in Oklahoma City ground away for several minutes at prodigious cost to the taxpayer and came up negative. Aforementioned Stanley Brill does not now hold and never has held a pilot's license. (b) Dorothy Bates Sommers, deceased, left a will drawn by her attorney Frederick B. Easby, Esq., in 1954, by which her estate is to be divided in equal shares among her three daughters or, should any one of them predecease her, among that daughter's surviving issue. No bequests. No conditions. No mysteries. No obscurities or eccentricities. It's been filed for probate, so it's now a matter of public record. They've estimated the estate for probate purposes at twenty-five thousand, but this is a formality. It might be much more, or possibly less. (c) Benjamin Harrison Sommers, who died in 1935, left everything—which, as it turned out, was nothing—to his widow. Also perfectly straightforward. (d) Harold James Bates, who died in 1924, left a considerable fortune. Half of it went to something called Last Judgment University, in a place called New Genesis, Ill. New Genesis, est. pop. seventeen, still exists, just west of Omega. But there's no mention of Last Judgment U. in contemporary works of reference, so I conclude that the Bates bequest wasn't enough to save it from such blasphemers as Charles Darwin and Walter Washburn Payne. The rest of Bates's money, still sizable, was divided between the daughters. Again, nothing mysterious or complex. A short will, and to the point."

He paused to take up a second sandwich. "I have also conducted further legal research into the residence of equity in dead bodies, their possession, disposition, and conversion. No new revelations. As I thought, (e) the mortal remains of Dorothy Bates Sommers, along with all clothing, jewels, chattels, and personal possessions thereto pertinent, are the legal property of her Estate, which means that while matters are *sub judice* they are in the charge of Maxie the Monster, as those in the trade affectionately refer to the Honorable Maxwell McManus, Judge of the Orphans Court. I am beginning to worry a little about Maxie the Monster—he is not a jurist who would lightly give up rights to corpses, jewels, chattels, et cetera. (f) The relevant statutes, ordinances and precedents dealing with body-snatching are, as I said the other day, old, rare, and obscure. But I found some, and as far as I can make out the snatcher or snatchers must have violated about four of them. (f one) Wrongful conversion and/or larceny of property belonging to Estate, as hereinbefore described. (f two) Violation of certain sumptuary regulations in the health and real estate codes of Van Buren County prohibiting unauthorized interments in any except such areas as have been officially designated as cemeteries or burying grounds, as may be by law established. None of this involves anything more than about fifty dollars in fines. (f three) Body-snatching is a common law misdemeanor, whether burglarious intent is present or not. The last penalty for it was imposed in 1873 and was a fine of sixteen dollars and five cents. (f four) An altogether more serious matter. The only important charge that could be brought against the malefactors involved, so far as stealing the body itself goes would be an action under Article Sixteen, Paragraph III, of a State Statute of 1917 entitled, '*Venerated Objects, Desecration of, an Act to Prevent The.*' It was passed with the idea of preventing the defilement of the American flag, but it has been interpreted as applying to dead bodies, too. Maximum penalties, five hundred bucks and a year in jail.

"(g) More important still, I took assorted jewelry and unset stones to my friend in Jackson Rapids. He informs me the sapphires are worth fully as much as I guessed. The trinkets are not much, although something. With the stuff that was actually on the body, we are dealing with pawn shops, not Cartier's. He tactfully explained that the trade-in value of used jewelry depends pretty much on how big a sucker the seller can be played for. He guessed at something like six or seven hundred dollars. But the sapphires are big. In both senses of the word. Probably nearer seventy-five thousand than fifty. They are, he says, extraordinarily fine ones. And they are in fashion at the moment, and hard to come by and hard to cut. If they *were* stolen, stolen by anybody besides me, it is very grand larcency indeed."

"It doesn't make things easier," Richie said. "Harder. Why would anybody bury seventy-five thousand?"

"For safekeeping, I suppose. You can see he'd rather bury precious stones than leave them lying around."

"Leaving precious stones lying around is what he does, though." Richie put his hand in his pocket and held out the diamond ring. "It must of dropped off. But you'd think he'd keep track. A careless cat."

Russ, who had taken a swallow of beer, choked on it. "Dropped off what?"

"Like a dead hand."

Russ took the ring and stood up. "At a guess, it's a good stone. O.K., Ace. What's your story?"

Richie frowned. He was in an odd mood, pleased at having created a mild sensation but not as pleased as he should have been. What had been troubling him the day before was troubling him still today. "I found it in Nine Seven Juliet," he said. "I gave it a going over yesterday morning. The ring's not all I found. I looked around the cabin, good. There was kind of smears on the floor. And in the crack at the edge of the carpet there was this." He produced the *Teen Male* envelope from his pocket and carefully shook out its contents. "From the woods up the hill, I guess. The guy threw in his shovel after he'd finished digging without looking to see whether it was clean or not. After he'd thrown in the corpse without noticing how many rings it had. Not too cool a cat, the Death Pilot."

Russ studied the loam and the rotted leaf. "If it's the same earth as that around the grave, which I'm sure it will prove to be, then it's evidence. It may not tell us anything we didn't know, but it ties one knot tight. What else did you find yesterday?"

Richie said tonelessly, "Nothing." He had made up his mind to lie and did so easily.

But Professor Payne, watching him with no suspicion that he was concealing important information, wondered about his uneasy reticence. Something uncomfortable had happened at the airport yesterday, and the impossibility of asking questions about it added Professor Payne's vexation to Richie's. The only thing he could do was to begin a report on his disastrous dinner party.

"You were wise to stay away," he told Russ. "It develops that Bergers and Custers do not mix. Glen and Persh gave a convincing performance of Cain and Abel. I couldn't say which is which though. They both of them seem type-cast as Cain. In any event, they both raise it."

"There was a fight?"

"There was. Or, more accurately, a series of skirmishes in what appears to be a sort of Hundred Years' War."

"What about?"

"That is the question. They were not precisely fighting *about* anything. Merry observed, gratuitously, that Persh had thrown Dolly's money away on the airport business —she attributed these sentiments to her Aunt Agnes, but I think they were purely her own. Then she accused Lisa of idleness and frivolity. Then Persh, who had been notably silent at the beginning, began to talk about the stock market. And this was construed by the Bergers as in some way a violent attack against Glen. Merry felt compelled to rush to his defense, although the way she did it was by becoming offensive."

"What did Persh say about the stock market?"

"He was describing, in a perfectly factual way, how he had just made a modest killing in United Gaskets."

"A killing?" Russ asked consideringly. "Are you sure he said gaskets?"

Professor Payne smiled. "I asked myself the same question. But he did. He repeated it several times. He gave us indeed a number of uninteresting details. The striking rise in Gaskets, he told us, is due to a recently negotiated merger with the firm of Wiley-Allardyce."

"G's and c's often get mixed up. It's true that Wiley-Allardyce manufactures electric switches, but perhaps they're planning to diversify. Move into the death field."

"I think not," Professor Payne said.

"It was gaskets," Richie said.

"Too bad. It would have been interesting if Persh were taunting them with some funny business connected with coffins. He would hardly have been taunting them about gaskets. Still, you had the idea that this was not the first time gaskets had come between the two families?"

"Decidedly not."

"So, what about Mr. Berger goofed in some deal in United Gaskets he was supposed to be doing for the old lady?" Richie suggested.

His uncle welcomed this contribution, although Richie's heart did not seem to be very much in it. It also struck Russ as useful. "Good boy. It's an operating hypothesis. Custer had recommended that Glen Berger invest Dolly's money in Gaskets. Berger tells them, perhaps, that it would be a foolish investment. But Gaskets prosper prodigiously. Recriminations ensue. Custer has done some private dealings and made a modest killing, and throws it in Berger's face."

"It is suggestive. But how it pertains to our concerns is doubtful."

"Everything is doubtful, except death and sapphires. Did anything else happen?"

"Not much. Merry told us a number of stories about people she'd met in Europe who were irresistibly moved to do her enormous favors. Then she told us about the enormous favors she'd done people. She has more quiet confidence in her own attractions and her own generosity than anyone I can think of. It makes her very happy. One is always being told how important it is to have a sense of one's true worth as a human being. This is quite wrong; what is important, to be happy, is to have a completely false sense of it. The true value of most people as human beings is negligible.

"In any case, none of Merry's experiences with all the wonderful people she met on her travels seems pertinent either. And I trust that the future course of our investigations will not involve any more direct contacts with her. I cannot—to put it bluntly—abide the woman. She patronizes me."

"That's not an easy thing to do," Russ said seriously. "How?"

"She claims to believe that I am more virtuous than I am. It is maddening." He paused and then vehemently went on. "A nation once trembled before my pen. And now a dismal bitch addresses me in my own house as a dear old teddy-bear."

"My God, did she really?"

"She also told me I was 'an old fraud' and had 'a heart of marshmallow.'"

"She doesn't know you."

"She doesn't know herself. She's one of those women who measures strength of character by her success in treating masculinity as an hallucination that she can dispel with a little will-power.

"I have always been strongly opposed to capital punishment. But I would not go to any great lengths to conceal evidence pointing toward Merry Berger as guilty of murdering her mother."

"Unfortunately," Russ said, "there is positive evidence pointing the other way. I checked with Air France. There's no doubt that Mrs. Merry S. Berger was a first-class passenger on their number 31, Paris–Chicago, last Sunday, and re-entered the U.S. with the other passengers on that flight. Air France looks at passports before boarding, so the identification's as definite as it could be. By the time she left Paris her mother had been dead for a day and a half in Buchanan."

"She couldn't have come here, strangled her, rushed back to Paris, and then returned in time for the funeral?"

"No. There wouldn't have been time."

There was a pause, and Richie said curiously, "She talked about coming home first-class last night, like she was the first person who'd ever done it. How come she was first-class?"

"It's a good question," Russ said. "I doubt if the Berger

resources run to first-class transatlantic trips. It's several hundred dollars extra."

"Their resources might not cover it," Professor Payne said, "but Dolly's might. Knowing her mother was dying she threw caution to the wind and soared luxuriously on the wings of expectations. I can hear her telling me, 'Walt, I've spent my life working for my boys, and I decided that I owed it to myself just once . . .'" He shivered slightly at the exactness of his mimicry. "And that reminds me of another development last night. Among her boys, as she puts it, is Stanley Brill."

Russ whistled. "That's what we were aiming to find out. How did you discover it?"

"I learned nothing except that she is a real good friend of Stan's and defends him against deprecations as ardently as she does her husband. I introduced Stan into the conversation, and that much came out. But nothing beyond that."

Richie said, "There was *something*." His mood was improving. There seemed no visible reason for this; the others did not realize that once he had crossed the hurdle of a flat lie he had begun to relax. "She said this Brill'd do *anything* for his friends."

"That's true. She thinks it is the most lovable of all his lovable traits."

"And before that," Richie went on. "You remember all that crap about confiding her body to him? *Then* about he'd do anything for his friends. Then—" He made a rude sound with his lips. "She stops. What stops her? She thinks she better not tell us what's anything."

"That's true," Professor Payne said.

"You infer from this that 'anything' meant taking Dolly out of her box?" Russ asked.

"Right."

Russ went to the refrigerator, took out another beer, sat down, and carefully decanted it into his stein. "O.K. Did sapphires come up at all?"

"No. And it did not seem feasible to work them in," Professor Payne said. "Or anything else of significance. Aside from Stanley Brill, I was not able to take the initiative without appearing suspiciously eccentric. I was suspicious enough as it was. So that while we found out a good deal, it is mostly inchoate. The messages were in code."

"Yes. All the messages we have received seem to be. We've tried research and we've tried taking them by storm, and all we get is inferences. And now we have given the alarm. They can hardly be unsuspecting. Both Merry Berger and Stan Brill, and probably everybody else concerned, must—in the peculiar British phrase—have got the wind up." He paused, looking unhappy. He had expected more from the dinner party. "What do we do next? Do I see any hands raised?"

There was silence.

"Well," Russ continued, "I must say, *I* don't know what the hell to do next. I must also say that while I've been having a better time in the last three days than I have in the last five years, I am beginning to worry a bit about venerated objects, desecration of. Or, to be exact, about violating Paragraph IV, Section Two, of the statute, regarding venerated objects, desecration of, willful failure to prevent the. Or to take all reasonable steps to procure the restitution of. I am also beginning to feel mildly apprehensive about having committed grand larceny. I perhaps should feel more apprehensive than I do. Still, now that I know what the sapphires are worth, I feel somewhat less lighthearted about having lifted them."

"What do you propose?" Professor Payne asked uneasily.

"The easiest thing would be for me to go home and for you to call Jim Fess and say you'd noticed some signs of recent digging while strolling in your woods, and you think he better look into it. A replay, with a new finale."

"And the jewels?"

"I'm not anxious to replace them where I got them. But as it's hard to think of a clearer case of grand larceny or a more tangible form of desecration, I suppose I had better. It seems a great shame," he said wistfully.

"Is there none of the information that we've collected that helps to make sense out of all this? I confess I can't think of any, but your mind is trained to deal with these matters."

"No. I do have some more information, but it doesn't help to make sense of the situation. It's about the finances of the Van Buren Flying Service, Inc." Russ looked obliquely at Richie. Like Professor Payne, he had gathered that something was wrong, and that whatever it was had to do with the airport. He went ahead very carefully. "I did some investigation into its finances. As we know, it has always been marginal, and recently it has become submarginal. Which would explain the trenchancy of the dinner-table conversation."

"Yes. One can see why there is a spirit of recrimination if the family business is failing." Professor Payne, as he spoke, also looked covertly at Richie. As he had feared, the boy was growing visibly tenser, trying with indifferent success to hide his feelings. Or, more precisely, to hide the fact that he had feelings.

"I talked to Charlie Knish," Russ said. "You remember him in school, Walt. He and I were frat brothers. He's a vice-president of the Corn State Bank now. He has a fantastic gift for what you might call statistical gossip. He knows every credit rating in the area. If you program Charlie properly and then push the right buttons, he can tell you anything you need to know about money and credit in Van Buren County. Well, I tracked him down in the Parakeet, across the street from the bank, where he takes a daily coffee break lasting from breakfast to lunch. It's where he meets people and gets his mental cards punched.

"I had a couple of cups of coffee with him and talked a while—'Gee, Brother Charlie, how's business' kind of thing—and inconspicuously pushed some buttons. And the tape came clicking out."

He paused. Richie said, "So?"

"Well, the corporation's in trouble. It owes everybody in town. Custer has just lent it a lot of his own money to cover the pay-roll, which it did, but barely. And there are some other items. (a) Dolly had bought a third of the company with her own money, a couple of years ago when it was also in need of some cash and capital, so the Estate owns a third of the stock. She was the biggest stockholder. So the other heirs may have some cause to complain about Custer's business methods."

"I can see why Persh would react so strongly, if Merry has been prodding him for years. And it explains all that stuff about Hog-calls."

"What?"

Professor Payne explained. "I conclude that Merry has

been doing a good deal of free-loading, and Persh ascribes the financial problems of the company to this. Or pretends to."

"No doubt it would add to the red ink. But there are other problems. Charlie says that after she bought the stock to provide some capital, Dolly borrowed a lot of money back from the corporation. And so has another stockholder. Bud Ramsey owes the company a good deal of money. It was legal enough—adequate security and all—but the company's short of cash because of Ramsey's loan. Custer asked Corn State for a loan and didn't get it, but he got one from Buchanan Trust, although not as much as he said he needed. Hence his own loan to the company. The books must be getting pretty tangled by now."

Professor Payne looked at Richie again. His face was as expressionless as it had ever been. Professor Payne went on quickly, "You don't know what Bud wanted the loan for?"

"No."

"Have you any idea how this would tie in with the desecration of the venerated object?"

"No."

"You haven't simply turned yourself off? Being ready to quit anyway?"

"No. I'm still smelling blood, and liking it. But I lack a plan."

Professor Payne was surprised to find how much the thought of calling Jim Fess depressed him. The smell of blood had had a markedly rejuvenating effect on him, too. For the first time in years, he realized, he had been engaged in action with some purpose larger than a crop of pest-free pole beans. Honesty obliged him to admit that he had, like Russ, enjoyed himself more in the last few days than for a very long time. It was embarrassing to find himself disappointed by the prospect of resorting to legal methods.

Richie rescued them. He had been staring fixedly at Russ during the final stage of his exposition, and now it looked as if he had come to some kind of decision. He squared his shoulders and leaned forward in his chair. "But we don't know how this financial stuff fits in, right?"

"Right."

"So the stiff and the stones are the only things we got. And since the stiff came from Brill, Brill's the only person we got. The only one for sure, anyway. It looks like Mrs. Berger's in, but we don't know that. Right?"

Russ hesitated this time. A strict regard for circumstance would have added Nine Seven Juliet, and the airport, to the list of sure things. But he decided to let it pass. "Right."

"So those two'll play it close since they know we've been trying to look in their hands. It's no good *talking* to Brill any more, but we could *do* something to him."

"What do you suggest? Thumbscrews?"

Richie frowned. "What it is is, we need to do a little more desecration."

"Of the venerated object? You don't think there's been enough already?" Russ paused. "You're not suggesting that we dig up Mrs. Sommers and return her to Stanley Brill with card enclosed, so that he can continue his operations in a more orthodox fashion?" He laughed at this. It had cheered him up more than anything so far today. "You could write on the card, 'Kindness of R. Payne.'"

"No," Richie said. "Not the stiff, the stones. How about giving the sapphires and stuff back to Brill? You want to get rid of it. He won't mind having it. It would surprise him, though. So he might talk."

The others stared at him. He was a little surprised at himself. He had been improvising, and he realized that there were some rough spots in his program. But it had been gradually dawning on him that, like the others and in spite of his own private embarrassments, he did not want to turn matters over to the sheriff's office.

So he improvised further. New elaborations occurred to him as he spoke. "We could go and plant the stuff in his office tonight. It'd get it off your back, and it wouldn't"—he was speaking very carefully, almost solemnly—"implicate anybody. Or not so you could prove anything. So we could trap Brill." He added in quite a different tone, "I don't know him, but I don't like him."

"I agree." Russ spoke respectfully. "Except about one point. I don't see how we trap him. Are we to hide in his office until he comes in tomorrow and discovers seventy-five thousand dollars' worth of star sapphires on his desk, and see what he does? Or do we install closed circuit TV along with the stones?"

Richie considered. He was getting enthusiastic about his idea, viewing it simply as an abstract design of great elegance. "Well, no. What'd be a good idea'd be, you make an appointment to meet him at his office tomorrow morning. Before the place opens. You want to talk private. You get there early. So you're waiting on the sidewalk when he gets there."

For a time no one moved or spoke.

There was a wall telephone beside the refrigerator. Russ

drained his stein, stood up, and dialed. The first words he spoke were into the receiver. "Hello," he said. "Stan?"

Russ Mallery was, in his way, a contrary-minded man. His career was the defense of civic propriety and security, yet he took satisfaction in doing things he knew were improper, and he liked to run risks. He accepted Richie's project as much because it was improper and risky as because he seriously considered it likely to yield results. He was also, in his way, a gregarious, cooperative man. He liked doing things with other people, and particularly with Professor Payne and Richie. He often remarked that he belonged to the most unhappy generation that had ever lived: "The last to be pushed around by its elders, the first to be pushed around by kids." The present venture satisfied not merely his hunting instincts; the teamwork involved in it was satisfying other, possibly deeper, instincts as well. He liked to be treated as an equal and to be able to treat other people as equals. Most of his life had been spent in either subordination or command. Both made him restive.

Contrariness and cooperation both played their part in the peculiar satisfaction he took in contemplating the hazards of the job that lay before them that night. Driving his colleagues into town, he reviewed in his own mind the tactical analysis he had made. There was no choice but to force open a window in Stan's office. He rather liked this prospect. The site was rather uncomfortably exposed, but the anticipation of Stanley Brill's forthcoming agitation obscured any possible disadvantage arising from the criminal nature of the project. He had no more hesitation in trespassing than in stealing sapphires. And he was reassured by the palliative thought that, while he might be breaking, he need not do any entering.

They reached Polk Street in silence and drove slowly past the Funeral Home. The floodlighting had been, as he hoped, turned off by now, and the building, dignified and decorously residential, was visible only as a faint white presence in the dark. But there was an illuminated sign near the sidewalk that still, at one A.M., informed possible customers that this was the Stanley F. Brill Funeral Home, assured them of DIGNIFIED PERSONALIZED SERVICES, and offered them A DISTINCTIVE FUNERAL WITHIN THE MEANS OF ALL. It also had an arrow pointing to FREE PARKING.

Russ went on around the block. Brill's had engulfed the lot behind it on South Grant Street, which was now entirely occupied by an asphalt parking area. It was overlooked, as he knew from his previous visit, by the windows of the Waiting Hall and Stan's office. He drove at the same steady pace, aware that anything slower would infallibly attract the attention of one of those predictable old women who sat up late at night staring out their windows and had infallible memories for license numbers. He was extremely alert, and he was enjoying himself. He had, when in public office, sometimes reflected that the professional dedication of any public servant—or any doctor or teacher or priest or undertaker—owed something to a gratifying feeling of committing acts of vengeance in reverse. But more than public office inspired him to willful mischief.

No house lights were on; Buchanan kept early hours. There was no other traffic, only the shapes of cars parked at the curb. The street lamps, widely placed and deeply embowered in the leaves of the elms, gave no light beyond a small green nimbus.

The dark streets were a subject for chronic correspondence in the *Courier-Bee;* nervous women found them dangerous, but Buchanan had remained serenely untroubled by crime in the streets.

"It's fortunate in a way that there's so much street-parking in this part of town," Russ said. "The houses are all big Victorian ones that have been divided up into flats, so they've run out of garage space. We'll be that much less conspicuous."

They had come opposite Brill's now. The screen of thickly residential shrubbery had changed to the empty expanse of asphalt, and across it they could dimly see the Funeral Home.

As Russ spoke he turned the car into an empty place by the curb and extinguished the headlights. Richie suddenly opened the door as he did so, and muttering, "I'll go look it over," disappeared into the dark.

The two men were startled by his unexpected action. "What's he up to?" Russ asked. "Do you think he's throwing himself into this adventure a bit too wholeheartedly?"

"No. No more so than we. He's merely reconnoitering. Very sensibly."

"But a trifle melodramatically. It's odd; the roles of the generations seem reversed. For us this is a lark, for him it's dead serious. Do you think it may be too serious?" Russ was having misgivings about his team. "Given that he's a sensitive youth, and it's a dark night?"

Professor Payne, his own hand on the door, hesitated. "I should judge not. He has his own kind of insensitivity as well as sensitivity. Boys do, different from ours. Darkness and crime may be alarming at eleven, but at sixteen they are pure glamour. And—" he went on, half-persuaded into equability by the sound of his hushed voice detachedly offering these abstractions, "I am inclined to think that Richie has more than his share of stamina. It is possible that stamina is not like a reservoir to be drawn on judiciously but a muscle that is strengthened by use. He has had plenty of occasion to exercise his. And in any event, he likes taking the initiative."

"He does. That's not to say it's always wise to let him."

"Perhaps not. But I think it is therapeutic. Adventure is a tonic for him. Quite as much as flying. As it is for myself," he added with unusual candor. He was generally relentlessly impersonal; the nocturnal outing had softened him.

Russ laughed but said nothing. Richie had come up silently, and he opened the door and leaned toward them. "We're in," he whispered, breathing heavily. He had covered the breadth of the parking lot very fast.

"In?"

"Window's open." He said it with an attempt at offhandedness, but he was jubilant. The shadows of lunchtime had passed, and he was justifying his great-uncle's hypothesis with the precision of an experiment in elementary chemistry. "Easy."

"Was it?" Russ had spent a good part of the afternoon giving pleasurable attention to the operation of breaking in. Richie seemed to have accomplished it without tools or preparation. "How did you get past the lock?"

"I didn't, exactly. It already was unlocked. I wanted to make sure."

"You knew it was unlocked?"

"I knew it had been." He had caught his breath and was speaking easily, with comradeship, not complacency. "I unlocked it myself. This afternoon."

There was silence in the car. Professor Payne asked, "How?"

"When I took the car this afternoon. Instead of going to the airport, I came here. To look the place over. But there was a funeral. So I joined in. Eyes on floor. Hands folded. Nobody noticed. Brill's office has his name on the door. Empty. So I unlocked the window. Air-conditioned and the blind down. I figured nobody would notice. They didn't."

Silence again. Then Russ said, "I congratulate you." He started to open the door. "Now I guess we better get on with it." He was dazzled, and a little disappointed as well.

"Give me the stuff," Richie said. "I'll put it in."

Russ started to get out of the car and then stopped. It was, in all justice, Richie's night. He handed over the canister of sapphires and a flannel bag which had once contained a silver platter, a wedding present of Professor Payne's from fifty-five years before, and now held Dolly Sommers' jewelry.

Richie took it and went into the darkness. He was back in a remarkably short time.

"It's O.K. It's good it's a night like it is. You can't see *any*thing out there." He climbed in and closed the door carefully.

CHAPTER VII

Emergency Procedure

Russ got up the next morning with a mild sense of annoyance at having been outdone by a sixteen-year-old boy in his determination to commit an impropriety. He faced the morning and Stanley Brill's sidewalk with an elusive sense of bafflement.

He kicked a small juniper.

But he was still enjoying himself, and he expected that the next scene in the drama would make him a star. The script was written to order, he thought, for his particular talents. He welcomed Stanley's appearance with pleasant anticipation. He liked dealing with Stan.

The mortician appeared around a corner. He strode briskly and looked spruce in fresh make-up and a gray suit which, like his expression, embodied the solemn without hint of the lugubrious. He carried an umbrella and swung it in a tastefully short arc. But all this was a matter of habit. Beneath the surface of a man skillfully embalmed and politely reanimated he was quivering. One side of his face twitched. Russ's spirits rose still higher.

"Hi there," Russ said with cheerful brightness. "I was early. It's a nice morning."

They shook hands. "Yes, yes, beautiful, yes," Stan said. His hand was cold and damp.

"I often take an early morning walk," Russ said untruthfully.

"An early morning walk, yes, an early morning walk. Yes." Stan paused, perhaps feeling that this was an inadequate commentary, and added in the manner of a drunk reciting randomly remembered snatches of verse, "It is pleasant to go strolling, so early on a summer's morn." He was looking sidewise at Russ as he said it, transparently wondering whether he dared to inquire the purpose of the interview. But he did not dare, any more than he had dared to refuse to grant it in the first place. Instead, he hesitated on the sidewalk and then started toward the portal.

It was a portal that at other times filled him with reasonable pride. He was a successful man, and he had translated into the physical structure of the Funeral Home, with ample means and tolerable ingenuity, his own dreams—of dignity, decorum, and beauty. A mini-Mount Vernon with aluminum columns and steel clapboards shining in white paint, green shutters fixed to the walls. An elegant palace of decease.

But this morning the enameled fulfillment of his dreams did not lighten his step or fill him with proud assurance. He skulked.

He skulked, indeed, to a point where Russ almost doubted the authenticity of his skulking. Was it possible that they had been seen and identified the night before, that Stan's furtive quivering was a form of guile prefacing an imminent accusation, with witnesses? Or was it that the tremulous approach to his own front door was a sign of neither guile nor alarm, but merely of genuine indecision about how to exploit his advantage? But at length Russ concluded that this was impossible. Whatever Stan looked like, it was not a man who had the upper hand. His bearing suggested an obligation to pay protection to pipers rather than to call tunes.

The colonial-type door had two locks. It took Stan an inordinate time to fit his keys in them. Finally they were admitted to a hall floored in vinyl, its walls painted a tactful turquoise, overgrown with jungly plastic verdure in plastic jardiniers, where visitors were faced with a large bronze plaque which said:

THIS IS THE HOUSE OF PEACE

Russ had seen it before and noted to himself that it was a vulgarity. Now he saw it also as an irony. Peace was as distant from a Funeral Home presided over by Stan Brill as from a zoo. He allowed himself to chuckle aloud.

He had intended this to discomfit his host, and it did. Stan looked over his shoulder, and his twitch became more pronounced. When he bent over to unlock his office door, it took him even longer than at the front door. They were exceedingly security-conscious here, with all these locks, Russ thought. Considering the ease with which Richie had inserted himself as a mourner, this augmented the irony of the House of Peace. And so many locks were not what one expected of an honest tradesman; particularly not one whose wares were of a sort so little likely to attract a casual burglar.

At length Stan pushed the door open and went into his office. Russ, intensely curious and alert, followed him, surveyed the room, and saw, to his alarm, nothing at all.

Or at least, nothing out of the way in the form of a small canister and a large flannel sack holding a king's, or at least a mortician's, ransom. The office was a large room, commodiously appointed. There were an arm chair and sofa upholstered in fern-green imitation leather, soft gray walls decorated with framed pictures and mottos, a Hepplewhite filing cabinet, a king-size desk of teak-finished steel bearing two fern-green telephones, and a large vase of artificial red roses. But there was no canister and no flannel bag.

For an unsettling instant he thought that a second jewel robbery must have occurred, some fantastically coincidental intervention by another trafficker in sapphires. But then he realized what had happened. Objects thrust through the window in darkness would fall in back of the large sofa, which stood a few feet out from the wall. In fact, unless Stan's janitorial arrangements were of exceptional quality, the presence of the canister and bag might well have gone unnoticed for a considerable time. Russ was glad he was there to draw attention to them.

But the baffling problem now presented itself of *how* to draw attention to them without inviting suspicion, or even supplying proof that he had known they were there all along. Stan, his morale apparently improved by a setting he felt became him, sat down at his desk and said with a reasonably exact facsimile of business-like authority, "Now, Russ, what is it you want this time?"

The disappearance of Stan's nervousness suggested a tactic to Russ. "Is anything wrong, Stan?" he asked solicitously. "You seem nervous?"

As planned, nervousness returned. "No," Stan said. "No, no, no, no, no." He paused, and Russ said nothing. "I feel a little out of sorts, yes out of sorts, the humidity, the humidity." He fingered a piece of paper on his blotter. Russ ostentatiously glanced at it. It was a carbon of a bill for $376.06 to a Mrs. Duane G. Heiser. Stanley, seeing Russ read it, picked it up and read it himself, put it down, and picked it up again.

"Have you mislaid something?" Russ asked.

"No." He was surprised and therefore apprehensive. "No, no, I have mislaid nothing at all, nothing." He drew a handkerchief from his breast pocket and carefully patted his forehead with it. He was beginning to sweat torrentially, but it was, in fact, very warm. The air-conditioning was not operating.

"Perhaps you would be more comfortable with the window open," Russ said with sudden inspiration.

"No, no. There is air-conditioning, air-conditioning, or whatever you may call it." The delay in coming to whatever subject Russ might be aiming to discuss was gradually reducing Brill to incoherence. But he was able to stand up and turn on a switch by the door. Faint distant roars were audible, and a surge of cooling air swept up through the register. "What was it, now, you wished to see me about?"

"Well." The plan of action had proved self-defeating. Tentatively he stood up. "Nice place you have here." He began to inspect the office. This was not, he realized, very convincing, but Stan was by now in a condition where it was not necessary to be very convincing. A measure of assurance was returning to Russ with his success in disrupting his host's morale. A leisurely inspection might be counted on to disrupt it further. He walked around the office and paused before a motto elegantly framed in gold and inscribed on artificial parchment in Old English lettering. Russ read it aloud.

"*The Mortician's Creed*

"Ah, lovely appearance of Death!
No Sight upon Earth is so fair.
Not all the gay pageants that *breathe*
Can with a dead body compare.

Charles Wesley 1768."

He continued round the room, pausing for some time before an original oil painting that evidently represented classical burial rites. Across a mistily Attic landscape epicene figures, exiguously clad, lounged sadly on the steps of a doric temple. Russ studied it carefully. Behind him, Stanley was breathing heavily.

When he judged that enough time had been allotted to admiration of the décor, he looked behind the sofa and said loudly, "What is this?"

Stan jumped. He was beside Russ, kneeling on the sofa, and staring down behind it in one movement. He looked in silence at the can and the large, lumpy bag on the floor.

Russ said, "We better have a look." He went down on one knee at the end of the sofa and reached toward them. Stan stopped him with a strangled cry and a hand laid powerfully on his wrist. He stared at Russ with wild surmise and then managed to speak. "No, no, no, no, I put them there. I *want* them there. They're *mine*, and I want them there." He paused, gulped and said a little more calmly, but still in a falsetto yelp, "You leave my things alone, Russ Mallery."

Russ stood up. He was taken wholly by surprise. Stan

was still kneeling on the sofa, sweating and trembling. But then, suddenly, he got to his feet, brushed his pants legs as if he had been kneeling in dust, and rubbed his hands. "And now, Russ, what is it you wish to talk to me about?" he said in quite an ordinary voice.

Russ stared penetratingly at him, professional habit reflecting the painfully acquired knowledge that penetrating stares covered a multitude of uncertainties. Stanley Brill was a man of unsuspected depths, and he was nonplussed. The lawyer's most conspicuous gift was for cutting losses, and the moment had come to do so. He had no *locus standi.* He could extract nothing more; he knew enough not to underestimate Stan's gift for further quick changes of psychological costume. At the door he said, "I have already found out what I came to learn. And I am sure that you can guess what it is, Stan." He put his hands in his pockets and walked away. Certain that Stan would watch his departure from behind a venetian blind, he went down the walk with the jaunty air of a man who has solved a perplexing puzzle in a particularly advantageous way.

His inward state was very different. He had sensationally failed as an actor in the scene where he had expected to triumph. It enraged and depressed him. It also perplexed him, which enraged him further. He could, at first, see only one explanation for what had happened. Stan had been quicker than he; Stan had immediately recognized the canister and seen how to deal with its presence, that is to get Russ out of the office before he had a chance to pick it up and open it. Russ had miscalculated all along the line except, he now saw with slight solace, on one point. When he started his car, he glanced at the

Funeral Home; Stan was separating the slats of a venetian blind to watch him.

It was the classic posture of a frightened malefactor. And it suggested an alternative explanation of his conduct. Perhaps all of Stan's behavior was equally classic, an archetypal posture of pure panic. Conceivably Stan had seen in the canister and the mysterious, lumpy bag nothing more than alien and therefore frightening facts. Conceivably he had not knowingly outwitted Russ at all; a man possessed by panic might act on a single, jungle principle: deny everything, conceal everything, insist that nothing was wrong. Instinct would urgently inform him that foreign containers behind sofas had better not be investigated by inimical lawyers.

He put the car in *Drive* and started off. The possibility that Stanley's response had been primitive, not intelligent, did nothing to comfort him. It might assuage his vanity, but it confirmed his failure. He could not now be sure that Stan *had* seen the canister before. And the more he thought of it, the more plausible an explanation panic seemed to be. Beneath his healthy tan, behind his shining white teeth, under the cosmetic crust of civilization, Stan was a very primitive creature indeed.

As he drove off, Russ punched his temple with his clenched fist.

Professor Payne's feelings, as he made ready to deal death to Liver Scale, Crown Rot, and Root Borer, suddenly epidemic among the vegetables, were similar to Russ's as he contemplated the personality of Stanley Brill. He generally found the massacring of pests a reliable palliative for malaise. But this morning the sight of writhing borers had no curing power.

No more than Russ had he been satisfied by the action of the night before. What seemed to be his better self (he was not absolutely certain of this) informed him he had been mistaken to support a program that combined the gothic with the illegal in undesirable proportions. He did not believe in the existence of conscience, but something like conscientious scruples troubled him. He should never have called Russ in the first place. Good citizenship should have led him straight to the sheriff of Van Buren County. He had been lured by unworthy motives into membership in that most odious of corrupt regimes, the republic of comrades. But still he disliked very much the idea of giving up the adventure.

Such conflicting impulses struck him as being as ominous as they were unworthy. He was afraid he might be observing a weakening of his moral reflexes, a failure of his powers of ethical coordination. Absolutes had always been his vital sustenance, so the prospect was fully as worrying as a palpable decay of muscle-power. But he had to admit it: he wanted to go on investigating the theft of Dolly Sommers and her jewels He wanted it too intensely; he saw with horror a vision of drooling regression.

If he worried about the balance of his mind, he also worried about the balance of Richie's. The boy had been (he had said) "scheduled for dual" at ten. He had asked for the car as his generation often asked for things, with a mixture of courteous formality and the certainty he had an inalienable right to it. And on consideration, Professor Payne was more inclined than he had been the night before to concede something to the theory Russ had advanced while they were waiting in the parked car. Richie's show of initiative had been almost excessively energetic. It gave his great-uncle the unnerving feeling that he might be raising a tiger in the belief that it was a tom-cat. It was true that a little earlier that morning Richie had discussed with trusting affability the problems of ways and means for financing flying lessons. He had dilated on plans, ambitious and vague, for finding a job. He had eventually negotiated, with a naïveté suitable to his age, a long-term loan without interest. The conversation had been conducted with mutual satisfaction and esteem.

It had ended on a less encouraging note, however. Something was wrong. Richie was being furtive. His initiative in opening Stanley Brill's window was not merely energetic but secretive. The failure of understanding, interrupted in the cabin of Nine Seven Juliet, was evident again. He had closed their talk that morning by saying, "I got to get out of here." He was not worried about being late. He was worried about being trapped.

Professor Payne hitched up the cumbersome tank of poison on his back, aimed the nozzle of its hose at an adolescent corn stalk, and declared war on the Liver Scale. But again, implications troubled him. The intimation of mortality, even for Liver Scale, was unwelcome. He was old and discouraged and perplexed by his moral uncertainty and the mystery of youth. Perhaps Richie was only growing up. Or perhaps he was too old to understand him.

Richie's state of mind, in point of fact, was at once simpler and more complicated than Professor Payne supposed. The oddest thing about it, the alternation of ebullient energy with brooding distress, was partly the sign of a returning spiritual elasticity. But there were more substantial causes for distress than the oscillations of psychic convalescence, and the symptoms were aggravated because he was not, by nature, much given to introspective questioning of his feelings. He did not know, or ask himself, why it made all that much difference to him that Bud Ramsey might be complicitously involved in body-snatching and jewel thievery. The evidence that he was, he realized, was extremely slim. But Richie's ability to appraise evidence did not include the control of his own reactions. He had lied about the evidence. He was aware of no conscientious regrets about lying, but the act of lying about it had somehow given importance to the evidence. He could say to himself, reasonably enough, suppose Bud had been snatching bodies or stealing jewels; so in a manner of speaking had Richie himself. Suppose Bud had been the skillful pilot who landed Nine Seven Juliet in a wheatfield; his burying the jewelry with the corpse might be construed of exculpating him of avarice which, to Richie's mind, was a more serious sin than theft. But he could work out nothing that explained his almost nauseated sense that anybody's complicity with Stanley Brill and the Bergers in any venture, even a legally innocent one, was dirty and disgusting.

He failed, in short, to see that he regarded Bud as the agent of his salvation, almost of his resurrection. Or that his standards for people, if a little ill-defined, were very high, and his standards for deities astronomical. In that, at least, Professor Payne had understood his problem very well.

But still his mood was variable, and these unpleasant concerns did not entirely dominate him as he drove to the airport. There were other, exhilarating, subjects to occupy him. He thought of Russ's interview with Stanley Brill, now presumably in course, with a confidence in Russ's ability to transact it successfully that would have touched the lawyer. He thought, with exhilaration of a different kind, about Lisa. He thought, with solid satisfaction, about the partial solution of his financial difficulties. He thought about airplanes. The intoxication of air began to work, and when he reached the airport, the familiar, electric elation had drowned all residue of melancholy.

In the terminal he found a variation of the familiar tableau. Norm was leaning against the counter. Jack was lounging in a wicker chair drinking cherry soda from a can. Lisa was doing accounts at her desk. Richie had a passing impression of a shopwindow, the composition slightly rearranged by a window-dresser for variety's sake.

Norm was talking to no one in particular, ". . . I had a little trouble when I was leaving this morning. This Sky King was taxiing ahead of me and he got to the runway, they were using three one, and the Sky King gets a little mixed up and tells the Tower he's ready at one three, so the Tower—some sarcastic son of a bitch—says 'if you're ready for take-off at one three make a one eighty and taxi south to the last intersection,' and this damn fool Sky King thinks he means it and by God if he doesn't start making the one eighty right the hell into my wing. Reminds me of one day back in fifty-nine when I was going into Meigs with a hell of a cross wind. . . ."

He went on. No one paid him perceptible attention, and no one acknowledged, or seemed even to notice, Richie's arrival. But this, he knew, was ritual. The code of airport etiquette forbade overhasty greeting. Indeed, it discouraged any greeting at all; it was a form of courtesy to treat newcomers as if they had been there all the time. And Richie was pleased by the unnoticing atmosphere. It certified him as a comrade. Self-confidence strengthened, his powers of critical observation revived. While waiting for something to happen he constructed and installed an imaginary sign with flashing lights, No Loitering. It would be the end of Buchanan Municipal Airport.

Lisa finished her accounts and consulted the top drawer of the filing cabinet. As she leaned over it she said, "Hi, Richie." She had been waiting for Norm to stop talking. "You were scheduled for dual with Bud."

"Right."

"He's not here," she said, her wide, luminous brown eyes very serious.

"I noticed that."

"I'm sorry, I've got bad news for you, my dear. He had to go off on a trip. I was going to call you, but I don't have your phone number."

"Bud off on a trip?" Norm asked of the countertop.

"He had to fly some deans or something from the university to a meeting in Jefferson City, Missouri, in the one eighty. They left at seven-thirty, and he'll be gone all day. Doc was scheduled for it, but he's still sick." She turned to Richie. "Cheese could have gone, but he had an accident this morning."

"Accident? He crash?" Richie asked it automatically, and then felt cold. He had not given any thought to the danger of flying, only to its security, but he knew now that a sense of danger was there, in his mind.

"No. It was on the ground. He hit his head on the bumper of a parked car. He's in the hospital."

"How'd he do that?" Richie felt much better. He disliked Cheese. An accident on the ground became him better.

"Nobody knows." Lisa was, as always, quick and noncommittal. "Norm found him out on the parking lot when he got in this morning. He was knocked out. The doctor says he probably has a concussion. He'll be all right, but he'll be away from work for a while."

"Must have stumbled," Norm said. "Clumsy son of a bitch." He spoke with languid malevolence, a little surprising. "Anyway, he's not hurt bad. Like I was saying, this Sky King this morning . . ."

He went on with details.

"Bud was sorry," Lisa said, when he stopped. "He was gone before I got here. But he left a note." She held up a clipboard. On it was a printed form-letter from something called *Integrated Control Systems Inc.* In the margin was a pencil message scrawled in big, slovenly script. "He says he's real sorry he couldn't make it but how about tomorrow same time. And then he says," she turned the clipboard sideways and frowned at the scrawl, "'ride with you Hayes if he wants?'" She looked up. "I have to deliver a hog."

He eyed her questioningly over the top of the Coke can. He was still being aloof, but he was grateful to her. In spite of her being much older, enough to belong, in his view, to the generation of Bud and Jack and Norm, she made Richie feel competent and confident simply by the way she spoke to him. She treated him like a man. And, he realized again with a small, hidden start, as a man she liked him.

"Yeah?" he said.

"Near Fort Hayes."

"They don't have enough hogs in Fort Hayes, or what?"

"You'd have to sit in the right seat. I'm not a CFI. But you can drive the plane if you want. And it won't cost you anything."

He was delighted. He said, "I won't have to hold the hog?"

"It's a crated hog. It can go in the baggage compartment. It's not very big."

"What do they use it for in Hayes?"

She stared seriously into his eyes. "It's a boar. A pedigreed boar. They're going to use it for breeding." She looked down and then up at him from under very long eyelashes and added, "When it's old enough."

He was taken aback. He seemed to have gone in rather deep. He said casually, "Right. When do we go?"

"I've got a letter to do. You can go preflight the one forty. It's on the ramp. Earl was going to top it, so it ought to be ready to go. I'll be out in five minutes."

He felt like a member of the ruling class again. But the sight of the 140 gave him doubts. He had preflighted a plane only once, three days ago under Bud's direction, and he was not sure he could remember all of it, what he was supposed to look at, or how it was supposed to look when he did. He recalled the headline in *Today's Pilot* which he had seen on his first visit, when it meant nothing to him: *Accident File: Careless Preflight.* As a member of the ruling class, a competent preflight was expected of him. He didn't like the idea of telling Lisa he didn't know what he was doing.

He studied the 140 speculatively. Now that he was responsible for it, it seemed to have grown large, complex, and redoubtable—and also fragile. He looked around, whether in hope of help or to make sure no one was looking he could not have said for sure.

There was a brown and white Cessna parked near him, and he noticed that on the ground, in the shade of its wing, Earl was again leaning against the landing gear with his comic book. Richie went to him with the half-formed idea of asking for assistance, and said, "Hi."

Earl did not look up but answered something like "Yump" that could be construed as showing awareness of someone else's presence. Richard Payne, Airman, looked down on Earl, the lazy line boy, and embarrassedly tried to ask him how to preflight his plane. "Lisa and I are taking the one forty to Hayes."

"Yeah. I know." His moistened finger-tip turned a page and resumed its progress through the text.

"It's set to go?"

"Guess so," Earl mumbled. "Topped it with ninety. Quart of oil."

Richie hesitated and turned away. He would rather face a faulty plane than Earl. In any case, Earl wasn't much better informed than he, and much less reliable. He went back to the 140 and concentrated on remembering Bud's lesson. Birds' nests. Prop blades. Test the wings to make sure they're fastened on tight. What was next? He thought and remembered. The gear. The struts and the tires. *If the gear falls off when you're in the air, it causes trouble when you try to land.* He grinned to himself. He wasn't sure what the exact symptoms of this disaster would be, but the gear looked normal. Sumps. Gas tanks.

He had done all right, he thought, and hoped that all right was perfect.

Lisa came out the door, lugging a crate. He relieved her of it and carried it to the plane. "I *think* I remembered everything. I wouldn't be too certain."

"I'll open the baggage door and you push the pig in," she said. He did so, and there were movements and subdued squeals. "He'll get used to it," she said. "They usually like flying."

"You fly a lot of hogs?" he was remembering her father's mention of this unexpected aspect of a romantic profession.

"Some." She was being a pilot now, terse and business-like. "It checks out all right? I'll have a look." She walked around the plane, looking critically at it, twitching the ailerons and the elevators. "It looks good."

She unlocked the door and climbed in. He followed her with a slight renewal of self-consciousness as he awkwardly hoisted himself up and then worked his way into the seat. But she was turning on the master and the magnetos and fastening her seat belt, not watching him. She was cool and crisp with the routine, checking the fuel pump and the radio, clearing the prop, cracking the throttle. They began to roll, and at the end of the taxiway she headed the plane into the wind, pulled on the brake, and handed him the typed check list. "Read it off, Copilot."

"Right. One. Run up to sixteen hundred . . ."

The sound of the engine drowned them as he watched her following his instructions. He was impressed by her business-like assurance, but not awed. He had done it himself, after all. She was a cool pilot-in-command. He was, for the moment, content to be her partner.

At altitude she leveled off and leaned back. He supposed

she was going to give him the controls, but she did not immediately do so. Instead she said to him, staring watchfully at the sky, looking for traffic, "You know, I don't think Cheese fell down. I think he got beaten up. Somebody hit him. He was already getting a terrific black eye."

He was startled. "Somebody doesn't like him, maybe?"

"I think you're right. It's funny. I don't know who could have hit him. There's never anybody around here. Any strangers, I mean. It's a long way from anywhere. Too far to walk. Nobody would come here unless they meant to. But somebody must have come. People don't fall down and hit their heads on bumpers and get black eyes. Not even if they're clumsy like Cheese."

"Nobody was in the terminal?"

"We hadn't opened up yet. Bud was here to get ready for his trip, but he must have left already before Cheese got here. Norm got in early. He was here when I came. But he didn't find Cheese at first. He was lying in the lot between two cars the deans had come in. Norm borrows the jeep when he comes. He found Cheese when he went out to get it."

"Why was Cheese here? He isn't, mostly, is he?"

"I don't know. Nobody ever knows why Cheese is anyplace. He's always going off on trips by himself in company planes without telling anybody. Sometimes he takes planes somebody else is scheduled for. It drives Pop nuts, but he can't say anything since Cheese's family pretty well own the place."

"Yeah?" Richie was cautious.

Lisa was silent for a moment, still searching the sky intently. Then she said, "I was kind of shaken."

"I can see you would be."

She did not, he thought, look shaken. She looked supremely capable of dealing with a crisis, including one of her own feelings, but her imperturbability gave added force to her words.

"He's not a bad guy, Cheese," she went on, "but he's mysterious. He's my cousin, you know, but I don't know much about him. Nobody does. And a lot of people don't like him. Including my father, and Bud. And Norm."

He knew more about this than she suspected, and the shade of duplicity his knowledge raised was embarrassing. He nodded. But she had said all she was going to say, and a moment later she gave him the plane and he forgot about Cheese and his being beaten up in the parking lot.

It was strange at first, flying from the right seat, with the functions of his hands reversed. He had to concentrate on it too hard to worry about anything else.

"Try holding a heading on the directional gyro," she suggested. He had not done that before, and it was harder than he expected: he tried to hold zero seven five degrees; he would fly what he was sure was straight for a few seconds; and the gyro had spun to ninety. He could not believe he had turned off his course—it seemed clearly a caprice of the gyro.

And there were other baffling things about it.

"Remember," she said, "it turns backwards."

He could remember it, but only after it had surprised him each time by doing it. When he went right the gyro swung clockwise away from him. Each time it happened, he said disgustedly, "Damn it," under his breath.

Lisa laughed. "It takes about ten times. Then you know. I don't know why. You have to unlearn your instincts. Like most other things about flying. When you start, what you know automatically is right is always the wrong thing. We're just about there, so I better take it and start letting down. We can try some more navigation on the way home."

He abandoned the controls. "O.K., Lisa, it's your airplane," he said. Now he could look down around him at the land, the geometric pattern of the section lines, the regularly spaced clusters of trees and barns and silos that marked the farmsteads. A design for wallpaper, the contours flattened, the gray-green and tan patterns repeated at intervals. Then, as the plane banked, there was a serpentine river lost in trees and flat meadows running to wooded hills that walled the winding valley. And in the sky, a long range of clouds lying flat, like more hills on a snowclad shoreline, miles away. This was his kingdom, his and Lisa's and the plane's. Infinity, and so freedom.

"I've been here before," she said. "It's a nice field to land in."

The plane banked into final. The field, its borders neatly aligned with the ends of the wings, rose to them. She was over the fence now, very low, holding back for the flare, leaning forward, her eyes on the ground, frowning a little, with her lips open, as the bright grass came toward her. They were inches off the ground, slowing fast, the nose of the plane rising as she held it off. Richie's glance was divided between her profile and the field. The sensual elation of coming home to the ground, smoothly, quickly, easily, but still with a feeling of overwhelming climax, until the gear were on the grass, and the plane was suddenly turned into a lumbering ground beast, awkward and heavy. She put on the brake and pulled out the mixture, then leaned back and smiled at him.

"Nice landing," he said.

She put her hand on his knee and smiled again, and then said, "We'll give Harry Gettelman his boar. Then we might go sit by the river for a while. It's pretty along here. If you're not in a hurry."

He was not. And it was indeed a pretty river, with willows and cottonwoods on the steep banks. They sat on a patch of grass almost at the water's edge, watching eddies form at the muddy brim. It was hot, and the river sounds were cool. Moving water, streams, currents, fascinated him. He remembered as a child watching beguiled for hours as streams washed by rocks and dug channels and fell in small white cascades over dams, displaying before him the mysteries of perpetual motion, the uncatchable, the unstoppable, like growing up.

He laughed at himself, and she asked what he was thinking of, and he answered honestly that he was thinking of water flowing, and airplanes landing in fields, and of how he admired her skill as a pilot. She said nothing, but looked instead at the water, as if she were seeing something in it she had not seen before. And after a moment she said, "Moving through time and space feels the same no matter how you do it. Water or air."

She was on her back looking up at him, smiling, eyes shining. He stared down appraisingly at her face. Her lips were parted as if she were about to speak, her breasts pointing up under her blouse. She lived in two worlds, he understood. He had seen her first as an attractive woman, the kind of woman, perhaps, that some of his friends claimed to have as aunts, whose perfume wafted a mildly illicit liking for guys his age. A liking with objectives quite different from Christmas presents or lent cars or clandestine cocktails. He was detachedly curious about such women and took a cautious interest in contemporaries who ostentatiously welcomed, or claimed to welcome, their attentions. He felt there was some danger and a little discredit in it, as in the more makeshift or esoteric drugs, and something of the same attraction. He saw her still in that class, a professional pilot, a divorcee, superbly confident of what she was. An era removed from the girls in his class whom he had gone out with, virgins who wore their make-up as a disguise and not a revelation.

But in her evident interest in him, her tactful show of initiative, there was nothing perverse. She belonged to his age, too, and that exempted her from danger and discredit. It was not at all that she was younger when they were together. It was that he was older or, more nearly, that they shared an age in a void of yearlessness. She treated him as an equal, and they understood each other's meanings. There was no need to explain things to her, and she did not need to explain anything to him. That was the talisman of equality, that explanations were never necessary.

He was excited, but his senses were not in flames. He kissed her, but rather absently, as an incident in a serious conversation, and stretched out on the grass with his hands under his head.

"When'd you start flying?" he asked.

"I soloed on my sixteenth birthday. The earliest you're allowed to, legally. Bud taught me to fly. My family thought it was a good idea. They thought it was safer than a car. At least, Pop convinced my mother that it was. Safer than most other things I could be doing, too." She laughed. "When I was fifteen my parents told me I was uncontrollable. They hoped flying would quiet me down."

"Did it?"

She considered this carefully, as an important but difficult question. "I suppose so. I didn't think about anything much but airplanes for a year or so. Then they made me go to college."

"Even if you didn't want to?"

"My mother had gotten tired of airplanes by then. She said I thought too much about flying. She decided it was dangerous. My parents told me I had a good mind and I ought to make something of myself. They wanted me to meet nice boys. So I went to college and met a nice boy and got married to him."

"So they decided they liked airplanes best?"

She smiled by way of answer.

"My parents never got in my way, much," he said. "At least they wouldn't have told me I ought to make something of myself." He saw this as a narrow escape from a major indignity. "What'd they want you to make?"

"They didn't know. Sometimes my mother would talk about having a nurse in the family, serving humanity. Except I faint when I see blood. Sometimes she'd talk about my being a librarian, to teach young people to love good books. Mostly she just talked about having a daughter who would be a lovely, gracious woman and a warm, mature human being, and who would lead a rich life as a useful member of the community."

"Why do they *all* talk that crap?" he asked thoughtfully. "I bet they believe it, too."

"It's noise. It's something to say when they can't think of anything else to say."

He thought about this and then asked, "But they thought getting married would get in the way of your being a warm, mature human being? Like people who get married when they're young may turn into warm, mature collie dogs?"

"As a matter of fact, my parents did hate my getting married, but they hated it worse when it broke up. They tried to make me stay married. It was Burt who got tired of it."

"The guy?"

"He began saying after a few months he wasn't ready for the responsibilities of marriage."

"He heard somebody else say that first."

"Of course. What he meant was, he hadn't really thought about what it was going to be like seeing me in the morning as well as at night. Neither had I. I simply liked playing tennis with him and all. And when you're at college, you have to have *something* to think about."

"Was he a pilot?"

She laughed, and hesitated before she answered. "Not *Burt;* he had a motorcycle. So I should have known better. But he had a guitar, too, and he treated girls as if he liked doing other things with them as well as going to bed. Like playing tennis. He was great at sports. If he'd been great at sports *and* liked playing tennis with me *and* playing the guitar to me *and* been a pilot instead of riding a motorcycle—well, he wouldn't have been Burt, so it's not worth talking about. But whoever he'd been, if he *had*, I might still be married to him."

Richie thought for a moment and then, without meaning to, said what he was thinking out loud. "I started to learn the guitar last year."

"Do you play tennis?" she asked with quick irony.

By way of answer, without the burning sense of desperation that he sometimes felt when he heard such questions, he snapped his finger against his brace. At the small metallic sound she turned her head and glanced down at his leg. "I'd forgotten about that," she said.

"I used to." He felt it important to make the point. "Play tennis."

"What happened to you? Bud said something about a car smash."

He told her briefly.

"Will you always have to wear that?"

"I guess so. Unless I want to go places on my hands and knees."

"Do you mind?"

"Not really," he said truthfully. "There's a lot of things I can't do. Like drive a motorcycle, I guess." He grinned. "But I can do most things. All the things that matter." He turned over, took her hand and kissed her.

It was a long kiss, and when she could speak she repeated, "All the things that matter," and sat up. Then she kissed him again, lightly, and said, "Which includes flying a plane, too. We better let you get more practice doing that, Richie. I've got to get back."

He did not answer, but lay silent on his back for a moment, staring at the sky.

On the way home, when he took the controls, he found that the plane obeyed his commands, and the laws of physics, with a new lightness. The world had subtly changed, but he felt no wonderment at the odd, triumphant contentment that replaced the anxieties of the morning, of the last days and months. As if the river had carried away his ability to be surprised at himself and at the world. He banked the plane smoothly to the left, watching the turn needle, to show himself how easily it was done.

He flew in silence for a long time, watching the gyro and the sky. And then he felt her hand touch his as it lay relaxed on the throttle.

"Richie, you better give it to me."

She said it with a queer tonelessness. He asked, "Is something wrong?"

"I don't know. I think so." She tapped the oil temperature gauge with her finger. "It's too high. And it's going up."

"What do you do about that?" He was himself instantly tense as he gave her the plane. The lazy satisfaction in the plane's response was gone, and he felt a touch of fear.

"We'll fly it slow for a while. And see what happens. It may go away."

But it didn't. The temperature rose higher. "The wall's getting hot," she said. "I can feel it. We better land. We're still quite a way out. Because you wanted to go dancing into space." She added it as a joke, to ease both their minds, but it didn't work.

"Land where?" He was looking out. The ground was three thousand feet below them, spread out in small squares.

"In a field. We've done it once today." She pulled back the throttle. She was very cool, but a little white. And he appreciated it that she did not tell him there was nothing to worry about.

"Nothing I can do to help, I guess?"

"No. Except when we are about to land, unlock the door. And after we're on the ground, as soon as the plane's slowed down, unfasten your seat belt and start climbing out."

She was circling down, the ground was nearer. "That one," she said, half to herself. "It's the biggest around, and it looks smooth. I'd like to turn the engine off, but I'm scared to, in case we have to go round."

As she spoke, he saw black smoke coming from under the cowling. "*Jesus Christ . . .*"

"Yes. I saw some on this side a second ago."

The airspeed was falling fast. The needle went down, 100, 90, 80. She turned again, pulled on the flaps, and played the yoke and rudder. The plane sank fast.

"It's a little short," she said. "But it will do."

Her right hand was still on the throttle, and he now closed his over it and squeezed it. She smiled sidewise, and he said, "You're doing great."

The field was on a grade, it now appeared, sloping upward away from them. It looked smooth enough, with a low crop of wheat. The engine was idling, and they were almost at the fence. Then across it, floating along over the field. "Too damn fast," Lisa muttered. And then, an instant later, "But we'll make it all right. It's touching down that's a problem—if there are rocks. Or a ditch."

He knew that. For a long moment it looked as if they would never touch the field. A third of it, then a half of it, was gone. And then, a jolt. It was not so smooth as it had looked. The plane bounced, was thrown sideways, rode fast and bumpily for a minute, and then, against the grade and the rough surface, stopped finally and suddenly. He was already out of his seat, half-expecting an explosion, cursing his unmaneuverable leg, pulling himself upright on the wing by the top of the door. And then he had jumped down and was on the field, and he fell, rolling in the grass.

Lisa was out after him. She had pulled out the fire extinguisher after her, and was on the ground running around the wing. Richie got himself on his feet and followed. "We've got to get it out," she said breathlessly. "We may get burned, but we've got to get it out." She put out her hand to open the fastening of the cowling, and then pulled it back, "God, it's hot. I should have thought."

He pushed in front of her and turned the bolts. His fingertips burned, but he felt none of it. One bolt stuck, and he swore before he got it open and pushed back the hood. Smoke surged out in a thunderhead, black with spurts of flame.

He held out his hand for the fire extinguisher. She gave it to him, and he began pumping. White foam went into the engine and the flames died, but the smoke was thicker than ever. He pumped, it seemed, interminably, wondering how much chance there was that the flames were creeping toward the gas tank, and how big an explosion it would be if they did. Enough, certainly, to kill them both.

A moment later he stepped back. "The extinguisher's empty. Anyway, I think the fire's out. But let's get a long way away, in case it isn't."

They climbed the hill. She wiped her hands on her skirt, and he rubbed his with a handkerchief. They were hurting furiously now.

"Did you burn them badly?" she asked.

"Not really." He paused. "What happened, do you think?"

"I don't know. I can't imagine. It seemed perfectly fine until about five minutes ago. And it was all right last night. Bud brought it in from Chicago and said it would be ready to fly in the morning."

He felt an appalling, formless anxiety in his stomach, much worse than the fear of explosions. But he quelled it and said uncertainly, "It was a beautiful job."

She kissed him. She was still very white, and her voice was uneven when she spoke. "I did what I had to do. You'll do it someday, at least as well. Now we've got to find a phone and tell somebody to come get us. Pop will be there by now." But she did not move, and for a long time she stood still, in his arms.

After they had phoned, from a farmhouse a quarter of a mile away, they went back to the field and sat near the plane waiting for rescue and talked of things that had nothing to do with flying. Where they had gone in the summers as children, what they had disliked most in grade school. They were nearer in age now than they had been before, sitting side by side holding hands. It had almost been worth it, he thought, for this long time with her. But then she stood up suddenly. "I expect it's cool enough to look at now," she said. "And safe enough."

They walked to the plane, and she peered down into the engine. Then, without speaking, she walked to the edge of the field and picked up a fallen branch. With it she fished under the hood, and then pulled it out.

"No wonder."

On the end of the branch was a blackened, half disintegrated lump. But parts of it were only charred. As Richie leaned over it, he could see that it had been a greasy cloth. It must have been a big one. When it dropped to the ground, it made a sizable heap of fragments.

"I can see what happened," she said. "It was lying in the cowling. It took a while to heat up, but then it got hot quickly, and when it started to burn, it made a lot of smoke. I don't think it did much damage. But it's a miracle it didn't."

"How'd it get there, anyway?" It had to be asked.

"I don't know. Bud was looking it over when he brought it in last night. But he wouldn't leave a rag in it. He's sometimes absent-minded about things on the ground, but never about anything to do with flying."

"It got there somehow." He persisted, grimly.

"I can't imagine how. Unless—" She stopped and frowned. "No. It can't be that." Then she looked at him and said, "Richie, you're not feeling so good, are you?" His face was very white and his eyes had a queer emptiness.

"It's been a big day," he said rather thickly. "I'm not used to walking so far." He leaned against the plane, looking away from her into space.

A moment later they heard the sound of a plane overhead, circling.

CHAPTER VIII

Climbing Turn

In the years since his wife's death Professor Payne had visited the city of Buchanan less and less often. He came generally only at the invitation of old friends, who had learned they could not count on his acceptance unless they first submitted the guest list for his approval, and even compliance with this crotchet did not assure his presence. He disliked the company of fools.

When he did come to town it was usually in the evening. He did not care for strolling the streets by day, and this for two reasons, apparently inconsistent: he disliked running into people he knew; and he disliked not running into people who knew him. The second reason he did not publicly mention. Indeed, he was—as he was of almost nothing else in his life—a little ashamed of it: it seemed a silly form of vanity. But he was chagrined by the realization that few people in the university would recognize him now. Of ten thousand students he was known to only a score; of a thousand faculty, to only a few dozen. Thirty years before, everyone would have known him.

The fact was disturbing; but he should have charged himself not with vanity but with a sense that obscurity was an early stage of oblivion. Indeed, he reckoned that most of the ten thousand, if they had ever heard of him at all, supposed him to be dead already. Having been first a social revolution, he had become a celebrity, then a legend, and now a historical figure. Candidates for masters' degrees occasionally wrote theses about him and respectfully dedicated them to his memory.

The former reason for staying away from Buchanan was more creditable in his view, although it might have seemed less so to public opinion. As if to balance the transiency of the university people, the townspeople formed a population stable to the point of atrophy. His acquaintance among them remained extensive. They tended to engage him in dull conversations on sidewalks, addressing him with gingerly awe, as they might an uncertainly domesticated bear who had achieved, through long residence, the right to wander the streets unleashed, a local curiosity.

A few days after the restoration of the jewels to the funeral home he was obliged to make a daylight trip to Buchanan. The time had come when an interview with Jeffrey Payne was in order. Jeff had a legal and possibly a human right to know of the new turn that Richie's affairs had taken. He was Richie's guardian and trustee, and, whatever his obtuseness, he must be honestly concerned for Richie's welfare. Moreover, Richie and Professor Payne both hoped he might be conned into providing the money for flying lessons. An appointment had been made by phone, and Richie had driven his great-uncle to town and then gone on to the airport.

Professor Payne arrived in Buchanan with more than his usual misgivings. He was pretty sure that Jeff was going to disapprove of Richie's project. He was aware, too, that his own position was delicate. Or so it would appear to Jeff; it was at the least controversial to have permitted, let alone encouraged, a highly unstable adolescent to take charge of an airplane.

A more compelling source of misgivings was that he himself was also beginning to question it. Richie's behavior was still developing in unsatisfactory ways, and airplanes seemed to have lost their therapeutic powers. He had gone off that morning as if he were approaching an ordeal.

It was conceivably, Professor Payne considered, loss of nerve. Richie had made it clear that he was resolutely, even obstinately, determined to go on with instruction. He had been determined enough in negotiating the loan and later he had intelligently plotted the possibility of extracting a loan from his Uncle Jeff. But it was possible that in a deeper sense he was frightened, not only of airplanes but of his own enterprise. As he had been, perhaps, frightened as well as elated by his enterprise with the window lock. He might be, as adolescents often were, unknowingly waiting for a command to call the whole thing off. Professor Payne appraised this theory and concluded that however true it might be, it could not be acted on. All his instincts told him that whatever else might happen, Richie must be paid the respect of being allowed to make his own decisions about his life. Considering his own misgivings, however, it would be hard to put this convincingly to Jeff Payne.

He approached the door of the building where Jeff's construction firm had its office. A loud voice interrupted him at the door.

"Well, *Walt!* I didn't expect to see you sashaying down Washington Street on a weekday morning. Why aren't you down on the farm keeping company with the plant lice?"

Professor Payne spoke an obscene word, almost inaudibly, and said, "Good morning, Merry."

She was looking her worst, like an old feather mattress. She shook hands and said, staring at him squarely, "Today is Tuesday."

He bowed. "I am glad to hear it."

"On Tuesday the Tuesday Club meets."

"One would not wish it otherwise."

"Tuesday we devote to group creativity. It's not too much to spend one morning a week being creative, I used to say to Mom."

"Certainly not." She was in a new phase, that of the cultured matron rather than the expansive old friend or the ferocious defender of her boys. It was not, Professor Payne thought, more attractive. "Most of us, as the poet Whittier said, lead lives of quiet desperation. Mom used to like to quote that."

"Whittier said that? Ralph *Wadsworth* Whittier?"

She overlooked this, and her manner changed. She abandoned culture for expansiveness. "It's a regular ladies' gab-fest," she said confidentially. "They all eat ten thousand calories worth of cake, Walt, and then they wash it down with quarts of gossip, and call it creativity. Alcott and Marguerite Fuller are on the program today. And maybe Henry Dean Howells, if there's time. But there won't be. There never is. Not after they've gotten done eating up all the chocolate cake and then everybody they know in town. And after that some old gal starts reading something she copied out of the encyclopedia but she hardly gets started before it's time to leave."

"Culture, like charm," Professor Payne viciously observed, "is relative. The lesser vulgarity looks refined beside the greater."

"You oughtn't to say things like that, that you don't believe, Walt. It's like joking about death. When Mom entered on her last rest, I realized what a sacred thing death is."

He wondered if Stanley Brill had been talking to her, and had put two and two together. Her tone was genuinely pained, as if he had subjected her to some grave indignity. It was possible. By now Russ would have finished his interview with Stan. Stan would have had plenty of time to call to Merry. She, hearing his story and remembering Professor Payne's probings at the dinner party, would have concluded that he and Russ were "in it" together.

What happened next strengthened his belief that something of this sort had in fact taken place. Merry's attitude of reproach abruptly altered. "There's something I want to talk about, Walt." She had become positively ingratiating. "Come have a cup of coffee with me." She had decided apparently to use her alleged charms as a *femme fatale* to disarm his enmity. If he had been twenty years younger he might have imagined that an elephantine flirtation was in course. As it was, her ingratiation could mean nothing but calculation, and he might learn something from it. Jeff could wait for a little while. "Fine," he said.

She took his arm and whispered throatily, "In here," steering him into Adolph's Gourmet Pizza Grille. Once they had been provided with coffee, she leaned forward and, glancing around, said intensely "Walt, I'm in trouble."

He almost jumped. Instead, he stirred sugar into his coffee and said in the kindly and reflective drawl with which generations of victims had been lured to syllogistic dooms, "I'm sorry to hear that, Merry. What kind of trouble could a gal like you be in?"

Again she looked over her shoulder. "I can't tell you, Walt. I wish I could, but it's something I can't talk about. It involves others."

He said, "It costs me the price of a cup of coffee to find out that you can't talk about it?"

"It's real trouble. It's—well, I wouldn't like to say, but a lot of people are depending on me."

He sat in silence as stony as he could make it. He was annoyed with himself for having been trapped as an audience for sheer self-dramatization. She observed that he was experiencing strong emotions. "I can tell that you sympathize with me, Walt. I knew you would. It means a lot to me to have your sympathy."

"You don't," he said.

She smiled—bravely, he thought—and studied his face. "Walt, I have to ask you a favor."

He was ready to welcome any communication that contained substance. Somewhat more amicably he said, "I never do favors."

"Walt, I happen to know about a lot of favors you have done for people. I know you are a very generous person." It was odd: she was combining incompatible pretenses, as indeed she often did—gravity, genial heartiness, sentimentality. "You were so sweet to me the other night at the farm. I really appreciated that, Walt. I understand *people*, and I have always known that you were a real friend, someone I could turn to when the going got rough. Mom felt the same way, Walt. Mom was always real fond of you. She used to say to me, 'Merry-girl, Walt Payne is someone I'd trust until hell freezes over.'"

He was stunned. Hysteria was showing like a sharp, dangerous rock beneath this folly. "Hell," he said, "froze over last night. I heard it on the TV weather report."

She put one hand on his arm. "I'm asking for something as an act of charity, Walt."

"I don't approve of charity."

"Walt." She was suddenly playful. "Walt, wouldn't you like to have me as your pet charity?"

"What do you want?"

"Two thousand dollars."

"I'll be damned."

Unfailingly, she misinterpreted his deflated expletive. He was more annoyed than ever and disappointed as well. All this was merely a build-up for a touch. But she thought that his blasphemy indicated sympathetic interest. "Walt, it's a terrible thing. I've come to my wits' end."

"Was it a long journey?"

"How did you guess?" she weirdly asked. "But it wasn't the distance, of course. The thing is, I came first-class." She was suddenly fluent. "I guess I was crazy, Walt. But I did it to please Agnes. Walt, Agnes said it would be a sin for me to go Economy Class, after Mother died."

"Naturally, you did not wish to commit a sin. Especially not at that time." He was always irritated by people who appended his name to each sentence when they talked to him.

"Yes, that's right. Agnes said she wouldn't be happy unless she could think of me, all by myself with my grief over the Atlantic, being perfectly comfortable. She said she wanted to pay for it. And I could see, she wouldn't be happy unless I let her. She said for me to charge it on my credit card, and she'd send me a check. But then I had a letter from her the other day, Walt—she writes a real good letter—and she has some business hang-up. All of a sudden."

He was electrified. "You don't say?"

"Of course it's only *temporary.*" She had misinterpreted his excitement as indicating reluctance to part with two thousand dollars on hung-up security. "She's got all the money in the world. Just some little thing happened to freeze her liquid assets—maybe Cartier's got huffy about her latest diamond necklace or something. But right now there's going to be a little delay sending me the check."

"The difference between economy and first-class isn't two thousand dollars one-way," Professor Payne said thoughtfully. "It isn't more than a tenth of that."

"There were other things, Walt. You see, when Agnes and I got word that Mom was gone, I was *real* upset. It was a pretty bad time for me, Walt."

"To lose a mother like Dolly. . . ." He was proud of this essay in total ambiguity.

"Agnes—she's a real understanding kind of person, Walt—she understood what I was going through. So I had to buy a fortune's worth of new clothes."

"I see."

"I mean—" She shook herself, perhaps realizing in a rare moment of awareness that the sequence of her thought might not be entirely clear. "Agnes thought it would make me feel better to spend that day before I left, shopping. It didn't mean anything to me, of course. But she *wanted* me to. And I thought I owed it to her, Walt. She said she'd pay for everything, and I could see that it was the only thing I could do for her to cheer her up. So now I'm stuck with a lot of clothes I didn't want and never will wear—mink stoles and stuff, the kind of thing Agnes likes. Boy, did that little shopping spree mount up." She had forgotten herself and allowed a gleam to come into her eyes. Then she looked demurely into her coffee cup. "I'm going to give all of it to Goodwill Industries."

"And now your Aunt Agnes finds she is unable to foot the bill after all?"

"It was all on my Diners' Club card."

"It will be quite a while before the bills come in. By then no doubt Agnes's affairs will have been straightened out." He was watching her closely.

"It won't be soon enough," she said emphatically, and went on quickly, "I'm getting a loan from House and Home Finance, but it won't be enough."

Professor Payne hesitated. The wise and honest course would be to say at once that he had no intention of supplementing the House and Home loan. But he was beginning to smell the odor of apocalypse. Some of this ridiculous story was true, he thought—quite possibly the part that seemed most ridiculous—although some of it was palpable eyewash. He asked, "When would you be able to repay me?"

"You don't know Agnes, or you wouldn't ask that."

"As a matter of fact I do, although I haven't seen her for years. Knowing Agnes, I repeat the question."

"Oh, *Walt*." The whine returned. "You can count absolutely on Agnes."

"I should be glad to. But I naturally would have to know *when* I could count on her. When will her solvency be restored?"

"Walt, I'm disappointed. I was sure I could count on you

to *understand.* It's a terrible thing to question the—the *integrity* of someone like Agnes."

"I'm not questioning her integrity. Merely her solvency."

She looked at him shrewdly and, he thought, for the first time with some suspicion about his real intentions. And then she shook herself again and evidently decided that if there *were* anything more in his behavior than met the eye, the way to handle it was with loquacity. "I don't know what could have happened, but whatever it was it can't be serious, financially, and of course those pearls of hers would cover twice what I spent that day, *and* the first-class supplement . . ."

"What did she say in her letter?"

"Oh, she said there had been a mix-up. She rode out with me, with the chauffeur, to Orly, to see me off, and there she was, waving and crying, when I left, but I know she felt better because I'd given her the pleasure of buying all those lovely things for me. . . ."

"I thought Glen handled her business affairs," he said innocently. "Doesn't he know when she'll be solvent again?"

"No, no. That is to say, he handles some things. . . ." She broke off. Her defensive impulses were sound, but she was not used to being on the defensive, and she had trouble forcing herself to say what was prudent. "Some things he helped her with, like grandpop's money, but mostly she does it herself." She was a little feverish, hacking her way through unfamiliar fiscal underbrush. "A man in Paris, taxes and all—you know, Walt, I don't understand any of this stuff. Anyway, I can promise you that. . . ."

"Have you seen Stanley Brill recently?" he asked pleasantly.

"Stan? No."

She was taken completely by surprise. And at last she despaired of his help. Perhaps she even interpreted his irrelevance as a symptom of senile decay. In any case she decided that her breath had been wasted. Her old friend was too old to follow trains of thought. He might even have forgotten, by now, all about Agnes and the shopping spree and the two thousand dollars. She got up decisively, took her handbag, and said, "I don't want to be late for the Tuesday Club." She laughed, and added in the interests of a plausible social manner, "If I'm not there soon, they'll start gossiping about my having coffee with an attractive man in Adolph's." Gamely, she laughed again. "I'll be seeing you, Walt."

"Possibly."

He watched her go and thoughtfully finished his coffee.

He faced the prospect of Jeffrey Payne in better spirits. Merry had aroused his combative impulses; he looked forward to war against his nephew with something like enthusiasm.

He had learned something from her. Or, more precisely, he had absorbed from her talk the sense of the emerging pattern, foggy but suggestive, of a rational universe. Certain points were perfectly definite now: Stanley Brill had not reported to her on the return of the jewelry; and something peculiar and important had happened in Paris—he was pretty sure that the story of the shopping spree and the first-class ticket was anchored in reality, although the sea-bottom was deep indeed.

His nephew's bland greeting sobered him by the reminder that Jeff knew nothing of what had happened since their last meeting. A revolution had transformed his cosmos and Richie's, while Jeff's, devoid of treasure trove and airplanes, was empty, out-of-date, incredibly square. It was hard to resist the feeling that this was Jeff's fault as well as his misfortune. As they shook hands Professor Payne thought, not for the first time, that the delightful surprises provided by phenomenological realism were among the things that made life worth living.

But they also made explanations difficult. Jeffrey, being both cautious and hearty, greeted him by saying, "How's the boy?"

It was a question of singular ambiguity. Professor Payne cautiously avoided it. "We're both well, thank you."

"Real good." This was a phrase from the local *patois.* Jeff interspersed his conversation with samples of it. He studied it as a branch of philological lore—and used it to show the world that although he was rich, successful, and cultivated, he was still a democrat who believed in equality before the lore. "Richie's well?"

"On the whole, yes. There has been some change. It's what I want to talk to you about. There's a problem."

"A change—for the worse?"

"No. Not for the worse. The problem is simply financial."

"What the hell kind of financial problems does he have? Did you take him to the races?"

"In a sense he took himself to the races. He bet his self-confidence on a long shot and won."

"What are you talking about?"

Professor Payne reproached himself for yielding to the habit of metaphor with a man who regarded it as a form of moral decay. "Tell me," he asked seriously, "did you ever notice that Richie, before the accident I mean, was interested in aviation."

"No." Jeff was impatient.

"Well, he is now."

"What's he doing? Building model airplanes? That can run into money."

"No. He's flying real ones. Which runs into more money."

"What do you mean, flying real ones? He couldn't be. They wouldn't let him."

"He's taken three lessons." It seemed discreet to omit the fact that he was at the moment taking a fourth. "He's apparently doing quite well."

"And you let him?" He sounded more hurt than angry. It was exactly what Professor Payne had expected. He did not blame himself for a wrong approach; no approach would have worked. "He'll kill himself," Jeff added, also expectably.

"I think the effect has been the reverse of that. He is bringing himself to life. He is intensely interested in it. You remember that at our last meeting, you pointed out what he needed was a new interest. He has it. And, of course, he only goes up with a qualified instructor."

Phrases like qualified instructor were the sort of thing Jeff liked. He said, "I don't know what the hell you were thinking of, Uncle Walt," but it sounded as if his belligerency was lessening.

"I was thinking of your excellent advice." This was both untrue and misleading; but it was not necessary to explain that Richie had given him no opportunity to think of anything at all.

"I naturally didn't have anything dangerous in mind.

Does he actually fly it himself? Handle the controls, and all?"

"Yes."

"I think you're both crazy. How much is it going to cost?"

Professor Payne hesitated. "You can't tell how many lessons he'll need. And there'll be ground school. All told, Richie estimates something like seven hundred dollars."

"You should have talked to me about this first." Jeff tapped his pen on his desk as he shifted his ground. "You had no business letting him go ahead with it, Uncle Walt. Legally, he's my responsibility." He was, quite suddenly, making himself angry by reminding himself that his authority had been flouted. "Goddamn it, I have a duty to Howard and Dolores' memory. I've got to protect the boy's welfare."

"I honestly think his welfare requires that somebody pay for more flying lessons. So, I may add, does he."

"It's none of his business, what he thinks. He's only sixteen, and he's sick. He's got to realize he can't decide everything for himself. I've got to make decisions for him, the same as I do for my own kids. I'd like to treat him like one of them, if he'd let me. I don't think he realizes what I do for him. He sure doesn't show it."

"It may be rather hard for him to realize it." Professor Payne was much annoyed at the turn for the worse the conversation had taken. "Parents seem to expect obedience and affection from their children as a form of income from an investment. Children are the only form of property I can think of where people think they can enjoy themselves with the capital while still getting paid interest on it."

"Oh, hell," Jeff said. It was the way many of his conversations with his uncle ended. He stood up and paced for a moment. After a long silence he said, "If he wants to go on with this foolishness, let him get a job and pay for it himself. At least he'd be learning something useful that way."

"I'll tell him you suggested it," Professor Payne said and left before Jeff had time to realize that his enthusiasm for self-help had won him a battle by admitting defeat in the war.

His next appointment was with Russ, and he approached it in a humor further improved. His partial victory over Jeff renewed his hope of total victory in the wider quest; his talk with Merry had left him with the sense of having caught a distant glimpse of what he thought was the quarry. He speculated vigorously about Merry's financial affairs as he walked along South Washington and east on Third, which led toward Buchanan's only skyscraper, a construction of the nineteen-twenties, in which Russ had his offices.

Passing briskly through the outer ramparts, manned by two secretaries, Professor Payne shook hands with Russ and seated himself in the visitor's chair, facing his friend across a wide and tidy blotter. Or rather, what he actually faced was not Russ but the spines of his reference books. Turned outward, Professor Payne noticed, so that their titles were facing the client rather than the attorney. *Capital Punishment. The Christian Idea of Contrition. Poison and Paranoia. The Horror of Our Prisons. Psychoanalysis and Guilt.*

Professor Payne stood up and took another chair. "You find it helpful to have those titles facing your clients?" he asked.

"It makes them less likely to boggle at the fee." Russ leaned back in his chair and put the ends of his fingers together with an air of ruthless despotism. It was not the first time that Professor Payne had been struck by the transformation that took place in old friends when he encountered them in their professional settings. He had met grim-faced doctors in their offices the morning after he had gotten companionably drunk with them, and he had known pretty girls who, joyously voluptuous by night, chastely disciplined ten-year-olds by day. He laughed a little uneasily, to rid himself of the impression that he was in the presence of an inquisitor. "You are impressive in your native habitat. As sheriff, did you extract confessions by pure impressiveness?"

"Sometimes. But a confession in itself means nothing. Most people confess to things they are not guilty of. Not in any legal sense, anyway. They do it for diversion. *Qui s'accuse, s'amuse.* I am about to amuse myself." He proceeded to describe his meeting with Stanley Brill that morning. "I accuse myself of incompetence, lack of foresight, and ruining Richie's brilliant tactic."

"It follows from your epigram that *qui s'accuse s'excuse.*" Professor Payne comforted him with equanimity. "I can't believe that anyone could have done any better, given Stanley Brill's slithy personality. And I have some small compensatory intelligence. I ran into Merry Berger by chance and had a talk with her over a cup of coffee at Adolph's. About money."

Russ violently tilted the swivel chair forward until he was sitting stiffly upright looking seriously at Professor Payne. "That is a curious coincidence. I have just had a cup of coffee with Charlie Knish in the Parakeet to talk about Merry and money. Tell me more about Merry's money. It sounds," he added, "like something jolly from *Iolanthe.* "Marry, prithee, more of Merry's money . . ." He was feeling better.

"The general burden of the conversation was that she has none and needs some badly."

"That is interesting. The burden of my findings was identical."

"It would have been more interesting if it hadn't been. Contradictory evidence is usually more enlightening."

Russ nodded. "Like a stereopticon. What did she say to you?"

Professor Payne neatly summarized the conversation while Russ, equally neatly, took notes on four-by-six cards. When the report was finished, he looked up. "There appear to be several separate but equal points of interest. The most definite and the most dramatic relates to Stan. We conclude that he has given her no inkling of the return of the jewels. We may infer, as a distinct possibility, that we were wrong in supposing that there was ever any connivance between them. If that's right, the removal of the body may have been all Stanley's work or not his work at all. Which is more likely, since somebody had to fly the plane. In which case, he must have gotten a real surprise when he opened up our Christmas present to him. Do you realize that if he *isn't* involved, we have just presented him with seventy-five thousand dollars with no imaginable way of getting it back."

There was a moment's silence, and Professor Payne answered himself. "But it isn't possible. Neither alternative is possible. You remember that when you first talked to him he showed gratuitous guilt about Dolly Sommers' funeral? And when I first talked to Merry, she showed unmistakable signs of guilt about her connection with Stan."

"It's true. And I am sure that Stan must be in a conspiracy with the family because there's no other reason in the world why he'd embezzle Dolly herself, though he might well have embezzled the jewels on his own authority. But he wouldn't have wanted them buried." Russ frowned and went on. "To come back to Merry, the same question is raised. If she's desperate for money, why would she want to arrange to bury it in an oak forest? The only possible explanation is one we considered before: Dolly's estate is zero, owing to the drain of the airport; the only assets are the sapphires, which only Merry knows about; she abstracts them in order to keep them from being inventoried and the proceeds distributed among all the heirs. It is perfectly logical. But why the body?" He lit a cigarette and stared into the smoke. "There's more to it than needing money. There must be. And her story to you about her debts is quite incredible. No rich aunt, however soft-headed, offers to outfit a niece she hasn't seen for years with expensive clothes, just to console herself for the loss of a sister she also hasn't seen in years. No wealthy woman suddenly finds herself obliged to welsh on promises like that. The only explanation that could reasonably include the basic elements of the story is that Merry got the old lady tiddly on white wine and cajoled her into loaning or even giving her all this stuff, and when the old lady sobered up and realized what she'd done she decided not to foot the bills after all, and cancelled payment on a check. Or maybe the whole thing was made up from beginning to end."

"But Merry did come home first-class."

"Yes. We speculated that she decided to splurge on the basis of expectations. Now it seems that instead of expectations she has debts. Then why did she come first-class? It's as queer as the body. Unless she is, after all, by some weird chance telling the truth."

"I have the very definite impression that she is. Not the whole truth, and certainly not nothing but the truth. But part of the truth. Something happened in Paris."

"Do you think it could have to do with her friend Carlton Ritz? A whirlwind romance under the chestnut trees? It seems unlikely *but:* suppose the debts were incurred in the normal course of purchasing a boy friend? She decided, let us say, to have herself a ball while in Paris, on the Diners' Club, regardless of consequences."

"God knows." Professor Payne, who rarely invoked the name of a deity in which he disbelieved, now registered a kind of desperate uncertainty. "On the basis of very long experience I would state as the only absolute truth in the universe that human beings, all without exception, are whited sepulchres. Merry's impulses have always seemed to me centered on controlling other people rather than indulging herself—a situation generally described as unselfishness. It's true that the sacrifices involved in wrecking the lives of everybody around her may have taken their toll: she may have developed a taste for orgies. But somehow I don't think that's what happened. I think what happened had something to do with Agnes. She talked about her with real feeling. I think Agnes is mixed up in the financial problem, and I think the financial problem is highly ramified."

"You're right on the last point. Old Charlie tells me

very confidentially that Merry has been looking for loans all over town. She ought to know that the bankers and loan sharks exchange notes almost hourly, but she doesn't. They didn't give her anything."

"Oh? She told me she had gotten one from House and Home Finance."

"She's lying. According to Charlie, everybody turned her down. Nobody wants to get mixed up with Van Buren County Flying Service Inc. At least, not until the estate is settled and some exhaustive auditing is done on the books at the airport. Everybody knows it's in trouble, and everybody knows that its stock is a considerable part, perhaps most, of the estate's assets, if that's the word. Another reason she got turned down was that she wouldn't say what she needed the money for. Instead of the tidy lie that most people go prepared with, she was full of dark dramatic hints about sinister drains on her resources. One loan agency man got the idea that she was threatened with some horrible brain disease requiring enormous outlays on medical care, while another concluded that her problem was termites. A third thought that Cheese was in trouble with the Feds for distributing pot by air."

"It's peculiar," Professor Payne said. "She started with dark hints when she was talking to me, but then she became forthright and down-to-earth as usual."

"It's not only peculiar," Russ said, "it's schizoid. But there are still plenty of realities around, even though *she* may be out of touch with them. There is one other item I got from Charlie that tends to confirm that Agnes is mixed up in some way with Merry's financial problems. Charlie says that Agnes Creston has had an account with the Corn State for years. A big one. What Merry said about Agnes's resources is true enough. She's a rich woman. For years, Berger has been depositing her dividend checks in the Corn State account. Then from time to time Agnes would transfer money to her account in the Broadway Trust Company Paris branch. In chunks of five or ten thousand dollars. She always had plenty left in the Corn State, though, and she sometimes used it to pay for things she ordered from stores in this country, or when she gave Christmas and birthday presents to people. Also, her commissions to Berger were in the form of checks on the Corn State."

"Ah-ha! That is quite striking."

"It is. What is more striking is that three days ago Berger went around to the Corn State to tell them that Agnes was going to close her account there. From now on he's going to send all her income direct to the Broadway Trust Company in Paris. He asked about her current balance, saying he was going to write to her, and later would draw a check to close out the account—he has a power of attorney, it seems. As it happens, the current balance is very low. Much lower than usual, and much, much lower than he expected. He seemed badly taken aback when they told him there was only a few hundred in the account. She'd drawn a biggish check—over a thousand dollars—to the order of a New York department store several weeks ago, and another for two thousand to the order of the Broadway Trust. He hadn't known about either of them."

"In a way it fits in with Merry's story to me. But something is wrong. Agnes would have known that the Buchanan account was low, as well as the Paris one, if that *is* low."

"I've been wondering," Russ said, "if there was any possibility of forgery. Merry buying stuff at New York stores and then putting her aunt's name to the checks. Agnes's bank statements are sent to Berger, not direct to her. But then she might have somehow caught on and raised hell with Merry in Paris. Fired Berger as her man of affairs and maybe threatened criminal action. Now Merry is trying to raise money to pay her back."

"Again, it's possible, but my instincts tell me it's wrong. I think Merry wouldn't do anything so likely to be found out. You can't hope to go on embezzling indefinitely without getting caught. She's a fool, but *her* instincts would tell *her* that." Professor Payne paused. The elements Russ had introduced offered no substantial clarification. But he had the feeling that clarification was nevertheless somehow approaching. These new pieces of the puzzle matched some others he remembered seeing earlier.

Russ was continuing. "There's one more item I got from Charlie. You remember I told you Bud Ramsey had been borrowing money from the company?"

"Yes."

"Well, whatever he needed it for, it wasn't enough. He went in to the Corn State to arrange a personal loan yesterday. Unlike Merry, he's getting it. He had a straight story—mortgage payments, down payments on a new car, the usual. He also had plenty of security. Notably one airplane worth about eighteen thousand dollars. The company owns most of the planes at the airport, but this is his personally. He rents it to the company as well as using it himself. He bought it two years ago. Charlie, naturally, remembered the registration number—he remembers all numbers. Nine Three Nine Seven J."

"I'll be damned."

"So shall I, probably. But his owning the plane means nothing. The only thing this definitely proves is that several of Dolly Sommers' heirs are in financial trouble. But we knew that anyway, and it proves nothing."

"Nothing does," said Professor Payne. But he said it with a grin that surprised the lawyer.

When he left the building, Professor Payne stood for a moment on the sidewalk in uncertainty. He was fitting into place the odd-shaped jigsaw pieces Russ had given him, and the outer margins of a design were coming clear. He thought he understood something of what had been happening to the Sommers family. He knew and understood what was happening to him. A compelling need for definite action, an almost physical need, was overtaking him. Like Richie, he found himself required to show initiative of a sort that might be more audacious than sensible. He thought for a moment and then, feeling heady and younger than he had for years, moved to gratify the need. He set out for the large Victorian courthouse, climbed its high steps, passed through a romanesque portal, and inquired of the receptionist the whereabouts of the Clerk of the County of Van Buren.

CHAPTER IX

Stalls

"You ready for a better view?" Bud asked.

The view was certainly limited; Richie could see nothing beyond the instrument panel. The rest of the world was shut off by a species of enormous plastic mask or vizor, worn like a cap. Or, he thought, more nearly like an elephantine trunk or an anteater sort of nose, belonging to some large mammal in a distant evolutionary stage, bestially primitive or futuristically spatial. Its effects were also queerly inhuman; it gave him a degree of intimacy with the instruments so intense that the directional gyro seemed to have attached itself to his own sensory apparatus. But the new senses, supplementary eyes and ears and fingertips, were terribly unconvincing in their messages. The white line of the "artificial horizon" had informed him that he was climbing; his stomach had informed him he was sinking fast, and he had jerked back on the elevators until he felt the pressure of Bud's unseen hand on the co-pilot's yoke, pushing it forward.

When Bud spoke he pulled off the hood, threw it over his shoulder onto the back seat of the 140, and brushed his hair out of his eyes. It was surprising to find the real horizon was still there; he spent a moment reintegrating it into his consciousness. "That was kind of great," he said, partly to disclaim impalpable charges of having disliked it, partly because it was true. His experience with instrument flying was exhilarating; the artificial horizon was in some ways more satisfying than the real one. The knowledge that human skill, and only human skill, was deciding his destiny, was alarming and delighting in about equal parts.

"We might as well try a few stalls now," Bud said. "Right?"

"Right." He did not know what would happen next. He did not know what stalls were; each stage in his instruction was announced by Bud as if it were the next course of a familiar menu; to Richie it came as a mystery to be unraveled. Whatever stalls might be, he was ready for them. For the moment, as always happened when he was in the air, the anxieties and perplexity that worried him on the ground had volatized and were lost in the cosmos.

"We'll take it up a ways. Climb to fifty-five hundred feet, say. Then make a couple of ninety degree turns, first right, then left, to make sure there's no traffic around."

"Right." Richie efficiently executed these instructions.

"O.K. Now let's see you do a power-off stall, Richie. What you want to do is to ease back on the power so it's idling, right? At the same time, start pulling back the stick, easy but not too easy. Steady and smooth. So the plane's nose is high. Keep pulling it back till the stick—the yoke—is in your stomach. Right?

"Now I'll tell you what's going to happen when you do that. The plane's going to slow down. Watch your airspeed to see it's doing it, right? When you got the yoke in your stomach and the airspeed falls to about sixty, the plane's going to start to feel soft, like it was on a feather bed instead of rolling along concrete. And the higher your nose goes and the slower the airspeed, the softer it will feel, and then it will stall. It will break, and begin to head down. And when it does that, what *you* do is to point the nose down—push the yoke forward, steady and even, and when it starts picking up speed, give it power and then gradually pull the nose back again until you're in level flight. Right?"

"Right." Richie hesitated. "I guess."

"You won't have any trouble. Stalling won't hurt you any when you're up this high. The reason we teach you how to do it is mostly so you'll get the feel of what it's like when it's getting near a stall—so you won't. And so you know what to do when you get into one when you don't mean to. The thing is, whenever a plane slows down beyond a certain point, it stops flying. Naturally. That's all a stall is. You got to be able to know when a plane's getting ready to stop flying. You got to know what to do when it does. As a matter of fact, if you leave it alone for a while it'll start flying again by itself. If you got enough altitude, it'll pick up the speed it needs to come out of a stall."

"Always?"

"Right." Bud paused. "Except now and then, maybe. Start easing back on the power and on the stick."

Richie started. Very slowly. What he was about to do did not much appeal to him. He went at it cautiously.

"It'll be all day before it stalls, at that rate," Bud said. "You got to be crisp. Steady, but crisp."

"Right." He pulled the throttle out from the wall, pulled back more vigorously on the yoke, glanced at the airspeed. It was falling to eighty, then toward seventy. He glanced outside. The cowling in front had risen steeply above the horizon. On his left the land lay, much farther down than when he had last looked, and the line of sky and earth met at an angle so strange that for an instant he felt the same kind of disbelief as he had a few minutes before when he was flying by the instruments. Then his mind admitted that his senses were accurately reporting the angle and protested it with fleeting sickness.

He returned to the instruments. The airspeed was down to sixty-five, and the V on the attitude indicator was high above the horizon line.

"Keep pulling it back, Richie."

He kept pulling it back. The nose went higher. The airspeed fell. And the yoke, which he had been working hard to hold back, began to go slack. The plane was riding soft, suddenly insecure and untrustworthy. And several things happened at once. Richie had an abrupt and urgent sense that he was about to go over backwards; sick dizziness washed over him. And then the plane fell.

He tried to follow instructions. He pushed the yoke forward. And suddenly the sickness was too strong, and panic drowned his memory of what he was supposed to do. He took his hand off the throttle and the yoke, thickly said, "Goddam," and went through a second of something between vertigo and unconsciousness.

Literally a second. Then he was back again in touch with the world of real things, his fingers back where they belonged, feeling Bud's pressure on the other yoke, watching the horizon turn level. "Goddam," he said again. He was humiliated, with a sort of humiliation that for the moment suggested death, perpetual, irretrievable.

Bud was looking straight ahead over the cowling, and he said, "It's your airplane, Richie." Then he went on, still looking straight ahead, "It's funny," he said. "Some guys don't mind stalls. Other guys don't like them. About fifty-fifty. Don't let it bother you. Right?"

"Right." But it wasn't. He was badly jolted.

"You want to try it again?"

He said "Right" automatically, and immediately wished he had had the wit and courage not to. He did not at all want to try again. The thought of it sent the dizziness mounting to his head and his heart to beating faster. He struggled with desperation, overcame it, and wiped his forehead with the back of his hand. Then he said again, a little more firmly, "Right. Let's go."

"We'll regain some altitude first. Then go through it again."

His hands were trembling, and he felt simultaneously hot and terribly cold. His bad leg had begun to twitch, and it hurt him for the first time in days. But he went on. Cutting the power, pulling back on the stick until he saw the nose pointing sharply up, waiting for the air under the wings to soften, and, with the plane heading—it seemed—almost vertically up, waiting for the appalling instant when it began to fall.

It happened, and this time he held onto the controls and did what he had been told to do. He felt none of the dizziness of the first time, but he did feel physical fear.

"O.K. Real good," Bud said. "You won't have any trouble." But for the first time since Richie had known him, his voice was false. And then Bud looked at him and said, "I guess maybe we've had enough. We can try some more next time. You'll get used to it, but there's no point in pushing it the first time. Right?"

Richie nodded.

On the ground he scheduled another hour of dual for the following morning. When he started out the door, Bud started to say something, and then followed him out to the car. "Kid?" he asked with a most unwonted show of indecision.

"Yeah?" Richie was starting to get in the car.

"You're not going to let that worry you? Everybody has a bad moment once in a while. Like me, I have them all the time."

Richie did not answer. Embarrassed again, and now in more complicated ways, he wanted nothing but to get away from the airport.

"I heard what happened the other day. Maybe that kind of upset you? When you and Lisa had that trouble . . . ? That could upset anybody. Like Persh, he's got nerves of steel, and he's been flying instruments for twenty years, but he got disoriented in a fog a few years ago. He came out from it in time to land in a field, but he had nightmares every night for a month. And nobody *likes* stalls the first time. Maybe I shouldn't have started you on stalls, right after that trouble. My fault."

He was more tentative than ever. He sounded not quite sincere. And this in itself had an effect on Richie.

"You'll be back tomorrow? We might try landing it tomorrow. Right?"

"I'll be back tomorrow."

"O.K., Richie. Take it easy—right?"

He closed the door and saluted, smiling.

"Yeah, all right, Bud."

Bud started to say something more, and then turned and walked off. He had given, very completely, the impression of a man thrown seriously off balance.

Richie started the car and backed out. His trouble now was worse than it had been before, more even than when they had found the rag under the cowling. And what was troubling him was not simply his own fright, though that in itself was sufficiently hard to take, but his all too clear understanding of what was frightening him. He was afraid of Bud.

Or, more precisely, he was afraid that he had grounds for being afraid of Bud. It was rarely substantial things that frightened him; it was doubt about his own bravery. With the stalls, as with his leg, he had uncertain confidence in his ability to face a trial without flinching. With Bud there was something of the same problem, the growing possibility that someone he trusted might be untrustworthy.

He was on the road to town now. His upper lip was wet with sweat, and he wiped his hand across it as he thought. He told himself that it was unthinkable that Bud had deliberately left an oily rag under the cowling. It would have been a senseless thing to do. Bud could have no idea that Richie was involved at all with reburied bodies or star sapphires. He would certainly not endanger Lisa's life, or anybody else's, or the plane. Richie knew these things to be true, but a nightmare assembly of fears and associations belied his knowledge. Bud had had the 180 the night the body was buried. Bud needed money and had been borrowing it. Bud had brought in the 140 early in the morning that Richie and Lisa had flown in it, and had suggested that she take Richie with her—and there had been an oily rag in the engine. Bud had been at the airport somewhere near the time when somebody had hit Cheese and knocked him out. Bud's family was mired in antagonisms, and some of them were mixed up somehow with Stanley Brill. Bud had treated him just now with a forced solicitude that suggested an effort to conceal something. None of it added up to anything, rationally considered, but Richie's psychic dizziness gave it a crazy coherence. He felt, and resented, the same lack of control over himself that he had in the months just past, as he had when the airplane began to fall a few minutes before.

He held the steering wheel tight and his foot carefully pressed on the accelerator, driving with undue precision. "Hell," Bud had said, "everybody overcontrols." Richie laughed to himself, relaxed his hands, and settled back in the seat. There was nothing to do but go on. He could not talk to anybody about this; he had cut himself off earlier from talking to his great-uncle or Russ. It was unthinkable to talk to anybody else. It was unthinkable to stop flying. When you started imagining things, there was nothing to do but to stop imagining them. To go back tomorrow and stop his imagination from making his hands clumsy on the stick and the throttle and from pumping fear through his veins.

By the time he reached town and found his Uncle Walt in the reading room of the university library where they had arranged to meet, he was feeling better.

At about the time they were leaving the library, Russ was lunching on a hot dog brought to him at his desk by his secretary. The hot dog both looked and tasted as if it had been manufactured as a plastic joke with which persons given to low humor might startle guests. It filled him with nameless resentment and heightened his strong sense of the futility of all things. A life sustained by fake hot dogs was not worth sustaining.

The unfinished business of the Sommers case gnawed, like the hot dog, at his intestines. Unfinished office business could be finished by yelling at associates or assistants who were trying to finish it, but the Sommers case was peculiarly and illicitly his own. He could yell only at himself, which he was inclined to do. His failure to solve it, or even to act like a responsible citizen in trying to, raised the ghosts of other failures. He resisted an impulse to knock his head against his desk.

The next day Richie went back for more.

He had reached the airport more relaxed than he had when he left it the day before. But the prospect of flying had not had its wonted exhilarating effect. He was afraid he was going to perform badly, and it did no good to tell himself that this was the surest way of guaranteeing that he would. They had a half an hour of flying circles around silos, and he did it raggedly. Then Bud said, "O.K., you're going to land it this time. Right?"

The prospect was disturbing because he knew he was going to do it poorly, and he was unnaturally unwilling to make a fool of himself in front of Bud. A sort of anticipatory shame made him tenser than ever. His hand was unsteady on the yoke.

The airport was in sight ahead of them.

"You know how to enter the pattern, Richie. Get down to pattern altitude. Eight hundred feet above the runway elevation, right?"

"Right."

"O.K., so what *is* eight hundred feet above runway elevation?"

He thought feverishly. "My arithmetic's poor. The runway's six hundred and sixty. So we want to be fourteen sixty."

Bud tapped the altimeter. "You've already broken altitude. You're down to thirteen hundred."

"O.K." He wondered how it had happened and pulled up the nose.

"Power controls altitude, stick controls speed," Bud said. "Take it easy, Richie. Don't make a monster of it. When we get opposite the end of the runway, start easing back on the power and let it glide."

Richie followed instructions; he was getting flustered, and he had the feeling that Bud was deliberately trying to fluster him. As if he were being told that he had done things wrong before he had done them at all.

"Keep on the altitude, Richie. You got to slow it down. Don't let it sink. And keep watching the runway."

Grimly, he tried to obey.

"Trim it up. You can't hold it up with your arms."

Richie looked up at the ceiling where the trim control was and started to turn it, when Bud said, "Look, you got to remember to fly the plane." He put his hand on the yoke as Richie looked out and saw the plane had banked steeply to the right while he was adjusting the trim. There was too much to do at once.

"When are you going to turn base?"

Richie impetuously banked left; he realized that he had turned too steeply and was slipping, and jerked the wings straight.

"Cool it. Richie. Watch your glide angle. Don't dive it, for Christ sake."

He was sweating now. He was angry rather than frightened at what was happening, but he had a growing sense of crisis. The plane was unsteady, and the ground was coming nearer. He felt a momentary impulse to abandon the controls and close his eyes, suppressed it, and made another left turn, more awkward than ever.

Bud did not immediately speak this time. But the runway was a long way off and the plane was losing altitude, and weaving clumsily. "Are you planning to land in the cornfield?"

Richie silently pushed in the throttle. The ground fell away again, but they were no longer heading toward the runway but veering to the left. And the plane was heavy and cumbersome and unresponsive. He had a fleeting fear of falling and a sense of desperate helplessness. Everything was happening too fast.

"Straighten your wings. And you can see you're going to make it now. Cut the power, Richie."

He felt the pressure of Bud's guiding hand on the other yoke and perversely resented his interference.

"Keep holding it off. You got to slow it down."

The plane had crossed the boundary and was over the runway.

Richie had an overwhelming desire to be on the ground and stop flying. But he pulled back on the yoke and saw the nose go up and simultaneously, while the ground still looked a long way off, felt the bump of the wheels on the concrete and felt the plane turn convulsively toward the grass at the edge of the runway.

"Get on the rudder. Quick."

But this time he did not try to obey. Now that he was on the ground he gave up. His hand dropped from the yoke, and his feet went limp on the control. It was Bud who steered it to the ramp.

They climbed out in silence, Richie shaken and sweating. Bud said, "I've seen worse, but not recently. It wasn't your day, Richie. What's wrong?"

"I don't know."

"That emergency landing with Lisa still bugging you?"

"I don't think so. I don't know. Maybe."

Bud shrugged his shoulders and turned to the airport. Richie limped after him.

He tried twice more in the next two weeks. Both times he knew in advance that he was going to do badly. At the end of the second hour, standing on the ramp, Bud said, "Richie, you got a problem."

"Right." He had a sense of dread, as if final and irretrievable disaster faced him, and he squared his shoulders to face it. He had been flying worse than ever, and he knew it, and he had felt again the corrosive despair of helplessness, the reverse of his first exultation, as if the airplane were out of his control. He thought now that some vast, volcanic disturbance of the natural order were about to take place. Bud's words sounded, when they came, prosaic and quiet.

"You know you got this problem. I know you got this problem. I don't know what it is. Do you?"

"No."

"You started out fine, Richie. Like you'd been flying all your life. Then something happened, right? I thought I was going to make a great pilot. I still think I might.

Maybe it's my fault. Maybe I ought to let you go up with one of the other instructors. I don't like a student to think we're taking his money without doing anything for him. And you're not doing good, Richie. You're regressing. You know that. Right?"

"Right."

"You got any ideas?"

"Bud—?"

"Yeah, Richie?"

"Nothing." There was nothing he could say. His misery was total. All he wanted was to get away from the airport.

"I'm willing to go on as long as you are," Bud said. "But maybe you should lay off for a while. Take a rest. Relax. Come back in a couple of weeks. A month maybe. Right?"

He put his hand on Richie's shoulder. Feeling very young, Richie muttered a good-bye and walked to the parking lot, going around the terminal building instead of through it, so he would not have to see Lisa.

In the season of his partners' discontent Professor Payne became purposeful. He also became taciturn and mysterious. He admitted to himself that what he was doing was mischievous. He knew that his plans had less to do with serious investigation than with the same taste and need for self-expression and adventure that had first carried Richie into the air. And both the taste and the need were as uncontrollable as Richie's. Spasmodically on the lookout for symptoms of disintegration, he wondered idly if such adolescent whimsies presaged second childhood as he proceeded, preoccupied, with his plans.

His preoccupation, misinterpreted, added to Richie's troubles. On the day after his last unpleasant hour of instruction, he was addressed by his great-uncle with a question that, in his distress, frightened him. And Professor Payne's manner was so odd that Richie, too, wondered if something in the way of decay might not be beginning to take place. After a long period of silence over a martini, his great-uncle had asked without preface, "Would you be able to take care of things here at the farm by yourself if I weren't here?"

Richie started.

"I don't mean permanently." Professor Payne laughed carelessly, but his carelessness was artificial, concealing a queer, manic quality. "I mean for a few days. Three or four, or five at the most. You know how everything runs. You wouldn't need to bother doing anything to the garden."

"Going someplace?" Lack of candor, an almost universal quality in adults, was one he had not previously encountered in his great-uncle. In others it made him suspect conspiracies. Now it scared him. There were several other things in the last few days that had given grounds for imagining something sinister. And so did the words with which Professor Payne now closed the conversation.

"Well," he said, "you never know what may happen."

The next day he borrowed the car and drove into town, allowing his great-uncle to suppose he was going to the airport. Instead he went to Russ Mallery's office.

He looked, Russ judged, both perplexed and troubled, and it was not easy to know how to encourage him to say what was on his mind. He wet his lips and began rather tentatively, "Is something up? Or, perhaps, down?" He extinguished his cigarette and leaned forward in his chair, giving an indication of undivided attention. "You don't seem to be brimming with high spirits."

"Something is down." Richie stared at the floor. "In the cellar. Under the cellar. Dig up the cellar and under it is where something is."

"What?"

Richie appreciated Russ's effort to treat him as comrade, but it was forced. Professional dignity was written all over the setting and, therefore, the man. Signs on doors; secretaries; prosperous clients waiting in the outer office. Pomp and circumstance automatically generated in Richie an impulse to treason. He hesitated on the threshold of rebellion—and retreated. The business at hand was too serious. He said, "Russ, you think maybe something's *wrong* with Uncle Walt?"

Russ started to say "no" and realized that this would be a condescending anodyne. Instead he said honestly, "I don't know. I haven't seen him for a week or so. What are the symptoms?"

"He's not there. He talks about going away and leaving me run the farm."

"Did he say when or why?"

Richie shook his head. "He's not going to take a vacation. He's really got something on his mind."

"You, conceivably." Russ ventured this a little doubtfully, but he thought Richie would receive it as a reasonable suggestion.

"No. He used to, but not now. He's stopped noticing me. Crown borers and that stuff, even, he's stopped noticing. He's stopped noticing everything."

"But he's—" Russ lit a new cigarette very deliberately. "He's clear-headed, I take it? He's not forgetting the names of things?"

"No."

"Is Mrs. Sommers' body, unexplained, on his mind?"

"Sure that gets him, but it gets me, too. It's something else. I think maybe he went to a doctor, and maybe the doctor told him he's really sick, like maybe he's got something you don't get over."

Russ, taken aback by this bluntness, said, "It's possible, of course. He's eighty. Do you have any evidence that he *did* go to a doctor? Generally speaking, he doesn't hold with doctors. As you know."

"No. But I think he may have, the day after he came here, to see you. That was when he got so far away. You remember that day?"

"Yes."

"What time did he leave?"

Russ scratched his head. "I think I can tell you. About eleven. He was late, but he didn't stay long. He left before my next appointment, just before, which was"—he pulled forward his big engagement book and leafed backward through it—"eleven!" He took pride in the reliability of his memory.

"Yeah? Well, I met him at the library that day at twelve, and he'd just gotten there."

"He had? Did he say so?"

"No. But he was reading a biography of Eugene Debs when I found him, *and he'd only read about three pages.*" Richie took pride in the precision of his observation.

"I'll run out this afternoon, after work. For a drink. Just drop in."

"It won't do any good," Richie sounded perverse in this, but Russ saw what he meant.

The boy was certainly upset himself. He looked thin and tired, and when he left the office he walked as if each dragging step were more effort than it was worth. It occurred to Russ that his anxiety about Professor Payne might be a projection of his own relapse into dismal discouragement.

But his visit to the farm that afternoon convinced him otherwise. Walt's manner was undoubtedly peculiar. He seemed a little febrile, and, Russ thought, at the same time sheepish. It was certainly something new. So was his almost provocative air of secrecy. When he spoke, it was with an odd, spasmodic excitement. After giving Russ a martini, he said, "I've had a very good day. I made a new will this morning."

"Why?" Russ asked.

"The old one was obsolete. There are certain things I do not want to happen when I die. One of them is for Jeff to get my money. I disinherited him." He seemed almost feverishly elated at this. "I've left everything to Richie. And—I perhaps should have consulted you about this before—I have appointed you to be his trustee until he's of age." He turned to Richie, who was staring at him with a resolute but perceptible effort to maintain his impassivity. "My death won't make you rich, but you'll have enough to pay for flying lessons. And I think you'd find it convenient to have Russ as a counterweight to your Uncle Jeff." He laughed with the same suggestion of excitement.

"I'll be glad to be trustee," Russ said. It was hard to know how to put it.

"Goddam, Uncle Walt," Richie said. "What *is* all this?"

"At my age one must face facts. One must, of course, face facts at any age, but at mine some facts are more imminent than at yours. Heirs," he said holding Richie's eyes with his, "are among them."

"Walt, are you ill? Or are you going to take up some dangerous pastime, like Richie? Water-skiing? Or parachuting?"

Professor Payne did not smile. Instead he said, "Possibly."

CHAPTER X

Breaking Out

After fifty years, the view was familiar. Astoundingly, almost paralyzingly, so. The brilliant light of recognition blinded Professor Payne to altered details. They were unimportant. He had come home.

The street below his window was narrow, but the opposite sidewalk was wide enough to hold three tables under an awning, electric blue with white letters announcing that it was the Café du Carrefour. Next to it was another, identical to all appearances to the first, to the point of having two identical clients seated at separate tables studying the apparently identical contents of identical small glasses under their noses. The only difference was that the second awning was cherry red and the name was the Café du Square.

Above the awnings, tiers of French windows with pale gray shutters, set in walls of freshly enameled ivory stucco, rose to the slated mansard. The street was crowded with a noisy confusion of bicycles, motor scooters, cars of an infinite variety of shapes and ages, and crowds of pedestrians. The late afternoon lit it with yellow luminosity, as if everything were freshly varnished. The air smelled of red wine and black coffee.

Professor Payne's emotions were stronger than any he

had felt for years. He had been refreshed by a nap, but the fatigue of transatlantic flight contributed to a heady sense of fantasy, like a painting by El Greco observed after four martinis. He felt, first of all, a bounding pleasure in Paris rediscovered. The amazing fact that it was still there, unchanged, was oddly, soaringly, rejuvenating. And so was the fact that he had reached it. He had committed a gratuitous act, an act of folly, an act to justify his existence, intended to achieve exactly such rejuvenation as this. He was surprised by his success. He had enjoyed his enigmatic planning, swearing County Clerks and travel agents to secrecy, revealing nothing to anyone until, the afternoon before, he had told an astonished Richie on the way to the airport. He had, with complete self-assurance, changed planes at O'Hare and reached Orly in a state of enjoyable anticipation. He had made his way, with a few but sufficient sentences of competent French, to the hotel where Magic Carpets of Buchanan Inc. had reserved him a room.

He had made up a precise schedule, which he had already begun to act upon. Prior consultation with reference books in the library had provided him with the name of a distinguished restaurant in the vicinity, and he had secured the services of the hotel concierge in reserving him a table at it. The hotel possessed what was called an American Bar, and there he proposed to provide himself with two dry martinis before dinner. He was not the kind of traveler for whom an affected desire to do as Parisians did would lead to sacrificing an habitual martini for one of the distasteful brands of cough medicine that he remembered, from 1918, as being what Frenchmen unaccountably drank before dinner. After it, he would take coffee and cognac in a café and then, fortified by gin, wine and brandy, he would stroll to Agnes Creston's apartment.

He had considered asking her to dine with him; he had even thought of writing ahead to suggest it. But he instinctively felt that the things he wanted to learn would be more readily found out if he took her by surprise. An unannounced visit did involve the possibility—even, if Merry's picture of her aunt's social life were accurate, the probability—that she would be out. But he could return as often as necessary until he found her in. He confessed to himself unabashedly that Agnes Creston was not the real reason why he had flown across the ocean, any more than high-speed transportation was why Richie flew airplanes, or an abstract concern for justice why Russ stole jewels. The affairs of Agnes Creston had stirred his impulses, but he realized that they could have been dealt with by a transatlantic phone call.

Merry had given him the address. He had arranged to meet her for coffee at Adolph's a few days earlier, insinuating that he might have changed his mind about her application for a loan. He had darkly hinted over the telephone at indescribably dramatic developments. ("It's not something I can talk about except in person.") He had referred vaguely to a Brazilian soprano he had met once at a party at Dolly Sommers', years earlier. Merry claimed to remember the soprano perfectly, and thereby had trapped herself.

When they met he followed her example further by making no reference to the soprano, who was indeed fictitious, or to the possibility of a loan, which was equally fictitious. Instead he asked straightforwardly if she had heard recently from her Aunt Agnes. She had looked surprised and said that by a curious coincidence she had had a letter from her that morning. Then, remembering the security for the fictitious loan, she went on to say that Agnes, while enjoying excellent health and spirits, remained—temporarily—in an embarrassed financial situation.

This gave him half the information he had wanted—that Agnes was in Paris and likely to remain there. He then extracted the other half. "Just out of curiosity," he said casually, pulling out his address book, "I wonder . . . 23, Rue de la Nouvelle Poule, sixteenth. I wrote that down years ago. Is she still there? Not that I mean to send her a Christmas card, since I never send Christmas cards."

"Oh, Walt, everybody *knows* that, but people forgive you your eccentricities. Yes, Agnes is still there. That apartment of hers is really something, Walt . . ."

When he got away from her, he asked Magic Carpets for a hotel in the sixteenth arrondissment.

He was convinced that Agnes held the key to the inner secrets of the Sommers case. Whatever climax had been reached in the affairs of the family, it had been reached when Merry was in Paris. He hoped he could startle Agnes Creston into saying what it was.

He was a little tight when he started out to do so. He had dined extremely well. He was an excellent cook himself, but he was now in the position of a student admiring professionals. A *blanquette de veau* could, with foresight and a friendly relation with a butcher, be successfully undertaken in Buchanan with tolerable assurance that it would bear comparison with the same dish made in Paris. *Quenelles de brochet* were a different matter. So were *tripes à la mode de Caen.* And a good Sancerre was not to be found in Van Buren County. He had drunk a considerable quantity of it.

Paris was stronger wine than that. The soft night shone with street lights as he turned into the Avenue Georges Mandel, where they whitened the green of its double rows of chestnuts and shadowed the majestic progression of great houses around its sweeping curve. At the end was a glimpse of the floodlit statue of Foch, the twin palaces of Chaillot, the *tour Eiffel* between them. It was all incredibly grand and suave, the finest urban landscape in the world. Across many years memory spoke to him in music. To its accompaniment he strolled to the Rue de la Nouvelle Poule.

The apartment building at number 23 duly testified to magnificence. But its entrance was presided over by a concierge who was slow to answer her bell. When she came at last, he saw with pleasure that she was the ancestress—and the descendant—of all concierges in all history. She was old and fat, she sidled in felt slippers to open the curtained glass door that gave onto the carriageway, she was wearing a long, shapeless dark blue dress with small white spots, a black sweater, and black cotton stockings. There were heaps of gray hair held in place on the top of her head with conspicuous hairpins, glasses on the end of her nose, and a hairy wart on her chin. She emitted a strong odor of hostility. She was, in short, a timeless type and model. Montaigne had known her, Professor Payne thought in awe, and Flaubert and Zola and Proust.

He inquired for Madame Creston's apartment.

"*Pas là*," said the archetype. Then, classically, she slammed the door in his face.

He was unsurprised. Literary history required precisely such conduct. He turned back, entirely content, to the city. He found that he was agreeably but decidedly tired, and he walked slowly back to the hotel and the most comfortable bed he had slept in in fifty years.

The next morning, early, he tried again.

The concierge recognized him without surprise, rather as if she had been expecting to find him again at her door. She asked whom he wanted to see, suggesting that she thought he was asking for tenants at random, merely to add to her chores.

He did not react to this with the impotent rage he supposed she hoped for. Instead, when he repeated the name of Madame Creston and she repeated the formula "*Pas là*," he laughed amicably and put his foot in the door. But the laugh had surprised her; she did not attempt to slam it.

He asked in very careful French, "Do you know, madame, at what time one expects the return of Madame Creston?"

He had rehearsed this and was fairly sure that it was intelligible. But the concierge answered by staring at him with eyes screwed up in mystified disbelief.

"*Quoi?*" she asked in contemptuous astonishment. "*Quoi, monsieur?*"

He repeated his question three times. Each time she looked at him with uncomprehending incredulity already spread on her face before he spoke the first word. At the end of the third attempt the frozen bafflement was permitted to thaw into understanding. She cried out, in very loud, very fast French, "Ah, monsieur wants to know at what time one expects the return of Madame *Creston.* Monsieur perhaps means Madame *Battess-Creston?* In the thirty-two?"

"*Oui.*"

She laughed. "Madame Battess-Creston," she repeated jocularly, as if he had asked for Madame de Sevigné, or the Duchess of Guermantes. Then, briskly, she reverted to an earlier theme. "*Pas là.*"

"Madame Battess-Creston is not there?" He barely stopped himself adding "either."

She shook her head. "*Partie.*"

"Madame Battess-Creston has gone away?"

"Yes, monsieur, Madame Battess-Creston has gone away." She spoke with pitying disdain. Everyone in the *quartier,* evidently, everyone in any part of the world that mattered, knew that Madame Battess-Creston had gone away. But she did not slam the door. She was enjoying her patronage of one so monumentally ignorant. "Madame Battess-Creston has gone to Australia."

"Australia?" he asked seriously. "It is far away, Australia."

"Oh, yes, monsieur. It is far." Her mood had changed to tragedy now. "One wonders if one will ever see her again. It was for her health that she went to Australia. She suffers. For a long time, she has suffered."

"When, exactly, did she go to Australia?"

"A long time ago, monsieur." She seemed positively cordial now, like a mourner finding herself beside a tearful stranger at a funeral. She reflexively wiped her hands on the hem of her skirt, as though preparing to shake hands. "You are a friend of Madame Battess-Creston, monsieur?"

"Yes. A very old one. How long ago did she leave?" His surprise was putting a heavy strain on his command of French, but she had no difficulty understanding him now that the curious camaraderie had established itself between them.

"Oh, it is at least three weeks."

"Three weeks? Do you know when she is coming back?"

"I do not know. She is keeping the apartment, but I have heard nothing of her since she left. I forward her mail as she asked, but I have had no news."

He missed this and asked her to repeat it, which annoyed her. She raised her voice to a shout. "Monsieur does not understand? Monsieur is perhaps deaf? Every Monday I forward her mail. It is not cheap, monsieur, to send letters to Australia. The postal rates for airmail are excessive, Monsieur. I assure you that I pay ninety-five centimes for each letter to be sent to . . ."

He had stopped listening in the middle of this. It was quite inconceivable that Agnes should have left for Australia three weeks earlier, since Merry had had a letter from Paris only two days before. But his thoughts were interrupted by the concierge's last word. She had said, it seemed, ". . . for each letter to be sent to Bew Shah Nah," and this destination, while it sounded more Persian than Australian, nonetheless struck an echo in his mind.

"*Where?*"

"A town named Bew, Shah, Nah, monsieur." It was now he whose face expressed stunned incredulity, and she screamed it. "*BEW SHAH NAH, MONSIEUR.*"

He staggered and put his hand to the wall. "Not Bew Shah Nah?"

"But certainly Bew Shah Nah. In Australia. She is visiting relatives there. A lady came here to see her, a niece, a certain Madame Bare Jay, an Australian lady. Madame Battess-Creston accompanied Madame Bare Jay upon her return to America three weeks ago. Since then I have forwarded her mail, but it is bankruptcy, monsieur . . ."

"America?"

She was impatient of these subtleties. "Australia. Perhaps America. In any case, Bew Shah Nah."

"And Madame Battess-Creston is now in Bew Shah Nah, in America?"

She answered in a voice suddenly gentle, which she might have used on concluding that a strange child who had addressed her was severely retarded. "I have told you, monsieur."

"Thank you, madame."

He turned away. He was very seriously shaken.

He thought of the common phrase, "I was so surprised, I thought I'd have heart failure." It accurately described his sensations, and he wondered idly if this state of affairs could have any foundation in medical fact. He leaned against a chestnut tree, breathing deeply.

A young girl, a very pretty girl, in high boots and a white beret with a miniature white poodle on a leash, glanced at him and unhesitatingly approached. "*Vous vous trouvez mal, monsieur?*"

He smiled, and felt a little better. "*Ce n'est rien, mademoiselle. Merci.*" Then, in English, he added, "I think I shall go have a small brandy."

She did not understand, but she had evidently decided

that his case was not critical for she nodded and moved on. He walked to the Café du Carrefour.

It was open for business, but it did not seem to be expecting any. The chairs inside were still stacked, and a boy in a denim apron with rolled up sleeves was mopping the sidewalk. When he saw Professor Payne, he brought a chair and stood it by a table under the awning. Professor Payne asked for black coffee and brandy.

"*Bien, monsieur.*" The boy was businesslike, indifferent to any oddity there might be in an old man presenting this order at nine in the morning.

Now that the first impact had been dissipated, the almost literal dizziness with which comprehension had dawned, he was feeling pleased with himself. The significant discovery had been made, with a vengeance. It was not what he had expected, but he had been, unquestionably, not only correct but remarkably percipient in supposing that the crucial information was to be found in Paris. A younger man might have felt a sheepish regret at having spent several hundred dollars to uncover a fact that could have been had for twenty spent on a phone call. But Professor Payne's appraisal of his venture was precisely the opposite; he was congratulating himself not only on percipience but on boldness.

The morning air sparkled bright and fresh, and the buildings and people in the lively street presented themselves to him in the light of age united with perpetual youth, two thousand years of civilization daily reborn in poise and vitality. The boy brought him his coffee and brandy, and he drank them with a young zest and ripe satisfaction that exactly matched the quality he saw in Paris.

Later that day, Russ Mallery was thinking concentratedly about Professor Payne. Knowing nothing of the events that had taken place in Paris, he was nonetheless thinking of similar matters and in not dissimilar ways.

The trip had worried him unreasonably. He knew where Professor Payne had gone, and he should have been relieved by Richie's report that he had departed in good spirits and proposed to be home in a few days. "Anyway," Richie had told him on the phone, "he hasn't got cancer or like that. What he's got is an idea."

There was nothing he could do about it. An elderly but robust man of independent means, responsible, clear-headed, and highly intelligent, had chosen to take a trip without discussing it in advance with family and friends. There had been no way to stop him. But Russ did not believe that he really expected to clear up the Sommers case in Paris, and he recognized that his concern was partly occasioned by a slightly sulky sense that a trick had been played on him. It was also, perhaps, the product of more general frustrations.

Frustration induced a need for action, and the only action he could think of was to call on Stanley Brill, to whose presence he was recurrently impelled after the fashion of a murderer to his victim's corpse. With the difference that Stanley was exasperatingly alive, a reptile who slithered with annoying efficiency and might venomously bite him. Still, he was moved to face him.

He entered Stan's office without appointment and said without preface, "All right, what have you done with them?" And as an afterthought added, "This time?"

"Russ Mallery, you are the limit."

"Of what?"

"Why can't you . . ." He checked himself. As usual, his defenses broke before the first onslaught. But Russ had no illusions now about his capacity for quick recovery. He tried to forestall it by completing Stan's thought. "You know very well why I can't leave you alone."

"I don't know what you're talking about. No, I don't. I'm very busy. I am obliged, yes, obliged . . ." He stopped, leaving the obligation unexplained, and looked at the door as if he hoped one might come through it. "If you do not stop this intolerable persecution I am going to. . . ." He stopped again.

He was shaking, and mopping his forehead. He had thought of something, and he said with cold assurance, "I know what you are trying to do, you are trying to plant stolen goods on me. I am going to call the police." He thought of something even better. "I already *have* called the police, as a matter of fact. I have told them what you are up to. You are planting stolen goods. *Where did you get them?*" He had risen to a crescendo and now broke off to listen, as it were, to the pleasant sound of impalpable tables being turned.

Russ was startled. But he was not intimidated, only further annoyed. He was determined this time to avoid any more slithering. There was no purpose to be served by denying that he knew what Stan was talking about. "You know where I got them, and I know where you got them. What I want to know now is, what have you done with them?"

"No, no, no, no, no. I don't know where you got them. Russ, you've got everything wrong." He was for the instant nearer the verges of sincerity than Russ had ever seen him;

his primitivism extended to an inability to conceal truth as well as falsehood. Then he recovered his poise with disconcerting suddenness, as he always did, but what followed was also convincing. "I have them in my safe, yes, in my safe, whose combination is known only to me. I am keeping them for the police. I regard them as a sacred trust, yes, a sacred trust. As a duty to the deceased. Yes, I recognized Dolly Sommers' rings and bracelet and necklace and earrings. I recognized them. I knew you brought them here to incriminate me, along with those sapphires. I have done nothing but my duty as a professional man, and you are guilty of . . ." He stopped again. It was clear that this was something that had been worrying him. "Of, of . . ." Then he screamed, "How did you get them in here, Russ Mallery?"

"I didn't. But I know who did. The window had been left open."

"I tell you I have done nothing but my duty. I don't know what you want, but the only thing I have done. . . ." He checked himself and moved away from the edge of a quagmire imprudently approached. "The jewelry belongs to Dolly Sommers' estate, and you stole it. I have it in my safe, and you can't get it again. And I have the sapphires too, but I never saw them before in my life. You must have stolen them, Russ Mallery, and planted them on me. You want to destroy me—why, why, why?"

"You'd never seen the sapphires?" The distinction Stan drew between them and the rest of the jewelry was queer enough to be persuasive.

"No, no, no, no, no." Stan said this with so much enthusiasm as to suggest he felt himself now on firm ground. "I never saw them before and I am going to get the police to find out where you got them."

Though it went against the grain, Russ decided he had better go on being honest. "They were in the same place with the rest of the stuff. And you knew it."

"No, no, no. I know nothing about them. Nothing at all."

"You knew they were in the same place, and you knew where that place was."

Stan stood up, angry now. "You're making it all up. We put those rings and things on Dolly Sommers when Merry gave them to us and said her mother always wanted to be laid out in them. It was a courtesy, yes, a courtesy, one of the many we perform. But I never saw those sapphires, *ever*. And I am going to make the police find out where they came from."

"And I am going to tell them we found them in the grave where Dolly's body was buried."

The climax of Stan's emotions was now reached. The climax, quite possibly, of a life of anxiety and torment. He cried out in horror and suddenly ran toward the door, as if his office had betrayed him with a false security and he wanted to leave it forever. But Russ caught him by the arm, aware as he did so of a discreditable, even a sadistic satisfaction in having precipitated this final disarray. "You forgot about Dolly's body for the moment. Because you were so anxious to tell me you really hadn't seen the sapphires before. I believe you hadn't. But you knew that Dolly was never cremated." He said it icily, a statement of fact irretrievably revealed.

Stan nodded. His lower lip quivered. He put his handkerchief to his mouth.

"Are you still going to call the police?"

Stan shook his head. And then his recovery began. "And neither are you, Russ Mallery, because you stole those sapphires. Neither of us is going to call the police." He was, incredibly, sly and composed again. "And you can ask all the questions you want, but I am not going to say another word to you." He closed his lips in pouting obstinacy.

He meant it, too. He had once more won a victory, but this time Russ had not been defeated. He had learned something surprising and crucial, and ideas were moving fast through his mind. He stopped to say one more thing as he reached the door. "You damned well *better* keep those things in your safe and make sure they stay there. As long as they're there, they can't get you for larceny."

Richie was driving to the airport. The last three days, since Professor Payne's departure, had been dismal for him. He was not bothered by being alone on the farm. He was notably untroubled by thoughts of fires, intruders, and tornadoes, or by noises in the night. He performed the chores competently, although with a somewhat increased respect for his great-uncle and all other householders. There was a good deal more to do than he had supposed. Carburetors, valves, fuses, rainspouts, recalcitrant screens, spilled milk, and refrigerators in need of defrosting, were things he could handle one by one, but taken together they suggested that a household was a chronic and complaining invalid, constantly requiring exhausting attentions. As he several times said out loud to himself, there were a hell of a lot of things that could go wrong.

What bothered him was not things going wrong but

lack of companionship. The farm was isolated. This was the longest he had ever gone without seeing another person. He found himself looking forward with an eagerness that surprised him to his great-uncle's return. It would ease, he hoped, the other source of his distress.

"I'll call you from Chicago on my return," Professor Payne had told him three days before while he was waiting to board the Midwest flight. "I don't expect to be more than a few days. I can find out what I want to know very quickly I think."

"It's a long way to go, and you might find there isn't anything to find."

"The same observation might be made of human life," Professor Payne had answered.

"So you have to live. You don't have to fly to Paris."

"And *you* don't have to fly at all," his uncle had answered and, with that, said good-bye.

This farewell speech, given the circumstances, was as unpleasant a one for Richie as he could have made. It inadvertently touched the sorest of all the numerous sore spots in Richie's psyche. The fact was that he now not only did not have to fly but, in his own judgment anyway, could not fly and had been trying for the past week, by not thinking about it, to avoid the pain that the thought of flying brought, a pain similar to that, borne in similar silence, that earlier had been brought by thoughts of footballs, ice-skates, and tennis racquets. He told himself that he would get over it, but he hated having to go through it again, and hatred sometimes bred something like despair.

It had lasted, increasing in severity, for three days. He had spent a bad night. He had had dreams of flying and of Lisa, the two indissociable and equally unattainable, and he had awakened to the third morning of a solitary life. Then, after lunch, the telephone rang. It was Professor Payne.

Richie was delighted. "You O.K.? Anything happen?"

"A great deal happened." He was alert and rather more terse than usual.

"I mean, anything bad?"

"Yes and no. Nothing bad happened to me, if that's what you mean. I had a very good trip. Meet me at the airport. The Midwest plane is supposed to reach Buchanan at five."

"It won't."

"Probably not, but be there in case it does. And call Russ. I want him at the farm as soon as I get back. Not later than quarter of six. It's extremely urgent, Richie."

He hung up, as if to foreclose argument. Richie stared consideringly at the telephone for a moment before he dialed Russ's office and delivered the message.

"Does he sound all right?"

"Yeah. Excited."

"He did find something then."

"I think so. But I don't know what. He hung up. But he really meant it when he said he wanted to see you."

"Worried?"

Richie hesitated. "Maybe."

So Richie was in a mixed mood driving to the airport, glad to know that his uncle had made it back to Chicago in good health and spirits, but not sure that he was going to welcome the new discoveries the voyager was bringing home with him. He had reached the stage of suspended curiosity where the prospect of explanations and solutions was alarming instead of stimulating. He had a precocious sense that almost anything that happened would be bad.

This feeling was heightened by the knowledge that, while waiting for Midwest, he was likely to see Bud and almost certain to see Lisa. In prospect the meetings were very considerable ordeals. He was so familiar with ordeals by now that he tended by reflex to expect them, to dread, while fighting his way through, each painful experience as it developed. This was like the first day he had gone back to school, on crutches.

He steeled himself to enter the terminal and found—what he had still not learned to expect—no one. It was almost time for the scheduled arrival of the airliner, but no activity was visible. This was not surprising; the daily flight did not attract a large custom. The airline served ten county seats on a zigzag course between Chicago and Kansas City; served them, Richie thought, right. The flying stock inspired no confidence, and it was almost quicker to go by car.

He limped out onto the ramp to scan the sky, and he saw Earl and Lisa standing by the 140. His heart jumped and then fell. The presence of the 140 made the encounter more difficult. He wondered what Lisa was going to say to him. She would know all about what had happened on his last lessons. She would have convicted him of incompetence and panic; he must seem to her absurd and very young, a crippled kid who had lost his nerve. He should never have tried, he should never have even dreamed . . .

"Hi," she called and smiled, and he knew that all his thoughts were baseless and preposterous inventions. She held out her hand as he came up to the 140, where she was standing with one foot on the step, and when he gave her his she pressed it tight and smiled seriously at him.

He said "Hi," to Earl, but the line boy, instead of responding, shambled off toward the tank truck parked on the far edge of the ramp.

Lisa was looking into Richie's eyes, her own dark ones asking silent, exhilarating questions. He was kicking himself for having been a fool in the last few days, the last few minutes. He said as a sort of disclaimer, "I have to meet somebody coming in on Midwest."

"It's going to be late."

"You're kidding."

"They called up a while ago." She paused. They were still holding hands, and she was still looking steadily into his eyes. "Cheese came back to work today, by the way. He's still got a black eye. And he lisps because he had a tooth knocked out. Somebody did knock him down. You can't hit the back of your head and get a black eye and lose a front tooth all at once by falling down onto a bumper."

"Does he say who?"

"He still says he stumbled and fell down. Anybody can tell it's not true, but he keeps on saying it." None of it seemed very important, but she went on talking of things that did not seem important as if she were trying to cover the things that did. "I was just chewing Earl out."

"What'd he do?"

"I've got to take the one forty to pick up Pop over at Pierce and I asked Earl if he'd topped it. He said he had, but when I preflighted it one tank was about two-thirds empty. Not only that, it needed oil. Which is why preflighting is important. Earl's a menace to mankind. If I hadn't . . ."

She glanced away now, looking malevolently in Earl's direction as she continued her listing of his defects. But Richie had stopped listening. He was thinking back to the day of the emergency landing when he had uncertainly done the preflight himself. Several recollections came back to him. He remembered that Earl had said he'd filled the gas tanks and checked the oil. But that time, like this, he had been derelict; and so, with a start, Richie realized had he. He had forgotten to check the oil himself. If he had done it he would have seen the rag. For Earl's dereliction that time had not been to overlook the oil but to drop a rag when he filled it and then forget it. Richie knew it, with instant, instinctive certainty, as a fact.

Lisa was saying, "I'm going to tell Pop we've got to get rid of Earl. He's lazy and stupid, and when he tells lies he's really dangerous. I guess I've got to go, Richie. When are you going to come fly again?"

He was already flying. She saw that something was happening to him; and something happened to her. He caught her in his arms and exultantly kissed her.

She was still in his arms when Earl drove up with the tank truck.

CHAPTER XI

Flight Rule Violations

Lisa took off. Richie waited for the Midwest airliner leaning against the wall of the terminal building, squinting into the brilliant sky, listening for the sound of its engines.

He was feeling fine, and this, objectively considered, was unreasonable; his high spirits were produced by a strong sense of guilt.

The emergency landing had been his fault. The fire that endangered his life and Lisa's, not to mention something like fifteen thousand dollars' worth of Cherokee, had broken out because he had failed to check the oil, and, what was worse, because he had been reluctant to admit to Lisa that he wasn't sure he'd remembered everything to do in a pre-flight. The responsibility might be partly Earl's, but morally and—he guessed—legally, the blame attached not to Earl but himself. Richie was the responsible authority. He was the airman.

He was going to have to confess. Lisa, and Bud, and the Van Buren County Flying Service Inc. would receive full apologies. But this did not at all weigh on him. On the contrary, it brought him a dizzy, soaring sense of relief. Everything was O.K. There was nothing to worry about. There never would be anything to worry about again. And Midwest Airlines solemnized his joy: at the moment he was congratulating himself and the universe on having nearly killed himself and his girl, a distant hum announced that the plane was less late than anticipated.

Professor Payne was the only passenger to deplane. The whole Midwest venture was random and rather speculative. There were no ground personnel to assist in disembarkation. The stewardess opened the door and unfolded the steps. The co-pilot handled the baggage. The plane itself gave the decided impression of having seen action in other continents and decades. Its red and silver paint was peeling, and it looked as if it might be dangerously tired of flying. So, when he emerged, did Professor Payne.

It had been a long trip. By Paris time, to which he had barely become adjusted, it was now midnight. He had spent ten hours in the air as well as two on the ground in Invalides and Orly, waiting for buses and PA announcements, and three more eating a club sandwich in a Coffee Shoppe at O'Hare. Boredom mixed with fatigue. When the stewardess on Midwest had offered him a snack consisting of Seven Up, he had irritably demanded Seven Down instead. This had made the stewardess look at him as if he were taking part in a protest movement.

His fatigue was not entirely physical. It was partly the product of his efforts to sort out the implications of *The Revelations of a Concierge,* as he entitled it, as if his adventure in Paris had been brought to life from a minor work of Lesage, or Dumas Fils. Most exhausting of all had been the judgment arrived at some twelve thousand meters above the city of Sydney, Nova Scotia: there seemed no alternative to the conclusion that murder had been done. And no alternative, thereafter, to the conclusion that his own position, and the positions of Russ and Richie, were uncomfortable to the point of danger.

It was some reassurance to know—assuming that his orders had been obeyed—that no one except his partners knew where he had gone besides the employees of Magic Carpets of Buchanan Inc. But this was a large exception. Their trail from the wheatfield to Paris and back was littered with blazing indiscretions. The result of these meditations was that he approached the Buchanan Municipal Airport with trepidations quite as great as Richie's a few minutes earlier. The evil centered there. It was quite possible that malefactors, apprised by Magic Carpets of his itinerary, might be waiting, armed, at the edge of the runway. As a consequence of these imaginings, so little in line with his usual sanguine and skeptical turn of mind, he was particularly relieved to see Richie, alone on the field, waiting for him, his hands in his pockets as he leaned against the terminal building with the lazy ease of a resident airman.

He looked, on closer inspection, older than Professor Payne had remembered. His mental picture, he supposed, must have been unconsciously distorted by elements of the Richie of an earlier summer. This was mildly disconcerting, but he sensed, and was pleased, that the boy reciprocated his own pleasure in seeing him. The words for shared affection and relief were, however, laconic. Richie made terse, polite inquiries as if he had been meeting a bare acquaintance returned from a banal visit to Florida. Professor Payne answered with precisely the terseness to be expected from such a traveler. He wanted to save what he had to say until Russ had joined them, and he was glad to learn that the lawyer had been notified and might be already waiting at the farm.

He had not yet arrived when they reached home—having reasonably counted, perhaps, upon the usual delay in Midwest's schedule. Richie, grown accustomed in three days to provide himself with food and drink, now politely offered to provide it to his host. Professor Payne was pleasantly amused by this innocent reversal of roles. He did not at all like being taken care of in the normal way of things, but at the moment he was not unwilling to avail himself of Richie's management of ice cubes. He leaned back and ordered a very dry martini. Richie, unselfconscious, bowed and produced one. With a Coke for himself, he sat down to wait for Russ's arrival.

The time and place were peaceful. Summer had reached middle age and shadows already lay across the golden grass. August had brought the garden to the summit of its fortune and filled the afternoon with richer scents than July's. But nothing besides the ripening summer had outwardly changed from that earlier night when they had sat, silently staring into glasses, and heard the engine in the air.

They were listening for the sound of Russ's station wagon on the gravel, and perhaps that was why they noticed another sound, as unexpected and elusive this time as it had been before. It was only a few seconds before they identified it. Richie stood up and walked to the edge of the lawn where he could have a clear view of the sky, free from the ceiling of leaves. He had developed the habit, in the last few weeks, of staring concentratedly at every plane that passed overhead, no matter where he was, and he had left the terrace now more out of reflex than with any conscious reminiscence of the earlier evening. He stood with the Coke can in one hand, shielding his eyes with the other as he studied the western sky. The plane, it was apparent, was low and coming closer but still hidden by the surrounding trees. Then, low and very loud, it broke into view and quite suddenly disappeared over the woods on the hill.

"Jesus Christ," Richie said.

"What?" Professor Payne had also stood up.

"You know, it's the one eighty. *Nine Seven Juliet.*"

"Are you sure?"

"I could read the numerals. Good eyes is one thing I've got. And anyway—" he hesitated and asked, with puzzled gravity, "what else would you expect it would be?"

It was a good question. Professor Payne realized that while he was surprised, he would have been a good deal more surprised if it had not been Nine Seven Juliet. It was odd, he thought with the reflexes of a man trained for forty years on the lecture platform, how deeply atavistic was man's expectation that destiny would provide him with symmetrical patterns.

But Richie, poised like young David with a Coke can for a slingshot, was unconcerned with atavistic expectations. The plane reappeared briefly over the hilltop, and its power cut out.

"Let's go," Richie said, and this time it was he who led the way up the track to the wheatfield.

And it was Richie who worried about Professor Payne. Mostly he was thinking, during the climb to the top of the hill, of what he might find when he got there, but at intervals he wondered whether he was setting too fast a pace. His great-uncle looked tired, and acted tired, and with reason. Richie suspected, with sharp insight, that Professor Payne had been greatly elated by the entire Paris venture. But elation itself could be, as he himself well knew, exhausting. And while his uncle might like drama, Richie had very definitely the impression that he was getting more of it than he had bargained for; at his age it was natural for a man to prefer drama mellow to melodrama. Further physical fatigue might impose a serious strain, so Richie moderated somewhat his fast if awkward lope.

They reached the gate almost together, both a little winded. Tactics, however, required a pause at this point, and exertion had no serious effects on either of them. Cautiously they approached the gate and surveyed the field.

"Same scene," Richie said.

It was, or nearly so. The plane was parked not far from the spot where it had been before. But the pilot had done an even better job this time than before, performing the not inconsiderable feat of using less of the full length of the field, so that the Cherokee was somewhat nearer to them than it had been before, and farther from the gravesite. The red figures on the fuselage were easily legible. It was undoubtedly the same plane. And as before there was no sign of a pilot.

"I think," Professor Payne said, "that we had better go back and wait for Russ. Who has a gun. He has probably already arrived. And I think we must call the police this time; there is no doubt in my mind that danger is involved. It is not a place for amateurs."

He produced this with the air of someone repeating a catechism. It was hard to believe that he meant it.

"By the time we get down and Russ gets up, that cat could be in the air. So what you think he's doing, digging?"

"Yes. It was expected that he return for the jewels. But for us it is a curious experience, isn't it? *Déja vu.*"

"You mean this is where we came in? Where we went out, anyway."

"What seriously alarms me is that this time we might go out permanently."

"I know what you mean," Richie said with complete honesty. "But—we'd better find out who it is. We can't risk letting him get away."

"Perhaps you're right." Professor Payne made the concession without notable reluctance. "We could hide in the bushes and watch for him when he gets in the plane. In the meanwhile, if we stand behind the bushes here we should be safe enough."

"But we wouldn't be able to see him from here. The door's on the wrong side. We have to get down opposite the plane anyway. And . . ." Richie added thoughtfully, as if he were contemplating tactics in a football game, "it would be much better to catch him, not just see him."

"No. It would be stupid and gratuitous. Whoever he is, I think he is quite probably a murderer. I have serious grounds for thinking this. It's not an eccentric imagination, Richie."

"I know." He was not at all disposed to doubt it. On the contrary, he was showing the rocklike spine of decision that had been so marked on Stanley Brill's parking lot. "I'll fight my way through the woods to opposite the plane. I'll keep out of sight. You don't have to come."

He did not suppose that this suggestion would be followed, but he hoped it might be. He had private reasons for wanting to be alone when the pilot came out of the woods. But as he expected, Professor Payne was following him when he set off.

He wondered, when they had gone twenty feet, whether it might not after all have been as quick to go back for Russ and call the police. The brush was thick, and brambles flourished along the margin of the field where the sun penetrated the woods. He shortly found himself walled in by thorns, and was reminded of the Sleeping Beauty. But this wall of thorns was not going to yield to magic. He stopped. The day was cool, but he was hot and dirty, bleeding from scratches, and out of breath. There seemed to be no way out—certainly there was no way forward—except through the thin screen of briars that separated him from the open field. Determined, made foolhardy by blood, sweat and thorns, he tore his way into the open and began to run—faster than he had run for ten months, swinging his stiff leg with a tremendous effort—along the narrow belt of high grass that divided the wheat from the woods.

He glanced back. Professor Payne, a long way behind him, had followed him out of the underbrush and was waving to him to stop. They were too near the end of the field and the gravesite to risk calling out, but his gestures were very clear.

But Richie went on, driven more by the impetus of wild forward progress than by any clearly conceived purpose. He had half an idea of turning back into the woods when he reached a point opposite the plane, there to wait, as previously planned, for the appearance of the pilot. But this stratagem was uncertainly conceived; and when he came abreast of the plane, he saw that it was impracticable. For the plane had been half turned out of its landing track, so that the pilot, approaching from the far side, would either be hidden by the fuselage or, if Richie pressed farther along toward the end of the field, display nothing but his back. And when he glanced at the margin of the forest, he saw that the undergrowth here was denser than ever; blackberries and sumac had built another rampart.

He paused uncertainly, realizing desperately that whatever he did had better be done quickly. He looked carefully at the plane, as if it might hold the answer to his dilemma, and saw that, incredibly, it did. On the tip of the left wing, he saw a man's jacket, as if the pilot, anticipating heavy work, had taken it off as he started away from the plane with his shovel and casually tossed it back onto the wing.

If he got his hands on it, it would be certain evidence of identity; it could hardly belong to anyone except the digging pilot. Ideal evidence, in fact, since it could be seized without any personal encounter with its criminal owner. He thought that all his problems were solved; and he started forward again toward the plane, aiming to cut in front of the nose in the direction of the farther wingtip.

The plane was some thirty yards from the edge of the field. As he crossed them, Richie realized that it was a long way, longer than it had looked from the shelter of the tall grass and the overhanging trees, and that he was very much exposed in the open stretch of cut wheat. He was, if not exactly a sitting duck, at least a swinging one. It crossed his mind to note that he was very easy to identify. His lameness made him recognizable to anybody who had seen him once, and it made him feel suddenly defenseless and foolhardy.

His great-uncle had started across the field after him. He had not, perhaps, seen the jacket; in any case he could have had no idea what Richie had in mind. So he was following him—probably with the intention of overpowering him and propelling him back to the safety of the woodland by force—following him into the heart of danger.

For danger, his hard beating heart now told him, was real and near. He was half-expecting a threatening yell from the woods as he came up to the plane. And he knew he could not run away if anybody tried to come for him. Even Professor Payne was gaining on him. He had gone remarkably fast in the last few minutes, but not as fast as any man with two good legs. If he was seen, he was trapped.

At that moment, as he reached the plane, with Professor Payne a few steps behind, danger materialized. But not in the way he had expected.

Somebody fired a shot at them.

There was no way to tell where it had come from. The surprise of it numbed their senses with shock, and it was followed by echoes rolling in from all sides. Nor could he tell where it had gone, or how close it had come, or whether, indeed it had been aimed at them. But logic, or at least supposition, worked faster than the message of his senses. He did not doubt that they had been fired at by someone in the woods at the end of the field. And his reaction, like that of a man slapped in the face, whose pain is nothing to his fury, was much less of fright than of outrage.

Richie shouted. Not in alarm or even defiance, but as a command. He had made a quick decision.

"Get in," he shouted to his uncle. Then he ran the last few yards to the plane and scrambled over the wing from the leading edge. He looked back, feeling, unreasonably, a little safer now that he was in the lee of the plane, as if it represented a friendly fortress in the open field. But he saw that his uncle was undecided. It frightened and alarmed him. To Richie the imperatives were so obvious and so powerful as to leave no choice. He shouted again, and still Professor Payne, standing three yards away, did not move to join him.

There was then another shot, and this time Professor Payne moved, and fast.

He was in the cabin in an instant. Richie had already jammed in the mixture to rich and switched on the master and the magnetos by the time his uncle was settling into the right seat beside him. He had trouble with the door; Richie wordlessly leaned across him and slammed it, pumped the throttle, pushed the starter, heard the engine cough and catch, and the propeller turn.

He was half-consciously calculating probabilities. The gravedigger would fire again. He might hit the wing tanks, which would not do much harm; the gas leak would be pretty slow, Richie judged. He might hit a tire, which would probably be more serious. He would probably aim at the cabin, in the hope of hitting the pilot through a window. The evidence so far suggested that their assailant was a poor shot, but the evidence was insufficient to prove it, and if he broke out of the woods running, he might be able to close the distance between himself and his target.

He had released the brake and was taxiing. What the gravedigger did was beyond Richie's control; but everything else depended on it, and his control was at best conjectural. It was important to taxi as fast as possible, but he had no idea how fast was possible, even on concrete, let alone a field whose uncertain surface might, for all he knew, be enough to trap the wheels, even to tip the plane forward on its nose and shatter the prop. He was not at all sure whether he could get the plane in the air fast enough and high enough to clear the woods. There were ways, he knew, of getting a plane off the ground steeply and safely, but he didn't know what they were. There was no point in worrying about what the gravedigger might be doing; he had quite enough else to worry about, but—he had instinctively weighed the matter before he made his decision—he thought he had better rely on himself as a pilot by flying away than on his bad leg by running away.

The plane was rolling, faster, jolting, and he had headed it toward the end of the field, when the third shot was fired. It was muffled now by the sound of the engine, but it was fully loud enough to show that their enemy had not given up.

There was, for the moment anyway, no hope of seeing who was shooting. The anonymous cat had presumably emerged from the woods and was following them—he would now be trying to shoot at a retreating target—and this meant that he was lost to view behind the plane. When they got to the end of the field and turned around to head for the take-off, they might have a passing glimpse, and there would be a moment of dangerous exposure. Richie was trying to hold the plane straight as it jounced along, the pedals kicking under his feet. They were making good progress. The bouncing was alarming, but the end of the field was close. In a moment they reached it, and his heart rose as he pushed the left pedal hard to turn the plane. He glanced at the instruments and the gauges and hoped they were in good order. There was certainly no time for the run-up and the check list.

As the plane turned, several things became evident. They *were* being pursued and—Richie saw it with astonishment—by two pursuers. The two figures were running along the course that Richie had followed in the opposite direction a moment before, at the edge of the field. They were in the shadow of the trees at the far end of the field, nothing more at this distance than moving forms. They were running fast. It did not look as if they were going to shoot again, for the next few moments, anyway.

But this did not mean that Richie was out of the woods. On the contrary, when he looked ahead at the length of the wheatfield before the plane, it seemed very likely that the woods were exactly what they would soon be in. The field was very short indeed, and the trees tall. He had taken a plane off only half a dozen times, and then always with a long smooth stretch of concrete ahead of him. He was vividly aware of the fact that once you got off the ground, if you pulled up the nose to clear obstacles before you had picked up speed the plane would stall. He shuddered, going back to the sensations of his dark day of stalls and had a moment's certainty he could not do it. He noticed that he had already made one mistake—he had not quite gone to the end of the field, and he had not turned as tightly as he could have, so he had lost several yards of runway. The observation, combined with his remembrance of what stalls were like, froze him in immobility. He pulled on the hand brake, as if to give himself an instant to recover from the passage of a brief storm of panic, and then he pushed the throttle to the wall and took the brake off.

Without knowing it, he had done the right thing. The plane lurched suddenly forward and picked up speed. He was holding the yoke back, waiting for the instant when he felt the plane lose weight and he could pull it off.

But the rough field slowed it. He was concentrating very hard, and he was tired, as if holding back the stick and riding the pedals to hold his course were demanding an effort of muscle so tremendous as to exhaust his remaining reserves of energy. He glanced at the airspeed, and watched it mount, slowly, maddeningly slowly, forty, fifty, sixty. He was covering the field frighteningly fast, losing space to climb, but the plane, bouncing violently, still would not rise. The trees were coming nearer. They could not possibly make it.

Desperately and dangerously, he jerked back on the yoke; and the plane came off the ground. He knew that he should level off, until the airspeed reached eighty, but this was now out of the question; it would mean hitting the tree trunks a few yards off the ground at seventy miles an hour. He held the nose up at an angle that he thought might possibly get him across the treetops. The red light on the panel, the stall signal came on. That was alarming, but the stick had not yet gone soft to give him the final warning, and he pulled it back a little further. The airspeed was falling, down to sixty. The white line on the indicator told him that a stall was very near now; and so were the trees. He could see nothing but a bank of green leaves in front of him.

But he had a fleeting, senseless instant of triumph. He had gotten the plane off the ground. His solo had begun.

Russ had reached the farm ten minutes after Richie and Professor Payne started up the hill. He shouted for them and then looked around the terrace. It would not at all have surprised him, given Midwest's reputation for punctuality, if they hadn't got back yet from the airport. But this, he saw, was not the case. It was he, not they, who was late. The front door was open, and a martini half drunk stood on the flagstones beside Professor Payne's habitual chair. He walked back to the driveway and saw that Professor Payne's car was there, pulled in by the stable, which suggested that they were not far off. They must be on foot, and neither Richie nor his great-uncle would be likely to go on foot for long distances.

He shouted again, shrugged his shoulders, and returned to the terrace. Availing himself of the privileges of a very old friendship, he went to the kitchen and mixed himself a drink. He started to drink it, wondering with perplexity and a little apprehension what had happened to his host. The time lengthened. The drink was half drunk. Perplexity and apprehension mounted. Then he heard a shot.

Like Richie he knew at once where it had come from, through the working of instantaneous logical processes rather than the evidence of his senses, and in the next fraction of a second his mind proceeded to further conclusions. The pilot had, of course, returned to the wheatfield to recover the sapphires that for some unexplained reason, he had buried with Mrs. Sommers' body. Richie and Walt must have heard the plane and had gone to the field to catch the pilot *in flagrante*. It was crazy, but it was what he would have done himself. And they had indeed encountered, if not caught, their prey, and he had shot at them.

At this point in his rapid construction of a skyscraper built from the lumber of the open door, a half empty martini glass, a parked car, and the sound of a shot, the gun was fired again. So far Russ's architecture had been faultless; but the second shot led his imagination impetuously to decorate the edifice with an inference too heavy for his logic.

His main weakness as a dectective lay precisely in the speed and flamboyancy with which his imagination operated. Hypotheses took fire and burst into conflagrations before he had time to check them. The second shot suggested to him that they had probably been hit. Two shots, two victims. Then, came a muffled roar, at first unidentifiable, and the sound of a third shot. A few minutes later he recognized the sound of an airplane engine. There was no longer any doubt in his mind what had happened. One shot had missed, or at least had failed to kill. The third one had struck its target squarely and the pilot had hastily departed. He would not have taken off had there been any possibility of his leaving living witnesses behind.

Russ was by then moving too fast up the track through the woods, reaching with his right hand for his shoulder holster, to reflect further on the accuracy of his conclusions and, in any event, no amount of reflection would have been likely to affect them much. He thought first, acted almost simultaneously, and felt things afterward. This sequence of responses obtained now; otherwise he would have suffered a good deal more than necessary.

He covered the length of the path much faster than Richie and Professor Payne. When he approached the gate, he cautiously slowed down and turned into the woods. For a man who looked badly out of condition, he moved with surprising agility, far more quietly and quickly than Richie or Professor Payne, through the brush to the edge of the field. He looked out from the undergrowth, and his first glance conveyed the horrifying impression that his expectations were in fact correct. There was no sign of the plane. There were, however, two figures at the opposite end of the field from the grave, and with surprise he saw that they were standing up, and they were strangers. Or at least they were sufficiently unfamiliar to be unrecognizable at that distance. But they were walking in his direction.

Before he had time to speculate on the whereabouts of Richie and Walt, the figures emerged as two men, one middle-aged and heavy, the other slight and younger. They were arguing, and before they noticed him they both stopped dead in their tracks and faced each other, shouting. They were still too far away, and their shouts were too incoherent, to be understood. The heavy man hit the slight one on the chin and knocked him down. And now his shouts were so loud that Russ, coming closer, could hear them.

"This time," he was yelling, "I'm going to knock *all* your teeth out, you block-headed little bastard." And he leaned down over the fallen man, who was struggling to his knees, and hit him hard in the mouth a second time.

Russ, revolver in hand, had come up to them. They still did not see him. The big man had his back to him, the other was beyond noticing anything. When he had come within a few yards, he quietly said, "As a citizen, I arrest you for trespass, assault, battery, larceny, using dangerous weapons with the intent to kill, and the desecration of venerated objects."

The big man wheeled around and stared in disbelief. Russ grinned at him, holding his revolver steady. He was more jubilant than he had ever been.

He had as yet no notion of how the situation in the wheatfield had come about. He realized now that Richie and Professor Payne must be in the relative safety of the air. He had no time to wonder how they had got there. But whatever the causes of this strange situation, he was indubitably master of it. The big man was still staring with inexpressible astonishment at Russ and his revolver. Then, his mouth still open, his hand moved toward his own holster. But he immediately thought better of it, and slowly raised his arms in the air. It was not the first time, Russ judged, that he had found himself in this position.

The man on the ground was still on hands and knees. His reflexes were stronger than his sense. He, too, tried to raise his hands, fell forward on his face, cursed into the stubble, and then painfully got to his feet. One hand went to his bleeding mouth, the other into the air.

"Start walking," Russ said. He was lost in confusion, but he was feeling fine. He had fulfilled his destiny.

CHAPTER XII

Home on the Numerals

"I congratulate you, Richie."

Richie acknowledged this judicious approval with the sketch of a salute. "Any time," he said.

A few seconds earlier they had cleared the treetops—or almost cleared them; leaves and twigs had brushed the gear. Until the last minute he had doubted that the margin could possibly be enough, but he had had no choice but to fly straight at the branches. He remembered the warning: you can't turn on the climb-out, because a plane stalls at higher speeds when it's banked; once you're committed to the take-off, you've got to take your chances with what's straight ahead of you. He had waited desperately for the yoke to go soft in his hands and then, incredulously, heard the leaves hit the gear and seen the wall of green replaced by open sky. An instant later the trees were far, far below them, and Professor Payne was congratulating him.

He continued to climb for a while, heading up into the sky in joy. He was very taut, but he was in command of his kingdom and his fate. He allowed himself a moment of exultation in celestial realms and then forced himself to abandon them. He knew he could fly best when he was thus cosmically translated, but he was still obliged to fly over the earth's surface, and there was a danger of getting lost. The airport was fifteen miles away. Less, probably, by air. Maybe five minutes flying time. About north, he judged.

He leveled off and professionally eyed the gyro, compared it to the compass, and found it accurate. He was on a heading of zero nine zero. He banked into a steep left turn, proud of his expertness and that he remembered what Lisa had taught him about finding and holding a heading.

The test, however, was nowhere near passed; it was much less than half completed. Landing was going to be a good deal harder than taking off, even considering the exceptional hazards of tall trees and an active gunman. Richie was also aware, more acutely at the moment than of the problems of natural laws of drag, lift, thrust and gravity, of problems presented by manmade laws against stealing planes, flying unauthorized solo flights, carrying a passenger without a license. These were all, he vaguely supposed, capital offenses.

But none of these drawbacks, although he considered them carefully, did any substantial damage to his self-satisfaction or, what was less easy to explain, his rapidly rising sense of safety. Half a mile up in the air in a plane he had never flown before, faced with the prospect of landing it, which he had never done successfully with any plane, he nonetheless felt safer than he had ever felt. It did not really occur to him that anything could go wrong.

Still, there *were* serious problems, administrative and technical. He briefly considered solutions. So far as legal problems went, there was no reason to go to Buchanan Municipal at all. He might fly to—say—Pierce City, land there, wave to a line boy to tie down the plane, and simply disappear with his passenger around the corner of a hangar, to bum a ride home on the nearest road. But the problem there was that the line boy would certainly pay particular attention to the odd pair; later he would be able to identify a very young and very lame pilot. There would be no advantage in going to another airport. If he were going to land in a strange place, it would be better to pick an empty field.

But that was fantasy. Good sense immediately informed him that he had neither Lisa's virtuosity nor her composure, in the matter of strange fields. The only reasonable chance of surviving his incompetence lay on a long concrete runway. If natural laws were to be obeyed, manmade laws could not be evaded. It was, he thought, irritating to be forced into malefaction in the course of apprehending malefactors, although guilty recognition of malefactions did not stop him from grinning as he shouted a comment along these lines to his passenger.

Professor Payne was remarkably composed. But he answered in measured clauses, a little pedantically, "It is a good deal better to be arrested *as* a criminal than shot *by* one. You have shown considerable resource and skill, Richie. I hope you are aware of it. It is important to have a just appreciation of one's qualities."

Richie said soberly, "O.K. Resource and skill. Not too much intelligence. I should of stayed in the woods and kept away from the plane."

"You can't stay all your whole life in the woods." His effect was weakened by the need to shout above the noise of the engine, but then proceeded with his eucharist. "Indeed, you can't keep away from planes all your life. You did something imprudent and dangerous. Imprudence and danger are necessary to living. It does not at all strike me that you were unintelligent."

"Yeah," Richie said with the appearance of skepticism. He was not displeased by his great-uncle's statement; indeed, he was convinced by it. But it had reminded him of another dimension of his problems; they were natural and legal, but also psychic. His great-uncle knew nothing of the crisis in his life when he tried to land a plane. He was, Richie thought, serenely supposing that he was in competent hands and that danger was now at an end. The thought of the responsibility he had assumed did not exactly daunt him, but it did fortify his normal reaction to praise, which was one of obscure embarrassment and mild annoyance. "So wait 'til we're on the ground before you say anything else."

As he spoke he reduced the power and let the nose drop a little. He had picked out on the horizon the familiar contour of Buchanan Municipal Airport, the white runway stretching across his path a geometric scar on the green land. The sight of it brought a chill of excitement with the certainty of approaching climax, and, a second later, fear. He felt adrenalin in his bloodstream. He was suddenly hot and tense, eager and scared at the same time.

He glanced at the altimeter. He would have to lose another five hundred feet. He would have to turn east, wide around the end of the runway, to enter the pattern. When he was parallel to it, on the far side, he would level out, eight hundred feet above the surface, and switch on the fuel pump. He would need to watch the airspeed and the altimeter carefully—they got away from you fast. Watch his turns, too—steep turns at low speeds were dangerous.

Keep the airspeed above seventy. Put on some flap before turning base.

All these instructions he gave himself tensely, but with pride in his memory and his skills. He was showing off, a little; the knowledge that he was acting before an audience lent reality to his pretense. He was flying better than he ever had before.

But still, not like a real pilot. He recognized some of the things he was doing wrong and wondered how serious they were. Overcontrolling, letting the plane drift sloppily from its heading. He knew there were a lot more things he must be doing wrong as well, things that he had not yet come to in his instruction. It was, he grimly judged, just as well. There was already too much to think about. He was downwind now, paralleling the runway. He cut the power, and trimmed it up as he had been told to do, when he was nearly opposite the end of the concrete strip. He knew he was supposed to watch it, to make sure he stayed at the proper angle to it at each stage. And while he was watching it, to watch everything else too, the speed, the altitude, the coordination of stick and rudder, the heading, the glide angle, the power, the trim, the flaps.

He put on the flaps and turned base. The runway was on his left now, suddenly too far away, too small, and as he turned final, a long way off line. He would have to get lined up, judge the wind, decide whether he was too high and too fast, or too slow and too low, whether to give it power, and how much, then remember to cut it at the instant when he saw, in Bud's words, that he "had it made."

Now, for the first time, panic replaced excitement. He was never going to have it made. It was inconceivable that he could put the plane down on that small, distant rectangle of concrete far below, that he could remember and do simultaneously a dozen things he did not know how to do at all. "*Goddam*," he said violently.

Professor Payne turned to him. He was perceptibly tense too. "Nothing's wrong?" he asked, his voice barely audible.

"No. Everything's great."

The reassurance, ironically intended, nonetheless helped him. The season of surrender passed; there was no time now for feeling anything. He saw the airspeed was too high, eighty-five, nearly ninety. How did you reduce speed? By pulling back on the yoke. The plane bucked. It was moving—too fast, terrifyingly fast—toward the runway, heading at the wrong angle. He twisted the yoke, and the plane bucked again, heading the right way now, but moving sidewise. And suddenly he was too low, much too low, hundreds of yards from the numerals at the end of the runway and going too slow toward them. This was what had happened to him before, with Bud, when he had found himself too slow and too far away and the plane uncontrollably heading in the wrong direction. He had no idea why it was happening, what he was doing to make it happen, or what could stop it. Instinctively he pushed the throttle toward the wall. The nose went up. The plane bucked again, more violently, and he thought he might be going to lose control of it altogether; it was rising, turning, with a demonic resolution of its own.

And then he saw the runway only yards away, almost below him, and he knew that he "had it made." Tension was succeeded by a surge of exhilaration. He knew what he had to do now. He pulled his right hand back. The power cut off. The plane was still sidewise; he jammed his right toe to the floor, and the plane jerked and headed around. He pulled back on the yoke. He heard Bud's words in his ears, "Hold it off, keep holding it off, keep holding back as long as you can, let it land itself."

The plane pointed up, and there was a long, breathless moment of suspended life, and then it sank suddenly and he felt the jolt as the gear hit the concrete and the pedals jerked under his feet. The climax had surprised him, coming before he expected it, over almost before he realized it had happened. He was working his feet to straighten the plane. His hands were no use now. It was just as well. His palms were so wet with sweat that he could not have held the yoke.

Sweat was running off his forehead into his eyes, and he wiped it with one hand as he pulled at the brake with the other. The plane slowed down, and he turned off at the intersection toward the ramp, thinking and feeling almost nothing but the certainty, thrust on him like a knife cutting deep into his consciousness, that he had known he could do it, that the flash of panic had been a nightmare of impotence, that he would never have trouble with a landing again.

On the ramp he put on the brake again and pulled out the mixture to weak until the engine choked. Then he switched off the master and the fuel pumps and the magneto, and leaned over to the door, to unlock it and push it open. Professor Payne did not at once move. Together they sat in silence for a moment before he climbed onto the wing. Richie, preparing to follow him, looked out for the first time since he had landed. Earl was standing by the terminal, talking to Bud. They both glanced without much interest at Nine Seven Juliet. As yet, Richie realized, they had no notion that it had changed management.

And it was a few seconds before he himself realized something as momentous as the fact that he had completed his solo flight and landed the plane by himself. If Bud were there on the ramp, he could not be the man they had left in the wheatfield. But that, like his ability to land the plane, was something Richie had known all along too.

Bud was standing, his hands in his pockets, as he leaned against the terminal building in the pose that Richie had unconsciously imitated an hour before. He wore though, as Richie had not, an expression of skepticism, coolly challenging the fates to produce any happening worse than he was prepared for, questioning a world whose answers could never surprise him.

But now he was surprised. Professor Payne was on the ground, and when Richie followed him Bud's poise melted. He jumped and said, "What the hell . . ." Then he settled back against the wall, lit a cigarette, and asked, "How'd you get the plane, Richie? Rub an old propeller and ask the genie for it?"

"No, I stole it."

"Right." Bud impassively considered the burning tip of the cigarette. "You also illegally soloed and carried a passenger. I watched your landing. I thought it was Cheese, and I was deciding he'd had a paralytic stroke on downwind. I've seen worse landings, but none where they could identify the bodies afterward. You're going to need a lot more lessons, Richie. After they let you out of jail."

He paused, scowling fiercely, but Richie, who knew him, realized that he was not altogether displeased. At that moment Lisa came out the door from the office. She looked at him in surprise and said, "You back again, Richie? Or still here? Didn't Midwest ever make it?"

Bud said, "Richie just soloed. He stole Nine Seven Juliet. When they let him out of jail, we're going to have to teach him how to land. But since he isn't in jail yet, I guess we got to observe tradition." He stepped forward and shook hands with Richie, and Earl followed him. Lisa kissed him, and while she was in his arms the telephone in the office rang, and Bud went to answer it.

Bud drove Professor Payne and Richie. Russ had urgently asked them to meet him at the farm. He had spoken briefly to Bud and at length to Professor Payne, and they had grimly made haste to leave. In the car, there was not much conversation. Richie cautiously explained, in monosyllables and incomplete sentences, some of the story that had led up to his solo. Bud asked no questions. He was engaged in calculation, and the silence with which he received the explanations had a dampening effect on the others. They had, moreover, their own thoughts to concern them.

Near the end of the trip, however, Bud spoke. "I wasn't joking, Richie." His voice was bleak but sardonic, as if he had been making a joke and decided it was a bad one. "We are going to have to report this. If we didn't, the company'd be in trouble. Right?"

Richie shrugged his shoulders.

"You don't even have a student ticket. You are as illegal as it's possible to be. You're more illegal than anybody I've ever known."

He thought for a moment, frowning, and said, "You're a

good guy, Richie, and you might make a good pilot. But I don't know whether we can ever make you a pilot at all now. When you took the controls of that plane without another pilot aboard, no matter how goddam extenuating the circumstances were, you not only went into the air, but into the soup too. Way, way in. You're about a mile deep in soup."

"There *was* another pilot aboard," Professor Payne said. "I am a pilot."

Nobody said anything.

"It's true," he went on, "that I haven't flown for almost fifty years. But I did have a private license. One of the first."

Bud turned to look at him. "Is that right?" He was making quick deductions with his neat, arithmetical mind.

"It certainly is."

"Then *you* were pilot in command," Bud said. "Once a pilot, always a pilot, if they don't take your license away. It puts Richie in the clear. Technically, I guess he shouldn't have been in the left seat, since you're not a CFI. But they'd overlook that. We may have to report you for flying without a valid medical certificate, or a check-out. The FAA may penalize you, sir. They might even lift your license," he said threateningly.

They had stopped at a light on the edge of town. The light changed; Bud pressed down the accelerator and they left the car beside them way behind.

Professor Payne said, "I am not planning to do much flying from now on."

"And as far as the other charges go," Bud went on, following his own chain of thought, "Nine Seven Juliet belongs to me personally. And I won't press charges of theft." He thought for a moment and then spoke over his shoulder to Richie. "Right?"

"Right," Richie said.

Of all the pleasant provisions of the common law, the one Russ Mallery liked best was the right of citizens to make arrests. He had never exercised it before. As he sat in a comfortable lawn chair, holding in his left hand the drink whose consumption had been interrupted earlier by gunfire, he fondly fingered his revolver with his right hand and reflected that life was good.

After a brief preliminary interrogation he had made four calls on Professor Payne's phone, ordered with a nice sense of civic and human responsibility. First he had called Jim Fess and was pleased to find the sheriff home, although asleep. It was the sheriff's custom to dine early and take a nap afterward, Mrs. Fess said, a fact that gratifyingly confirmed all Russ's suspicions about his successor. Mrs. Fess, reluctant to wake him, agreed to give him an urgent message. He was to send two of his men to take possession of criminals caught, *in flagrante delictu,* in the commission of an extensive series of felonies and misdemeanors. Next Russ called the airport and found that Richie and Professor Payne had arrived safely. He found out a good deal more besides, and what Professor Payne told him led to his next telephone call, which was to Mrs. Glendenning Berger, whom he also summoned to the farm with a message that her son, painfully but not seriously injured for the second time in two weeks, required her presence. Finally he called Stanley Brill and threatened him.

If the untangling of criminal plots and the apprehension of malefactors was the most driving interest in his life, another almost as strong, now discovered for the first time, was for stage direction. He awaited the arrival of those he had summoned with the satisfaction of someone whose blocking out of a performance was proceeding with unexpected success. He filled in the time with further interrogation.

The heavy man was obstinate. He refused to talk in the absence of his lawyer, a constitutional privilege of which Russ had carefully reminded them both. There was no reason for them to talk at all, of course; having arrested them, he had no subsequent *locus standi.* But he had, almost without being aware of it, reassumed the manner of power. They both acted as if they were in the presence of authority, in their different ways. And Cheese Berger was willing enough to show that there was no honor among thieves. He talked. He talked, it was true, almost unintelligibly. His companion had not had time to make good his threat to knock out the rest of his teeth, but he had knocked out several. This made communication painful and sometimes nearly impossible, but it was also what made Cheese willing to attempt it. He was enraged by the additional loss to the point of garrulity. Some of it was understandable, although none of it was sequential. Russ, having finished his drink, took notes.

A good deal of it was aimed against the other man whose name it appeared was Norm. "How the hell could I tell it was going to clear up the next morning?" Cheese rhetorically asked. "All the weather reports said Chicago was going to be fogged in for another week. Did he expect me to carry the damned stones around in my pocket another week? I did what anybody would have done. When I had to find some place good to bury the damned body, I buried the damned stones too. It was the only sensible thing to do. I knew I could get them back whenever I needed them, and they were safe there."

Norm stirred. He, too, was enraged, and he started to speak, but caution, born it seemed of experience, restrained him. He reacted instead with a singularly eloquent sound that committed him to nothing but contempt for his colleague. "So then," Cheese went on, holding his hand over his mouth as if it were necessary to use his fingers to operate its movements, "he gets mad because I couldn't find the damned field again. I told him I'd find it in time. But a damned field like this is hard to find."

"You were, no doubt, rather tense during your first visit here," Russ said kindly. "Anyone might forget his bearings, under the stress of burying a body and a small fortune in illegal jewels."

"Tense, hell." He spit some blood. His bearing was one of fused defiance of the world and total surrender to it. "I looked out from the damned woods and saw two characters climbing in the plane. Who the hell wouldn't be tense?"

"You had no idea whose property you were on, of course? Or that there was a house at the edge of the woods?"

"There're a thousand wheatfields in woods, and you couldn't see the house. I knew I could find it again, but it would take some time, that's all. But this bastard gets mad and gives me a hell of a punch when I wasn't expecting it."

Norm's eyes, shifting around the terrace, now focussed again on Cheese, with even greater malevolence.

"Then when I get out of the damn hospital, he says he's

going to come with me when I look for it because he doesn't believe I ever buried them there anyway. And we find out some bastard's dug the whole place up and taken them, and then those other bastards steal the plane, and Norm tries to kill them. I told Norm he was a fool to fire at them."

His spirits seemed to be rising as he said this. He took his hand away from his not very attractive mouth and looked up at Russ. It was as if somebody had handed him a key and he was slowly realizing that it would open the door of his cell. "I told him he'd get himself hung with a murder charge. He's a god-damned murderer. He tried to kill me, too," he said, now almost cheerful and much more fluent. "It's a good thing you came along when you did, sir, or I'd be a dead man now. I'm going to charge him with three attempted murders. Mine and the old man and the kid." He was sneering, jubilantly sneering. But he paused. "And I'm going to charge that damned kid with a lot of things, too. How the hell did he get here, anyway?" He was speaking with a queer, toneless vehemence, as if these recriminations owed more to dreams of vengeance than to an urgent sense of reality.

"He and Professor Payne live here. This is Professor Payne's house."

This momentarily erased the jubilation. "Jeezus, wouldn't you know. Wouldn't you know I'd pick a field next to their house—"

For the first time Norm spoke. He said stonily, "Yeah, I would."

"I'm going to get him charged with three attempted murders, and get that kid charged with—man, you don't know how much trouble you can get into violating FAA regulations. Besides getting killed. Maybe he *did* get killed." He brightened again. "He can't fly worth a damn. Bud says . . ."

He was interrupted by the sound of a car, and by Bud, followed by Richie and Professor Payne. And this sight crushed him again. Bafflement was more torturing to him, or at least more real, than the prospect of criminal charges. He looked at them briefly and said, "How the hell did you . . ." and then broke off and put his head in his hands.

Professor Payne deliberately went to his half-empty martini glass and swallowed it. Bud and Richie stared at Norm. Russ, disregarding their arrival, spoke to Cheese, "What I want to know is where the stuff came from. I can guess where it was going. I take it that our friend here–" His voice, insinuating, took on the soft guile that a hundred juries in the county had heard. "Is in part of a big operation in Chicago. No doubt the police will be able to get on to it, with suitable methods. I imagine Norm is in for very serious trouble on that score, selling hot stones. Quite aside from the trouble you will put him into with charges of attempted murder. Yes, I think we can guess where the sapphires were going. The question is, where did they come from."

Cheese looked up. "The question is, where are they now. Did the kid take them?"

"They are in Stanley Brill's safe."

Cheese writhed in astonishment. He started impulsively to ask a question, stopped himself, and spit more blood.

"That is where they are now. Where did they come from?"

Cheese showed no disposition to answer this. His moment of garrulity passed. He looked around desperately at the other silent men and leaned back in his chair. "I'm not talking," he said.

But he did, and almost immediately. For another car had come in the driveway, and when its driver got out and started up the walk Cheese got to his feet. "Oh my God, what the hell are you doing here?" he said to his mother.

As she approached, Russ also rose and said, which was not true, "I have the duty to inform you, Mrs. Berger, that your son is charged with grand larceny of jewelry to the value of more than seventy-five thousand dollars."

It was not his duty to inform her of it, but it was his pleasure, and it had upon her an effect as large in magnitude, though quite different in nature, as any he had expected.

Merry Berger had driven to the farm with a high degree of irritation which was, like her son's, much intensified by confusion. She didn't know why Russ Mallery was at the farm, or what her son had been doing there, or how he had gotten hurt, but it was, in her judgment, exactly the sort of thing that was to be expected of him. She was not worried about him. She thought he was probably malingering. He had spent a notably healthy boyhood malingering. She had arrived instead in a mood of dudgeon, prepared to put up with no nonsense from either Russ Mallery, whom she barely knew, or her son, whom she knew too well. But Russ's words had completely deflected this resolution. She was astounded.

"Seventy-five thousand dollars! Why Russ Mallery, Mom never had anything worth anything like that. That diamond ring that granddaddy gave her was real pretty, but I never suspected it was worth much. Granddaddy was a generous man, but it never occurred to me for a minute that—*seventy-five thousand dollars!* You can't mean it, I mean . . ." She broke off in exuberant delight and sat down heavily. "Walt," she said, "I think you might offer me a drink."

"It was not your mother's jewelry that was worth seventy-five thousand dollars," Russ said. "It was some sapphires that your son stole and buried at the same time he buried your mother's body."

She did not take all of this in; she was busy with her own thoughts, and only the last clause reached her. Then, in strident horror, she said, "Beaufort, I don't know what I'm going to do with you. Do you mean to sit there and tell me that you've told these people everything. I always said you don't have the sense you were born with." She turned to Russ and went on, "You know Russ—you don't mind my calling you that, do you, I don't know you real well, but I remember you from when you were a little boy and Mom always said to me, 'Merry, I knew Russ Mallery's mother, and there wasn't a finer woman in Van Buren County,' so I know you won't mind my calling you Russ. Anyway, I was saying, I don't know what to do about this boy of mine. And his father's the same way. I always say to them, I think they were both born with something *lacking*. I swear they can't do a thing right. I've said it to Walt and I'll say it to you, I think if it weren't for me we'd all *starve* to death. You know, I could hardly get Beaufort to take Mom's remains in that plane to go inter them. I practically had to force him to do it. He's just a bad boy, he'll never do anything I tell him."

She was going on, unaware now of where she was, or whom she was talking to, saying things whose meaning she was not aware of, talking with a feverish fulfillment in merely uttering them.

Russ stopped her. "I said, your son will be charged with stealing valuable jewels."

"Don't be absurd, Russ. He didn't steal anything. If they're that valuable of course we'll go get them back. But nobody stole anything, people are so silly, and I think you better be careful about the way you say things like that. I know nobody is going to arrest Beaufort. I was saying to him only the other day when he got out of the hospital . . ." She stopped, on the verge of lying. But lies had no meaning to her; she was deeply convinced that if she told lies with enough emphasis they would be believed as truth, that indeed, because she told them, they became truth. The universe ran by laws decreed by her needs. "It was all Persh Custer's idea," she said. "Nobody stole anything, and I don't know what that foolish boy of mine has been saying to you, but when Gay first married that man, Mom said to me . . ."

"Mrs. Berger, your son has stolen some sapphires, which have nothing to do with your mother's body."

"I didn't steal them, you bastard," Cheese said, his face in his hands. "I never stole nothing."

"Where did you get them?"

"I got them," he said.

"Now Beaufort, I've been through enough with you," his mother said. "Nobody's going to arrest you. You tell him what he wants to know."

"I'm not talking."

"You better not," Norm said.

Merry Berger, who seemed to be seeing him for the first time, turned on him. She looked like a monstrous hen, her feathers ruffled for combat. "I don't know who you are, but if you're the one who knocked my boy down. . . ."

She was interrupted by another car, and Stanley Brill. He came onto the terrace sidewise. If Merry Berger looked like a hen, he looked like a lizard emerging from primordial ooze. He had not known what to expect, and he was intensely nervous. What he found was evidently worse than anything he had imagined; when he saw Cheese Berger and his mother, he stepped back, started to cry out, put his hand over his mouth, and then looked around not so much in terror as hope, it seemed, of a path to escape. Russ raised the revolver in his lap and tapped it lightly on his knee. "Sit down."

"I am afraid I don't know these gentlemen." Stan's pliable veneer could cover even this predicament. He nodded at Bud and Norm in formal, somber style, as if they were the relatives of a man he had just embalmed.

"Mr. Ramsey and Mr. X," Russ said. It added nothing to Stan's peace of mind. Then he said to Mrs. Berger, "I asked my old friend Stan Brill to come along so he could assure you of something that might worry you. He will tell you that your mother's jewelry, along with the stolen sapphires, are in his safe. Safe," he said meditatively, "and sound."

"I have held them in trust, yes in trust," Stan began, but Mrs. Berger stopped him with a cry. For once she had been paying attention to someone else. She shook her finger furiously at him. "Stanley Brill, I see what happened. I see exactly what happened. I'm not surprised. The last thing Mom said to me before she went into the coma was, 'Merry, don't ever trust Stanley Brill.' Mom was always right about people. When I think of you crawling out and taking the rings off her poor fingers. . . ."

His instinct for survival was as strong as hers for dramatics. He broke in. "A simple act of trusteeship, yes, trusteeship. It is wrong of you to make charges like this, Merry, yes, very wrong. I would be very careful what you say to me if I were you. Yes, very careful. Very careful."

She looked at him menacingly; her large, frowzy form hovered over him like an unkempt storm cloud. "It wasn't enough for you to charge a ridiculous price just because you knew I was helpless, you had to go out in the woods . . ." She stopped. She had noticed a gap in the sequence of events she was imagining. "I don't know how you ever found out where . . ." She stopped again, having filled in the gap. "Beaufort, I don't know what I'm going to do with you. You must have told *everybody everything* you did that evening. When you got back to town you must have gone straight to Stan and told him, and Walt, and Russ Mallery, and everybody in the world. First you forgot all about the jewelry that Mom especially wanted *me* to have, and then you go tell Stanley. He must have *paid* you, Beaufort. And then he goes out and steals the rings off . . ."

For the third time she stopped in the middle of a sentence. This time it seemed as if her sense of injustice had strangled her, but she added hoarsely to Stanley Brill, "After all the money I paid you, you go and do a thing like that."

Russ had listened with attentive satisfaction. The culprits in their confusion were hanging each other. His self-confidence mounted further, and the odd result was to diminish a little his air of autocratic dominion and to restore to his manner an unstrained quality of mercy. "Your son didn't tell Stan Brill anything, Mrs. Berger," he said quietly. "Stan didn't know where the body was buried. He never went near the grave. When he turned the body over to you, he hoped he'd seen the last of it. He certainly never tried to find out where it was. How much *did* you pay him, by the way?"

"It was an act of friendship," Stan said. "A simple act of friendship. There were expenses, of course, but there was no fee."

Merry cut him off. "Two thousand dollars."

Russ seemed to disregard this. "Let me assure you that you are mistaken about Stan's intentions regarding the jewelry. He was doing something much as he says, acting as trustee. We wouldn't want to make any mistakes that might damage Stan's reputation. He didn't steal the jewelry, Mrs. Berger. He didn't even *want* the jewelry, I imagine. He found it. He found it in his office one morning, together with some mysterious sapphires. How they got there, no one will ever know."

His manner was one of leniency, but his words were provocative. Merry Berger responded with an expression of curiosity so overt and so intense as to be almost painful. Her punishment had now begun.

Bud had been looking on skeptically through all this, scratching his head from time to time. Now he said, "I don't know where the hell Cheese got the sapphires. But I know how long it took to get there, and I know how often he went there."

"Listen, Bud," Norm said, and then he stopped. "I'm not talking. And you're not talking either, Cheese, you hear me."

"Whenever he went, it took him six to seven hours there and back. He was always taking planes without telling anybody, mostly at night. It was costing us money, and Persh and I began to check up on him. We checked the tach time every day on the planes. He'd go out once a month for six hours or so. Right? So Persh told him to stop. For a while he did, but then he started up again. He went out one night when Merry was abroad, just before she got back. Persh chewed him out, but he wouldn't say what he was doing."

It was Russ's turn to be startled. He had, until now, been in what looked like thorough command of everything. "He went out on these trips *regularly?*"

Bud nodded. "I guess always to the same place. The tach time was always the same, give or take an hour."

"You've been making a *career* of stealing sapphires?" He turned incredulously on Cheese.

"Don't pick on that boy," Merry said. "He wouldn't steal anything. He hasn't got the nerve to steal anything. He's like a naughty little boy. . . ."

Cheese looked up. "Shut up," he said to his mother, with a fury that made it plausible to suppose it had been accumulating for a lifetime. He gulped hard and then shouted at her. "I've stolen a lot of things in my life. I've done a lot of things you never even dreamed of. And this time I was stealing. I was picking up the stuff in Canada to deliver to Norm. . . ."

Norm, immobile, said, "You better shut up, son, or . . ."

"He's been paying me five hundred a trip. To a field in Canada. They gave me the damned stuff in a can. I never knew what was in it. Then . . ."

"Where do star sapphires come from to begin with?" Russ asked.

"Pakistan, I believe," Professor Payne said. "Sailors, perhaps, on ships to Vancouver. Then Cheese. Then Norm."

But Cheese had not finished. "I met this bastard in L.A., and he got me hooked on this then. I can get him for blackmail, too, along with attempted murder. He got me in jail out there once for smuggling. Then I got here and started working, and he found out where I was, and . . ."

"And *you* had the nerve to bury smuggled gems in the same grave with your sainted grandmom," Merry Berger said. "I don't know what I'll do with you, Beaufort Berger." She stamped her foot.

"I know things that some other people will, though," Bud said. "Right?"

"Right," Russ said.

"And I'd say they might know some things to do to you, too, Merry. For a lot of different reasons. One is conspiring to steal your mother's jewelry. It wasn't your fault Cheese forgot to bring it home that night—you meant to steal it. That stuff belongs to the Estate. And boy, can the Estate use anything it can get."

"She was, in fact, conspiring to steal your money," Russ said. "And the rest of the heirs'. And the Van Buren County Flying Service's. Right?" He asked it quietly.

"Right. And we all need it. I've spent a hell of a lot of money recently. Mostly paying Glen Berger for expert advice on how to lose a fortune on the stock market. He's the world's leading specialist in making fortunes disappear into thin air. You probably know the Estate my mother-in-law left has a total value of just about zero zero. In fact, it has a negative value, right? It owes everybody in town. Glen's been buying the wrong stocks for about twenty years. It's like the law of gravity: Glen buys something, and it goes straight down. There's one thing you can say for him. Once you get the knack, you can make money by watching what he does. Persh and I did pretty well now and then, buying what Glen sold and vice versa. We made like a thousand bucks a year while he was losing twenty thousand."

"What was everybody living on?"

"Me, mostly. Me and Persh. The company makes some money, even after Merry gets through free-loading and Cheese uses up our gas flying off to Canada. But it still took everything we had to keep Mrs. Sommers going, with nurses and all, and then some more to keep Glen and Merry fed and pay Cheese a salary he didn't earn. We've borrowed on everything we own. A few months ago we got sore as hell and told Glen, 'No more.' Right? So Merry goes off to Paris to con Aunt Agnes. She paid her fare with money I'd borrowed, with my own house as security."

"Bud Ramsey, you are *mean.* I'm not going to make any more allowances for you. When I go to Paris to try to *help* Agnes, you throw it in my face. You are a cynic, Bud Ramsey, and if there's one thing I can't stand it's a cynic. Agnes *needed* me. Everybody's always needed me."

"Like Red Ridinghood's grandmother needed a wolf." Bud spoke equably. He was, evidently, used to this sort of thing. "The way Agnes needed Merry is like this," he said to the others. "Agnes is not in good shape, right? So Merry goes off to do a snow job before she can conk out. It would not be advantageous to Merry or the rest of us if Agnes conked out before the snow job, so Merry beats it to Paris at supersonic speed."

Merry screamed.

She screamed, it was clear, from frustration, because she could think of no other way to stop Bud. More than that, she screamed to prevent the utterance of a monstrous obscenity. Self-defense was, for her, preeminently a form of delicacy.

It was stunning unsuccessful as a tactic. No one moved. No one even seemed surprised. They behaved as if they had heard a distant fire siren that interrupted but did not interest them. They merely waited until she stopped and then, as she looked around, incredulous that her screaming could have so little effect, Bud went on.

"The thing is," he said seriously, "we all knew what was in Agnes's will. She was leaving all her money to some orphanage in France. And it was considerable. *She'd* never taken Glen's advice. The Berger Law of Gravity did not work on her money. She told him what to buy. If he'd listened to her instead of listening to himself or Merry, we'd all be millionaires."

"Agnes was a great gal," Merry whined. She had recovered. She was breathless, but her confidence in her ability to inspire confidence had returned. "All I wanted was for her to have a little fun before the end. You know me, I've always said there were a lot more important things in the world than money. It was up to Agnes to use hers for something she would *enjoy*. I wouldn't dream of trying to interfere with . . ."

Bud broke in, not so much interrupting as merely beginning a conversation, as if hers were inaudible to him. "What happened, I figure, is that Merry talked the old lady into coming back here. God knows how. Probably yacked all night until the old girl was ready to agree to anything just to shut her up, telling her she has a duty to come to the funeral. Anyhow, she calls Glen one night, running up about forty bucks on her phone bill, and says she's bringing Agnes back. Glen tells the rest of us Agnes is coming. I guess they were going to lock Agnes in the cellar and starve her until she signed a new will. Right? And she told Glen to get Cheese to take a plane and go meet them in Chicago. So he takes the one eighty, without telling me, but Lisa saw him leave in it. And that night Merry and Cheese turn up at the Viewing. No Agnes. Merry says she changed her mind. But no one eighty, either. It's my plane, right? Cheese checked in by car, and he tells me the engine was sounding funny so he'd landed over at Pierce and rented a car while he left Nine Seven Juliet to get looked at by the mechanic over there. I was scheduled to fly some hogs somewhere with some guy, when it never comes in I took the one forty, which I didn't like because they were big hogs. Cheese brings back the one eighty Monday night and says it's been fixed up. It seemed O.K., but it's my bird and I wanted to know what was wrong with it and what they'd done to it, since I wouldn't trust those boys at Pierce with a hay wagon that belonged to me. And Cheese keeps saying not to worry, and he'd paid for the repairs himself. Which is not like Cheese, right? So I called the boys at Pierce. And they tell me that Nine Seven Juliet had never been near Pierce, and neither had Cheese, or any passenger of Cheese's, or anybody. Not that Sunday night, not any night. Right?"

He was looking at Cheese, who repeated, in his flat and inexpressive drawl, "You bastard."

"I see what you figured," Russ said. "You began to see it would be more convenient for them to arrive with no Agnes than to arrive with Agnes. With no Agnes, in either Buchanan or Paris, Berger could go on handling her money as he always had, except he could now keep it for himself instead of depositing it to her account. Which is certainly what he did try to do. Did you know he closed her account at the Corn States?"

"I'm not surprised. It figures. But the main point—at the moment anyway—is not that it was better to have no Agnes than to have Agnes. What I worked out, except it took me about three weeks, was, it was better to have no Agnes than a dead Agnes. Right?"

Russ started to speak and then checked himself. He said, very slowly, "Right. It's not the way I worked it out, but I see you're right. Considering Agnes's will." He was slightly aggrieved at being deprived of a murder, and more aggrieved at having miscalculated. But he understood Bud's logic, and took the demolition of his theory with good grace. "I hadn't considered the will. Not knowing about it. I was assuming that Agnes's money would go to her nieces. I realize now that was an inexcusably vague guess. I see what the order of preference would have to be: (a) Agnes alive, (b) no Agnes at all, (c) least desirable, Agnes dead."

"Right. That's what I finally figured when I found out he'd never gone to Pierce, and Merry was being calm and collected about Agnes's changing her mind. Which is not like Merry, when a couple of million bucks are at stake, right?" He turned to Cheese and asked, "Right?"

"Yeah," Cheese said grudgingly, but with something less than his usual reluctance. His supreme battle was being fought, and it was being fought for him by someone else. He glanced covertly, but with notable malice, at his mother.

"I don't know what everybody is talking about," she said. "Agnes is fine. I had a letter from her just a few days ago, and Agnes is there in Paris, safe and sound. The only thing I want for her is to have some fun with her money in Paris. If she has some fun, she could live forever. There's a lot of life left in that gal."

This, Russ thought, was self-centeredness carried to lunacy. She could not believe that the others would not believe her. She was right because she had to be right: the classic mark of the psychopath. But there was more—or less —than that to it. She was classically stupid as well.

Professor Payne attempted to instruct her. It was his corresponding blindness that he believed everyone else to be as capable of rationality as he. "It happens," he said, "that I was in Paris myself yesterday morning. I spoke to Agnes's concierge. She told me that Agnes and Mrs. Berger left together for Buchanan three weeks ago." He was very matter-of-fact, as if he were correcting a widespread misapprehension about the private life of Ralph Waldo Emerson.

"So," Russ said, "Agnes is not safe and sound in Paris. She is safe and sound in one of Stan's urns, marked with her sister's name and buried in her sister's grave. And where her sister is is in the woods up at the top of the hill."

"Do you mean to tell me, Beaufort, that . . ." Merry stopped.

"It's easy to see what happened now that Bud has told us. Agnes dead was an infinite liability, but Agnes fictionally safe and sound in Paris could be an unlimited asset. For years to come. I take it she died between Chicago and

Pierce City. To preserve the asset, Agnes had to be cremated. There must be no trace of Agnes dead if Agnes were to be missing and presumed alive. It took," he said, "some ingenuity to plan. Ingenuity, and two thousand dollars as a fee for Stan. But why the substitution?" He turned to Bud. "Why not cremate both bodies at once? Why the awkward removal of Mrs. Sommers? Why the ceremonial burial by Cheese in the oak woods?"

Bud scratched his head. "And why, since you raise the point, the oak woods?" He said to Cheese, "Why the hell didn't you bury the body in some other damned oak woods? Why not bury it wherever you landed the plane after she died? You didn't land at Pierce. You couldn't land in any airport with a corpse in the back seat. It must have been in somebody's field." He turned back to Russ. "I kept asking him what the hell he'd been doing with my plane. Just like I've been asking for months where the hell he went when he borrowed planes and went off for six hours. He's good at not answering questions. He doesn't react much."

He wasn't reacting now. He was staring glazedly at the floor. Russ said, "We know all the answers to the big questions, Cheese. You won't lose anything by doing a little reacting."

"He can't react. Merry won't let him," Bud said. "Right?"

He said it very coolly, but there was brutality in his voice. And his calculation was correct. For the second time that evening Cheese Berger's gelatinous resolution melted. He looked up with soft hostility, lit a cigarette, and spoke in his slurred mutter that was half an affectation of manly arrogance and half, it seemed, a fear of being understood.

"Ma thought he was going to cremate them both at the same time. Part of the two grand package deal. He *said* he was going to." Cheese nodded to Stan. "The dirty little bastard. So I took the car and went out to the field where I'd left Nine Seven Juliet as soon as it got dark Sunday night, after Ma had talked the family into getting Grandma's body cremated. I brought it back to Stan's. He puts it in Grandma's casket and puts it in the furnace. Then he asks for two thousand more. Two thousand for shifting stiffs, two thousand for cremating the second one."

"There were expenses," Stan said. "It was of course necessary to consider the cost of a second casket. I naturally insist on showing due respect . . ."

"He figured he had us cold," Cheese said. "But Ma wouldn't pay." He fingered his damaged jaw. "So she tells me to take Grandma's body out and bury it somewheres. I got it in the car, but I didn't have a shovel and anyway you can't dig a grave at night, since I didn't know where the hell to dig it. So I took it out and shut it up in the plane. At least animals weren't going to get it. I put a blanket over it and locked up the plane. And I was still carrying the damned can of stones I'd brought back from Canada two days before which Norm couldn't come get because he was socked in. I was tired of carrying it. So I threw it in with the body and left it in the plane."

"My plane," Bud said to himself.

"I'd landed in a field that belongs to some guy I know, about five miles from Pierce. He was away somewhere for a while, took his family camping or some damned thing. He told me he was going, which is why I landed there after Agnes passed out on the way in from Chicago and Ma started screaming about how we got to do something. So after the funeral Ma drives me back there with a shovel, and then she says she can't face watching me bury Grandma so she goes off and leaves me there. And I begin to see I can't dig a grave around there. No woods, and this guy's house is right there, and if I dig the place up, his goddamn kids are sure to start playing around. So I take the shovel and fly around till I see a field I could land in that had trees around it with no house you could see for miles. So I get the body buried, and I throw Norm's can in because I don't know where the hell else to put it. The way things were going, it looked like he might be socked in for another month. I didn't know what the hell was in the can, but I knew it was something I didn't want to be found with. It makes me laugh, the way the blackmailing bastard got caught. Because when he turns up the next day, his can is buried, and I go out looking, and damned if I can find that field again. That made me laugh."

But he didn't laugh now, and neither did Norm. Instead they stared at each other with common loathing, as if each hoped silently to transfer the totality of his own guilt to the other. And Cheese, talking on with a curious, toneless intonation that made it sound as if he were repeating in hypnosis formulas of revenge he had first spoken with bravado to himself, continued, "Another thing made me laugh. Ma told me to strip the jewelry off the body, but I didn't feel like doing it. I tell her I forgot, and then she gets mad. Like Norm when I couldn't find the field. Man, did she get mad. Just like she was when she found out Agnes was dying on the back seat when we were flying in. She got so mad then she'd have killed Agnes for dying if she hadn't already been dead." And now he did laugh, grimly, as if he had finished at last the reenactment of an old play.

Throughout his story, Russ had been watching his mother. She had sat, her legs apart like his but sitting stiffly erect instead of leaning forward, with intimations of emotion in which, Russ thought, impatience predominated. It was intensely irksome to her to have to sit through so long a discourse from her son. She had not been listening to it, merely waiting until she could make her own speech. Once or twice she had started to speak and then thought better of it. Now she burst out, more, it sounded, from a desire to talk than from any strong feeling of a need to defend herself. She sounded, in fact, almost normal, as if the scene had suddenly dissolved and been replaced by a congenial cocktail hour on a peaceful patio.

"Mom's death was pretty hard on me," Merry said. "I can't go into it now, but I went through a lot more with her illness than anybody realizes. I had to take all the responsibility, and that was pretty hard on me, since she and I had always been so close. I guess it's just my job in life," she said, bravely covering tragedy with patio-type cheerfulness, "taking care of people who can't take care of themselves. Trying to get Glendenning and Beaufort straightened out. Making that long trip to cheer up poor old Agnes because she was so upset when she heard of Mom's being sick. Having to buy all those darned clothes in Paris just to please the old girl. Then chaperoning her back to Buchanan when she insisted on coming home for the funeral. I tell you, I was about dead by then myself, and when I looked over my shoulder and saw Agnes was . . . well, I'm not kidding . . . the first thing I thought of was all those bills she'd said she was going to pay, *including* two first-class tickets, and there she was passed out on the back seat, I thought to myself, Merry, this is what you have to put up with when you're trying to help other people."

She was lost now in her own performance, delighted by the mere fact of possessing a stage. "But you know, even then, there was one thing that made me feel good about the situation. The poor old gal was *really* enjoying herself when she went. You know, I offered to rent a car in Chicago and drive her all the way to Buchanan, but she insisted on having Cheese *fly* us. She'd never flown before until that trip, and boy she really took to it like a duck to water. She loved every minute of it, until she died. If there's one thing I'll always be glad of, it's that I was able to help bring joy to the poor old gal in the last few minutes she was alive. There she was, a woman sixty-nine years old and she'd never been in a plane before that day. It gave her the biggest kick she'd ever had. She was just *crying* from the thrill of it, all the way from the time she left Chicago until she died. You know, that was how I knew something was wrong, when I couldn't hear her any more. I'll always say Agnes died of plain, simple happiness. That's one thing I'll always be able to say to myself, I really did something for that old gal. . . ."

"Shut up, goddamn it." It was Cheese who spoke, softly, without looking up, but with a suggestion of authority that surprised the others. Certainly it surprised his mother. "Agnes died of fright," he said. "She was half dead when I met them at O'Hare. She said she wouldn't get into the one eighty, she couldn't stand any more flying. She was yelling, and gasping for breath. But Ma pushed her in and said she couldn't afford anything else because the company was paying for my flying them. I thought when we took off the old woman wouldn't make it back to Buchanan probably."

"Still, she died a natural death? In a technical sense?"

"Yeah, sure. She'd been in terrible shape for years. Everybody knew that. I was surprised she'd gotten as far as she did."

The fourth car was in the drive. When the sheriff's deputies came onto the terrace they nodded to Russ. They knew him well from earlier days, and their manner was deferential. It was clear that they would do what he told them to and believe what he said.

What he said was, "Take that man there." He nodded to Norm. "Have him charged with two attempted murders."

Norm stood up slowly, in a ponderous rage. "Goddamn," he started, and then, remembering lessons learned the hard way, he checked himself.

The deputies handcuffed him and turned him around. He kicked one of them in the calf as a non-incriminating release for his feelings. The deputy kicked him back. Then he said to Russ, "Is that all, sir?"

"That's all. I'll talk to Jim Fess later."

"I thought there were going to be two of them."

"No," Russ said slowly. "Only one. Mrs. Fess misunderstood."

They left, and there was silence on the terrace for a moment before Merry began, "Russ, I tell you I was fit to be tied when those two . . ."

After Bud and the Bergers had gone, Stanley Brill lingered. He said tentatively, "I am most upset, yes, most upset and confused."

"You needn't be," Russ said. "I don't think anything is going to happen to you. It may, but I don't think so. There are going to be some formalities about Agnes Creston's body, but if you're helpful with them, your role in the business need not be made public. You're going to have to pay me a fee for professional services rendered as your attorney, though. Payment in kind. You've got another cremation to perform, personally and privately."

"With the greatest reverence," Stan said. "Yes, reverence."

"And promptness, too."

Stan nodded with majestic solemnity. His reaction to salvation was as opaque as his reaction to terror.

Professor Payne had been staring into space. "Very well, Russ. It's fair enough. But the others, Merry and Cheese? You let them drive off without warnings. I don't know what, precisely, they are guilty of in law, but by any conceivable standard of justice they should be dealt with in some fashion."

"They will be. So far as Cheese goes, I'll see that his pilot's license is lifted. Out of a decent regard for the safety of the flying public, if not of justice. He may be charged with smuggling, too, if Norm talks, but I doubt if he will. There's no reason for him to entangle himself with smuggling charges as well as assault with intent to kill and distributing stolen goods. And Jim Fess wouldn't be much interested in the desecration of venerated objects. He wouldn't know what the hell it was. But Cheese will get quite a lot of retribution from other quarters. He's getting quite a lot of it in the car with his mother now, I imagine."

Professor Payne considered. "I agree it is better not to try to remedy the irremediable. It merely costs money and wastes time. I have always thought that the law, which is unbearably oversubtle in its processes, is unbearably crude in its results. Retributive justice is quite as indefensible as crime. The problem is, what will he do next?"

"God knows. But I think it's possible he'd like to keep out of trouble. And, by the time this little drive with his mother is finished, out of Buchanan as well. And so far as Merry goes, losing him will be part of her punishment. It will be painful to be deprived of her punching bag. A bigger part will be losing her mother's jewels. A still bigger part will be losing Agnes's money. We'll have to work out some way to notify the authorities that she is deceased, so that the French orphans can get their reward. But the biggest part is going to be that from now on nobody will pay any attention to Merry's advice. In fact, nobody is going to listen to anything she says. I think Bud will see to that."

"I can see that jail sentences would not cure their folly. Still, it wouldn't do any harm to frighten Merry."

"It wouldn't do any good, either," Richie said.

"But justice is an ethical notion, and she is guilty of murder."

"Do you really think she killed Agnes?" Russ asked. "In the technical sense of strangling her, or socking her with a wrench?"

"I'm quite sure she didn't. She may even think, by now, that she was really just intending to show the old gal a good time. But she has murdered two men."

Russ looked at him questioningly.

"Her husband and her son."

Stanley Brill laughed nervously.

October. On a gray afternoon Richie was crossing the wide expanse of asphalt behind the high school, where a bored generation bred to opulence parked its sports cars. He was limping more than he had three months earlier, not because he was lamer but simply because he had stopped trying not to limp. His mind was on higher things: he was appraising the gray sky. It was overcast, but the ceiling was certainly way above minimum. Halfway across the parking lot he paused, wet one finger with his tongue, and held it up to the breeze. Just about two seven zero, he thought. At like twenty. Steady wind, and down the slot. There wouldn't be any problem. Satisfied, he continued toward his car.

He had almost reached it when he saw another boy coming from the opposite side of the lot and recognized him as Gary Wayne who, before Richie had lost his year, had been a classmate and a football team-mate as well. They had not met before, this autumn. Now they greeted each other with the sidewise, laconic impersonality that constituted the cautious courtesy of their kind.

"Hey, Rich."

"Hi, Gary. How you doing?"

There was then a moment of slightly awkward silence. Richie noticed detachedly that Gary's manner was in fact somewhat more than cautiously impersonal: he was embarrassed. Trained by experience, Richie realized that Gary had been watching him as he limped across the asphalt and that his eyes had traveled involuntarily down to Richie's foot.

He said, in an effort to sound natural, "Hey, Richie, you want to go over to Western High with us this afternoon? Some guys from the team are going over to watch them play. We have the game the week after next. . . ." He checked himself and asked out of frank curiosity, "Maybe you don't like watching football now?" He hesitated. "You going to be able to play again?"

Richie was relieved. It was much easier to deal with questions than with questioning glances. "No, I won't. And I don't mind watching football, but I can't today. I got to go to work."

"What you do?" Once again his curiosity slightly exceeded the conventions of courtesy.

"I got a job at the airport. Line boy."

"Line boy."

"It's like working at a gas station, only for airplanes. Plus some other things. I been doing it since last summer. As a matter of fact, I'm not on the line this afternoon, though. I got to fly somebody somewhere."

"Fly?"

"Yeah. I got to fly my great-uncle to Chicago. He's leaving for Paris on a trip."

"You fly the plane? You got a license and like that?"

"Yeah. I got my private. They give me free instruction as part of my pay for the line work. I'm working on instruments now, for my rating." He saw no need to add that he had had his license for only a week, and that his instrument work had consisted of an hour of dual.

Gary was uncomfortable with this. "Hey, cool," he said.

"Well, be seeing you. I ought to get started. It takes four hours to Chicago and back and I got a date afterwards."

"Seeing you," Gary said, and he stood watching emptily as Richie got into the car and backed out into the lot. For reasons he could not explain, Gary was feeling resentful and a little disappointed.